Buck's strong arms wrapped around her, hauling her close.

She should have resisted, but that embrace felt so good, and those arms felt so strong and protective. It had been way, way too long since anyone had hugged her, and her throat tightened as she realized how much she had missed that kind of comfort.

"I won't let anything happen to you," he murmured. "That much I can swear. Not one bad thing is going to happen to you."

"You can't promise that," she said weakly into his shoulder. "Nobody can." Life had certainly taught her that lesson the hard way.

"I can. It used to be my job. Nobody's going to hurt you. They'll have to get through me first."

Conard County: The Next Generation

Dear Reader,

This book started as a game. I was having a terrible time coming up with a story idea, so a couple of friends and I played an improv game. One set a scene. Then each of us added to it, none of us being able to change what came before.

The game is called, "Yes, and..." Each subsequent person builds on what came before.

And while the game didn't give me the whole idea, it raised a question: What did Haley see in the parking lot that was so dangerous?

From there other ideas occurred to me as I tried to answer that question. Among the things I wanted to do with this book, other than tell a suspenseful love story, was revisit Conard County in a way so many readers asked for. A lot wound up being cut for length, but I feel I've at least added to the sense of homecoming for those who asked for more.

I hope you enjoy *What She Saw*. Because what Haley saw bought her a whole peck of trouble and a whole lot of love.

Hugs,

Rachel

RACHEL LEE

What She Saw

⟨H⟩ HARLEQUIN® ROMANTIC SUSPENSE

Recycling programs
for this product may
not exist in your area.

ISBN-13: 978-0-373-27813-8

WHAT SHE SAW

Printed in U.S.A.

Books by Rachel Lee

RACHEL LEE

was hooked on writing by the age of twelve, and practiced her craft as she moved from place to place all over the United States. This *New York Times* bestselling author now resides in Florida and has the joy of writing full-time.

Chapter 1

Nothing hinted that a man would die that night.

Haley Martin arrived at the truck stop for her shift at eight in the evening. The place was open round the clock, and was busy enough at any hour because this was the only big truck stop for nearly a hundred miles in any direction.

Big enough for rigs to park and idle while drivers slept. Big enough to have hot showers and other amenities. And the restaurant itself was famous for good down-home cooking.

That night the lot was almost empty, but she knew this would change. Traffic always seemed to come in waves, maybe because the truckers liked to travel close together so they could keep in touch by radio and chat.

On her way in, she noticed two trucks parked back-to-back. That was unusual. They usually parked side by side. One of the trucks was smaller, a box truck, not a trailer rig like the other. It didn't seem important, though, and she quickened her step so she wouldn't be late. She'd taken a small role in a college play and the rehearsal had run over.

She liked the job. It was tiring, being on her feet for hours, but she liked it anyway. As a college student, it fit her perfectly, and when it got quiet the boss didn't mind if she studied.

She was only taking one class this summer, and working full-time, but the class had more than an average amount of reading and homework, so a quiet night would be welcome.

She breezed inside, waving to the other waitress, Claire, an attractive thirtysomething redhead, and the skinny short-order cook and owner, Hasty. He tossed her a grin as she passed by on the way to her locker, then returned to his cooking.

After getting her purse and books stowed, she tied on her apron, starched and white, over her pink uniform, checked that her blond hair hadn't escaped its bun, then punched the time clock and headed out to work.

"Coffee's fresh," Claire said as she returned to the restaurant. "It's been slow since I got here at four."

"That'll change," Hasty remarked as he slipped burgers onto buns and scooped them onto plates with fries. He turned and put them on the counter for Claire.

"Might as well study, Haley," he said. "You'll know when to hop."

Yes, that was part of why she liked this job. Hasty seemed to care as much about her education as she did. But she also liked the truckers who came in here. Most of them were nice enough, and some even told great stories about the places they'd been.

There was one driver in particular, she thought as she

went back to get her books and a cup of coffee. One guy who seemed to stand out, although she wasn't exactly sure why. It wasn't just that he was awfully good-looking, or that he seemed to have a body honed to hardness, unlike many other drivers who had been softened by the endless hours at the wheel.

No, it was something else, she thought as she took a seat by the window. Something about his manner. Quieter and more respectful than the others, not that many gave her a hard time. He was the only one who didn't address her by name, even though it was plainly written on a badge above her breast. No, he always called her *ma'am*. And he tipped generously.

But that wasn't it, either, she decided as she opened her book. It was his eyes. Dark, dark eyes that seemed to hint at danger while reflecting a good helping of sorrow.

Almost without fail, he was here three nights a week, and unless she was mistaken, tonight was his night. For some reason, she had begun to look forward to seeing him.

She chided herself. She'd already made up her mind that she wouldn't let anything get between her and completing school, and there was nothing like a relationship to do that. She'd seen enough people drop out to get married. Besides, what did she know about him except that seeing him made her heart skip a beat? That he wasn't married and drove a truck, and his last name, embroidered on his gray shirt, was Devlin. Not a whole lot, even for a fantasy.

Shaking her head at herself, she burrowed into her text. She was discovering very little real interest in diet and nutrition, maybe because she had had to juggle so many diets during her mother's illness.

Interested or not, she still had fifty pages to read before class tomorrow, and there would probably be a pop quiz, plus the final loomed on Friday morning, so she dove in.

A noise from the lot caught her attention and she looked out through the plate-glass window. The brightly lit restaurant didn't help her view any, nearly turning the glass into a mirror, and those two trucks she had noticed were parked at the far end of the lot in near darkness. But she heard a clang, and then squinted. Were those two trucks transferring something?

She stared for a minute, thinking that she saw a crate or two passing between them along a metal ramp, but unable to make out any real details.

What did it matter? Maybe something was scheduled to be off-loaded here. Just because she'd never seen it happen before didn't mean it was unusual.

She turned her attention back to her book, but discovered her mind wanted to play games. She was acting in a mystery play, and the role had gotten to her enough that she sometimes found herself imagining nefarious things in ordinary activities. Like those two trucks out there.

Almost grinning to herself, she tried to return to nutrition. *That* was almost enough to put her to sleep.

About ten minutes later, the bell over the door sounded and two men entered. Goodness, was that Ray Liston? She hadn't seen him since high school, after he'd had a run-in with the law. So he was a driver now.

She glanced over and saw Claire was busy with the table in the far corner. "I'll get this, Claire."

Claire waved her thanks, and Haley stood, going to the counter where the two men stood. "Can I get you guys something?"

"Two large coffees to go," said Ray. Then his eyes brightened a bit. "Say, I knew you in high school."

She pretended not to have realized it, though she didn't know why. "Really? Oh! You're Ray."

He grinned. A tall, lanky guy with a thinly growing beard, he had crooked teeth. His family had always been dirt-poor, though, so no orthodontics for him. That poverty hadn't made his school years any easier, and Haley had often felt a twinge of sympathy for him.

She felt Claire slip behind her to get to the coffeepot as she rang up the two coffees and accepted payment. "You're driving now?" she asked.

"Yup."

"Good for you. It's a great job." She couldn't help noticing how the other driver, a short, burly man with a balding head, kept looking the other way, as if he were uncomfortable for some reason. Nervous? Shy? What did it matter? She shrugged it off.

Claire surprised her by reaching around her to put the two coffees on the counter in front of the men.

"Thanks, Claire," she said as she closed the register.

"I was already here," came the response as Claire slipped past her again and headed back to her customers, pot in hand.

"See you around?" Ray said, almost hopefully.

She had no interest in him, but she managed a smile. "Sure, nearly every time you come in here now."

Ray laughed, then he and the other guy went to the condiment bar to add sugar and creamer to their coffees. A few seconds later they were out the door and headed across the lot.

Twenty minutes later, almost as if a signal had been sent, the lot started filling with the big rigs coming from the west, all of which had made a perilous trip over the mountains from the West Coast. She put her books away and went to work, hoping that the driver called Devlin would show up again.

He wasn't in the first wave, and soon she was busy serving everything from burgers to breakfast—large stacks of pancakes, lots of eggs and home fries, and gallons of coffee. She joked and chatted with those who were feeling friendly tonight, and kept the coffee coming. Coffee was essential, and the restaurant had four double-drip coffeemakers working constantly.

Then the place started emptying out. She filled a dozen takeout cups with coffee, and listened as the throbbing engines revved up and began to roar out of the lot.

Sometimes she imagined getting on those rigs and traveling to places she'd never been, from Denver to Chicago to St. Louis. These guys were headed all over the map, and in a small way she envied them. They had to feel free, out there on the road, aside from the need to keep to a schedule. Maybe that was part of the charm.

Just as she and Claire finished wiping the last table clean, readying for the next wave, a police car pulled up out front. Haley didn't immediately pay it much attention. Being the only all-night place operating around Conard City, they saw cops almost as often as they saw truck drivers.

But somehow, the instant Deputy Parish and Deputy Ironheart walked through the door, she knew this was no ordinary visit. They didn't go to the counter. They looked around, then focused on her and Claire.

Both deputies were of Native American descent, with dark eyes and equally dark hair, except for Micah Parish, who was starting to show some gray streaks in his raven hair. She had known both of them nearly her entire life.

"Hi, ladies," Sarah Ironheart said. "Can we talk to you?"

Haley felt her heart skitter. Something bad must have happened, but it hadn't happened here. Her mind started running over anything that might have to do with her, and discarded possibilities as fast as they occurred. She lived in a cheap, run-down apartment and all she owned was a twelve-year-old car and a laptop computer. No, it couldn't be something like that.

She and Claire dropped their cleaning rags in the bin and joined the deputies at one of the tables. Claire looked excited by the change of pace. Haley couldn't help feeling dread.

Life had taught her to dread. Words from a doctor, words from a cop, they weren't often good news.

Sarah Ironheart started, "We were wondering if either of you know Ray Liston."

"I knew him in school," Haley answered promptly. "Most everyone knew who he was. Is he in trouble?" At least this didn't have to do with her.

At that moment, the deep throbbing of another rig alerted her and she looked out to see a solo truck pulling in. Her heart jumped a little, hoping it was the Devlin guy. Why had she gotten so attached to seeing him?

Sarah's voice called her back. "Did he stop in here tonight?"

Claire looked at Haley for an answer.

Haley nodded. "He and another driver came in to pick up some coffee to go."

"Did you talk to him? Did he seem all right? Alert, not under the influence of something?"

"He seemed fine, actually," Haley said, thinking back. "He recognized me even though we hadn't seen each other since high school. It wasn't much of a conversation. I asked if he was driving now, he said he was, and I said I was glad he had such a good job. Something like that."

"So you didn't notice anything off about him?"

Haley shook her head. "No. Why? Did he get into trouble?"

Sarah sighed. "He ran his truck off the road about ten miles east of here."

Haley's hands tightened on the edge of the table. She felt her heart race with shock. At that moment Devlin walked through the door and headed to his usual table. "Customer," she said almost automatically, still trying to absorb the news. *Ran his truck off the road?*

"He can wait," Micah Parish said. Then he glanced over his shoulder. "Buddy, can you wait a few?"

Devlin nodded. "No problem."

God, he looked good, Haley thought. Better than usual, though she couldn't say what it was about him. But she forced her attention back to the two deputies because another question, one she wasn't sure she wanted answered, hammered at her. "Is he okay? Ray?"

Sarah and Micah exchanged glances. "No," Micah said. "He's dead. That's why we need to know if you noticed anything at all unusual about him."

"He seemed fine," Haley repeated. "Not much different from high school, except maybe thinner. He's dead? He's *really* dead?"

It fully hit her then. A man she had been talking to a short time ago, a man she had known for her entire childhood, was dead. Tremors started to run through her and a tunnel seemed to grow around her vision.

"Focus," Sarah said gently. "Focus, Haley. We need to know if you noticed anything at all unusual about Ray."

"He seemed fine," she repeated, hearing the flatness of her own voice. Her mind was trying to draw into a cocoon, she realized, just as it had when she first heard her mother's diagnosis.

"So there was nothing off-kilter, nothing unusual?"

The restaurant, which had seemed to be receding, suddenly snapped into sharp focus as she remembered. "Not really. Not when he came in here. But beforehand…" She hesitated because it seemed so unimportant to a man's death. An accidental death.

"What?" Micah prompted.

"I'm not sure exactly. When I came to work there were two trucks parked back-to-back. That's unusual. They usually park side by side."

"So he didn't park normally." Sarah scribbled something in a notebook.

"It's probably meaningless," Haley said. "It's unusual, but there weren't any other trucks out there at the time. They could have parked sideways for all it mattered. I thought I caught sight of them moving crates between the trucks. Just briefly, but I can't be sure because it was so far away and with all the light in here, the parking lot isn't easy to see."

"Well, that wouldn't have caused an accident farther down the road," Sarah said and closed her notebook. "Thanks, Haley. If you think of anything else, just let us know, okay?"

"I will."

The deputies rose, leaving immediately. Haley jumped up, still feeling shaken, but needing to take care of her favorite customer. *Her favorite customer?* What an odd thought, considering he didn't talk all that much. But he was nice. Then it struck her that he never came in with the rest of the waves. He always came alone.

Move. She needed to move. She felt as if news of Ray's death had tossed her brain like a salad, if only because she had once known him and he seemed so young to end this way. Keeping busy seemed like the only antidote.

She grabbed the freshest coffeepot, a cup and saucer, and headed for Devlin's table. "Hi, Mr. Devlin," she said, trying for a smile as she poured his coffee. "What'll it be tonight?"

"An omelet with green peppers and onions, and rye toast, please."

Unlike others, he never imagined she would remember his usual order. He always told her, and rarely did he change it.

"Coming up," she said as cheerfully as she could.

Then he startled her by calling her by name. "Haley?"

She turned at once, surprised, and found those deep, dark eyes fixed on her. "Yes?"

"There was an accident?"

"Yeah. A truck went off the road east of here. One of your company's, I think. At least it looked like your truck."

He nodded slowly. "I heard some of what you said. Mind telling me about it?"

She hesitated, then decided there was no reason not to. The place was nearly a graveyard right now, and there was no reason not to chat for a few minutes.

"Sure," she said. "Let me just put your order in. Want me to leave the coffeepot here?"

For the first time since she'd met him months ago, a faint smile touched the edges of his mouth and sparkled quietly in his eyes. It seemed to reach out and touch her, and made her tingle. "Sure. And bring a cup for yourself if it's okay with the boss."

Hasty, as usual, didn't have a problem. "As soon as I make his meal, I'm heading out back for a smoke. Go ahead and take a break. Damn, ain't that some news about Ray? Used to go to my church before the family fell away."

After serving his meal, Haley got herself a cup and joined Devlin at the table. He stuck out a large hand. "Buck Devlin."

She shook it. "Haley Martin."

"Wild night, huh? Do you want something to eat?"

She shook her head. "Thanks, I'm okay. Hasty lets me eat whenever I want."

"One of the perks of working here, I guess. He sure makes a great omelet."

"You should try some of the other things on the menu sometime. He's good at them all."

Again that faint smile in the corners of his eyes. "So you've noticed I'm a creature of habit."

"When it comes to what you eat here, anyway."

"I guess it comes from all the years when I didn't have any say about much." He fell silent, eating his omelet, munching on a bite of toast. She refilled his cup when he half drained it.

"So," he said a couple of minutes later, "you knew the driver who was in the accident?"

"I went to school with him. This is the first time I've seen him in a few years. Do you know him? It looked like he drives for the same company. His shirt was like yours and his truck, too."

"I didn't know him. I don't spend a whole lot of time hanging around the terminal."

"Oh." She wondered what that meant about him. Maybe he didn't have a whole lot of time between trips. Or maybe he wasn't like the other drivers who, when they came in here, at least, seemed to crave the company of other drivers. He *did* seem self-contained.

"Must be a shock for you," he said.

"I guess." She hesitated. "I don't know, Mr. Devlin—"

"Buck," he interrupted.

"Buck," she repeated obediently. "Honestly, I haven't seen Ray in six years. It was a surprise to see him again tonight. I thought he'd left for good. So, yes, it was a bit of a shock, but not a huge one. If you know what I mean."

He nodded. "I understand."

Something about his face suggested he did.

"Maybe he fell asleep at the wheel," she said when he remained quiet. "Not that he seemed sleepy or anything when he stopped in for coffee. But I guess it's possible."

"Could be. Some drivers push it too hard and too long."

"I thought there were regulations about that."

"There are. And for every regulation there's a way around it. So…you said you saw him doing something before he came in here."

She turned her coffee cup in her hands, looking down. Something about the intensity of his gaze made her a little self-conscious, like she should be patting her hair to make sure it hadn't fallen from the bun she wore to work. "I'm not sure what I saw." She nodded toward the window. "You can see how hard it is to see the lot from inside here. The odd thing was the way the two trucks were parked. Back-to-back. That's something I haven't seen before."

"Anything else?"

She wondered why he was so curious about it when the cops seemed to think it irrelevant, but then figured there was no harm in telling him. He worked for the same company, after all. Maybe he figured the company would have some questions for him.

"Well, I was sitting at one of the tables studying when I heard a clanging. I glanced out and thought it looked like they were moving some crates around, like there was a ramp between the trucks. But honestly, Buck, I'm not sure. I wasn't paying close attention and I couldn't see clearly. I don't see what that has to do with his accident, anyway."

"Maybe nothing," Buck said, returning to his meal. "How's the pie?"

"I recommend the cherry cobbler tonight. Hasty makes the best in the world."

His face suddenly blossomed into a smile, and the expression took her breath away. My God, he was gorgeous.

"Then I'll break tradition and have some cobbler a little later. Tell me about yourself, Haley Martin."

"Why?"

"Because I'm curious."

Being the object of Buck Devlin's curiosity made her heart skip a little. Why in the world would he be interested in her? But when she considered the story she had to tell, she figured the interest wouldn't last. Not that it mattered, she told herself.

"Not much to tell," she tried to say lightly. "I grew up here, I've never been farther from home than Laramie. My mother got cancer when I was a senior in high school, so I took care of her until she died last year. Now I'm going to the community college. A very boring little life. What about you?"

"Well, it hasn't been boring," he said, pushing his empty plate to one side. "Sometimes I think I'd like boring. Maybe that's why I like driving so much. It's peaceful."

"Have you always been a driver?"

He shook his head. "Nope. Army. I traveled all over the world, but take it from me, it wasn't the stuff you'd put on a postcard."

"I suppose a lot of it wasn't," she said carefully, wondering if this man was troubled by nightmares. The notion gave her an unexpected pang.

She rose and went to get him a generous serving of the cobbler. She thought he was done talking with her, but instead he motioned her to join him again, his brow arched questioningly.

So she slid into the chair, refreshed her cup and waited to see what was going on. She didn't think he was interested in her, particularly, but this was so out of character compared to the quiet way he usually came and went that her curiosity began to stir. Not to mention her hormones. She couldn't evade her attraction to him, but it wouldn't do her any good. It might cause her more problems.

"I'm going to Denver tonight," he said. "I'll be back in a couple of days."

"What exactly do you do?"

"I carry shipments from Seattle to Denver. Usually there's a load leaving Denver for Seattle. Tacoma's a decent-sized port and a lot of stuff leaves there for Japan and other points east, and we get stuff from there in and out of our terminal."

"What exactly do you carry?"

He smiled faintly. "A little of this and a little of that, honestly. Everything from bikes to camping gear to coffee. Coming back out of Denver it can be a mix, or it can be an entire container of something headed overseas. I'm not much interested in my loads. I just need to get them delivered in one piece."

She nodded. "How is it coming over the mountains?"

"A thrill and a half when the load is heavy, that's for sure." He rose, pulling out his wallet and putting thirty dollars on the table. A huge tip for her.

"I'll see you in a couple of days, Haley. Thanks for the company."

She stood, too, ready to clear the table, sorry to see him go so quickly. But he never lingered. He had a schedule to keep. "Have a safe trip."

"I intend to."

Then he paused and said something that sent a chill to her very bones. He kept his voice low, so low she was sure Claire couldn't hear from the other end of the restaurant. "Haley? Don't mention what you saw in the lot tonight. Not to anyone. I'm going to check with my company, but...just don't mention it to anyone."

She stood frozen, wondering if that was a threat or a warning.

"Promise," he said.

"I promise."

He smiled again. "Good. I'll talk to you when I get back. Stay safe."

She watched him walk across the lot and climb into the cab of his rig. It was definitely a warning. But whatever for? The cops hadn't even thought it important.

What in the world did he think might be going on?

Then she realized Claire had come to stand beside her. "Look out," Claire said.

Haley tore her gaze from the truck that was now pulling out of the lot and looked at the other waitress. "What?"

"These guys are rolling stones, Haley, and we're only a stop on a long road. Don't waste any interest on them."

She knew Claire was right. "He just wanted to ask some questions about what happened tonight. Same trucking company."

"Sure." Claire shook her head, but a wicked little grin seemed to dance around her mouth. "That's why he was eating you up with his eyes."

Haley couldn't prevent the shiver of pleasure that ran through her. "Don't be silly."

"I saw it, and I've been around the block more than once." Claire's grin faded. "Just watch it, Haley. The guy's probably got a life somewhere else."

He most likely did, Haley thought as she cleared the table and wiped it, just as another wave started to arrive. She owed it to herself to keep her eyes on her goals. That was the only sure way to build a future for herself.

But throughout the night she kept remembering how good Buck Devlin looked, and how nice he'd been. And how she'd responded to him as a woman.

Oh, well. Claire was right. He was just another rolling stone.

Chapter 2

Two nights later, Haley raced into work, her face burning. Hasty was sitting at his stool behind the cash register and his eyebrows lifted. "What the heck happened to you?"

"Dress rehearsal is a great time to find out I must be allergic to stage makeup."

Hasty's jaw dropped and then he let out a belly laugh. "No!"

"Oh, yes. Is there any still left? I scrubbed it so much with cold cream, but it still burns."

"I can't see it, but dang, girl, you look like you spent too long in the sun."

"And I have to do this again on Friday and Saturday night," Haley answered. "I can't believe this."

"Can't they let you use something else?"

"I'm not sure it would work. Besides, I never wear

makeup because it's an expensive waste of money. For all I know, I'm allergic to all of it."

"Go back and wash up some more. I got some of those over-the-counter pills that might help. It'll make you sleepy, though. Maybe you should just take the night off."

"Not unless you think I look that bad. I got bills, remember?"

Hasty chuckled a little and shook his head. "Soap and water, then I'll give you one of them little pink pills. If you're slow tonight, I won't hold it against you."

Haley took his advice, scrubbing well with soap from the hand dispenser, and leaning close to the mirror to check for any remnants of makeup. She couldn't find any, but her whole face looked red and just a bit puffy.

When she got back out front, Hasty and Claire were seated on opposite sides of the counter, drinking coffee and chatting. Claire took one look and shook her head.

"Can't you get someone else to fill in for you? What do they call them? Understudies?"

"Not for my role. It's too small. No, I'll just have to get through this."

She slid onto a stool beside Claire with a cup of coffee and accepted the pill Hasty popped out of a blister pack into her hand. "I didn't know I was in trouble until after the rehearsal had started. I wanted to scratch my face off."

"You need to be careful," Claire said. "I had a cousin who had an allergic reaction and it put her in the hospital the second time she had it. The first time wasn't that bad."

"I should be able to get the makeup on and off in about fifteen minutes Friday night. And everybody knows what happened."

"That's good. They'll know what's going on if it gets

bad. Maybe it would help to put some petroleum jelly on your face before the makeup."

"That's an idea. Thanks."

Hasty poured himself some more coffee, then came back to lean his elbow on the counter. "Ray's wake is tonight and tomorrow night. Funeral Friday morning. I'm thinking about going to the funeral."

"I guess I should," Haley said reluctantly. The last funeral she had been to was her mother's, and she wasn't sure she ever again wanted to see the inside of Meeker's Funeral Home. "The wake, anyway. For a few minutes. I have a final Friday morning."

"Ray had his troubles," Hasty opined, "but the family's never been a problem. Being poor ain't a sin, despite what some think."

"You're talking to a couple of waitresses," Claire said, a touch tartly. "We know."

Hasty flashed a grin. "You girls get better tips than my day girls. They got you beat on poor."

Claire sniffed. "Your day girls don't work as hard. If they want more money, tell them to work nights."

Hasty was still looking amused. "I think they get that."

A short while later, the night's first wave rolled in. Haley and Claire jumped to work, and after a little while, even though she noticed she was a little slower than usual, Haley felt her face calming down.

At least nobody asked her about it. She joked casually with some of the drivers, but it seemed like an oddly quiet night. She wondered if news about Ray's death had gotten around and they were all feeling a little more sober than usual.

The place sure didn't feel quite as energetic as it usually did when it was full. Or maybe that was the little pill Hasty had given her.

She was working her way back through her section, clearing some tables, handing out tickets and picking up cash and change, serving latecomers, when Buck Devlin walked in. It was so unusual to see him when the place was crowded that she froze for a split second. He got his usual table, though, despite the crowd, and she worked her way toward him.

It wasn't easy. The night turned unusual in that another wave arrived before the first was done. Hasty was cooking with both hands as fast as he could, and Claire was looking a bit frazzled. What was going on?

Then someone asked her for directions to the funeral parlor and she knew: these men had heard about Ray's death and that his wake started tonight. Whether they'd known him or not, at least some were going to pay their respects, however briefly.

Because of the hour, most ate quickly, then headed out to walk to the funeral home, only a couple of blocks away.

"Isn't that something?" Claire murmured to her as they brushed past each other.

Haley nodded. It was the last thing she would have expected.

At last she made it to Buck's table. By this point her apron was showing signs of wear and a tickle at her neck told her some of her hair had escaped from the bun.

"The usual?" she asked him.

"Not tonight," he answered. "What do you recommend?"

"Anything," she answered promptly. "It's all good."

"Then surprise me." He smiled, but the expression didn't quite reach his eyes.

"Anything you don't like or can't eat?"

"I've never been picky."

"You're so helpful," she said tartly. "I'm a waitress,

not a wife. Pick something from the menu. I promise you'll like it."

So he pulled the plastic card from the holder. "You going to Ray's wake?" he asked casually as he scanned the menu.

"Tomorrow night. I'm surprised so many drivers are going."

"Yeah. They've been gabbing about it on the radio since it happened. It bothers them."

"I guess I can see that. Did many of them know him?"

"I don't know. But I do know it doesn't make any sense."

"When does it ever?"

He looked up and his eyes seemed to bore into her. "Something wrong?"

She caught herself, wondering why she was being so prickly. "Sorry." Then a thought occurred to her. "I took an allergy pill. I guess it's not agreeing with me."

He nodded, dropped his gaze to the menu and said, "I'll take the steak, medium rare, side of mashed potatoes and broccoli."

She scribbled it down then tried for a lighter note. "A man who eats broccoli. I hope Hasty can remember how to cook it."

"Nuke it for three if it's frozen," Buck said and winked. "Otherwise, I'll take it raw."

That drew a laugh from her and she felt some inexplicable tension seeping away. Maybe it was just from the unusual burst of traffic. She was used to one level of activity, but tonight had been almost double. Then there was her face burning up and the allergy pill. Enough to make her just a bit irritable.

Hasty remembered how to make the broccoli, of course. She carried the plates to Buck's table, refilled his coffee and went to take care of the remaining handful of drivers. In another half hour, the place had quieted almost to desolation, and, one by one, trucks started pulling out of the lot. She figured that might be the last of them for a while if they'd hurried to get here for the wake.

"Time for a smoke break," Hasty announced. "You gals take some time, too."

"I'm joining you," Claire said.

"You don't smoke," Haley remarked.

"I used to. And right now I want one."

Hasty eyed Haley. "You going to be okay?"

"Like I can't hold the fort for ten minutes?"

So the two of them headed out back. Which left her alone in the restaurant with Buck Devlin, who was taking his time with his steak.

"Join me," he suggested. "It wouldn't hurt to rest your feet."

She supposed it wouldn't. "Are you going to Ray's wake, too?" She glanced at her watch. If she remembered correctly, wakes ended at nine, and it was already past that.

"Tomorrow night," he answered.

All of a sudden everything zipped into clear focus. The faint fog left by the allergy pill was gone. Her heart even remembered how to speed up. "You're staying in town?"

"Over at the La-Z-Rest. I'm on vacation."

She almost gaped at him.

He caught the expression and his eyes danced a little. "What?"

"Why in the world would someone on vacation stay *here?*"

"Where would *you* go?"

"Any place. Denver. New York. Paris. Miami. I don't know. Some place with things to do."

"So you want action?"

"I wouldn't exactly put it like that," she admitted. "There's nothing wrong with this place. I like it. It just doesn't strike me as a vacation spot."

"That's because you live here. You can't see its charm."

A little laugh escaped her. "We roll up the sidewalks at nine, except for here and the roadhouses. You're going to get bored."

"I doubt it. It's quiet here. I like that. Plenty of nice places to walk. I like that, too, especially when I spend so much time driving."

She supposed she could see that. Maybe. "Well, if you're into hiking, there are some nice mountains."

"They probably look different when you're not behind the wheel of a heavy rig," he allowed.

"Well, I'll be interested to see how long you last. Most people who visit here wonder how we can stand it."

"What makes this place work for you?"

She thought about it. "People. Great people. There's something nice about knowing almost everyone. But that's not going to work for you."

"Maybe not. We'll see. It's sure some pretty countryside."

She looked down at the table and realized she didn't believe him. She was right, nobody picked this place for a vacation. Not even someone who was tired of driving. People who vacationed here—and there weren't a ton of them—came to camp up in the mountains and hike.

"So, looks like you got sunburned." He pushed his plate to one side.

Suddenly self-conscious, she put her hand to her cheek. "I wish. No, I had a dress rehearsal for a play I'm doing at school, and I discovered I'm allergic to the stage makeup."

A smile crooked one corner of his mouth. "I bet that's miserable. And you have to do it again? When's the play?"

"Friday and Saturday night."

"I ought to come to see you."

"I'm on stage for less than five minutes. You won't see much. But it *is* good play, a mystery. One of the students wrote it."

"I'll definitely come."

She laughed. "See, you're already looking for stuff to do around here. If you stay long enough, you'll go crazy." She started to get up as she saw another truck pulling in.

But Buck stopped her by reaching out and touching her hand. The contact felt almost like an electric spark, a zap that ran through her entire body. Before she could react, he'd withdrawn his touch. "I need to talk to you," he said. "About what happened to Ray. Not here, though."

For the first time, a real shiver of uneasiness ran through her. What was going on? And why should she trust this guy she didn't know? Was he some kind of stalker?

All of a sudden, she had major doubts about the kind of person Buck Devlin might be. About the danger he could represent.

"I don't think so," she said briskly and stood. "I don't see customers outside of work. Ever."

Then another driver came through the door, ending the conversation. For the first time, she was relieved to get away from Buck Devlin.

Haley felt a little silly for asking Hasty to walk her to her car. She didn't tell him why, but she also couldn't forget that Buck was in the motel just across the way. At least Hasty didn't ask any questions. Maybe he didn't think it unusual for a woman to get a little nervous from time to time about crossing that huge parking lot where almost anything could lurk.

And maybe it really wasn't. All kinds of strangers came through that lot, people with no roots and ties here. Maybe she should have been afraid all along of walking out there alone in the dark. She just wasn't used to thinking that way.

But Buck had made her think that way, and ever since she'd told him off, she'd been wondering if she had overreacted. He wasn't the first driver to make a suggestion and he wouldn't be the last. So what had set her off? Disappointment that he was no better? Or his reference to Ray?

She honestly wasn't sure. Overreaction, she decided finally. She was still upset that someone she knew had died, her face was a mess because of an allergic reaction, she'd taken a pill that had left her feeling off-kilter all night and then Buck had wanted to talk to her away from work.

Well, it wasn't the first time some driver had made that suggestion, but it was the first time she'd gone into hyperdrive over it.

Thinking back over it, she almost felt embarrassed. It wasn't as if he was a total stranger, in the sense that he'd been coming into the place for many months now. People knew who he was and who he worked for.

Now if it had been some guy she'd never seen before, that might have been reason to get upset.

Or maybe she had reacted oddly because he said he was vacationing here. At the ends of the earth. At a truck stop surrounded by a small town and a lot of wide-open spaces and distant ranches. Most definitely not a place on most people's vacation lists.

That, linked with Ray and Buck's interest in what

had happened in the parking lot before the accident, seemed odd.

But odd was not the same as evil. And maybe his company had asked him to check around. How would she know, since she hadn't given him a chance to explain anything?

Standing before her mirror, washing her face yet again and feeling some relief that most of the redness and swelling had gone down, she decided she had probably overreacted.

She didn't work tomorrow night, but she might run into him at Ray's wake, and if she did, she promised herself she was going to ask some questions.

Because the simple truth was, she didn't want to put Buck in the category he seemed to be sliding toward: just another creep. She didn't want to put him there at all.

Especially when she finally crawled exhausted into bed and realized that his face was floating in her mind's eye, and that all she could think about was what it might be like to feel his arms around her.

Stupid, but private, she thought as she drifted away. No one would ever know.

And she was too smart to get herself into trouble over a rolling stone.

The wake the next night was surprisingly crowded. Or maybe not, Haley thought as she stood to one side and watched a swirl of local people she knew and truckers she recognized. All spoke in the subdued voices that seemed to go with the solemn situation. Her mother's viewing had been less crowded.

People she had known at least by sight for most of her life. People who hadn't forgotten her mother or her through all those terrible years of illness, even though the two of them had gradually withdrawn from most so-cial contact.

Good people.

This was different, though, with those truckers coming and going in a fairly steady stream. She hadn't realized that they formed such strong bonds just from being on the road. But they were all drivers who'd been coming through Hasty's truck stop for a long time. Maybe they felt a link with this little town.

She was surprised, though, by how elaborate the funeral was. Her mother's had been much less so, simply because after her illness there were few resources left. She would have thought Ray's family would find it even harder. That looked like an awfully expensive casket, for one thing. And there was a ton of flowers. Plus, having a two-night viewing cost more. She'd had to shave it for her mother, having a relatively short wake right before the funeral.

"Hey," said a familiar voice, and she turned to see one of her high school friends, a girl named Debbie. "Sad about Ray, huh?"

"Very. I have to admit I hadn't seen him but once since high school, though."

"I had." Debbie shrugged. "He asked me out a few times in the last month."

"Oh, Debbie, you must be devastated!" Haley at once reached for her hand.

Debbie shook her head. "Not really. I didn't take him up on it. It was just kind of sad, though, because it sounded like things were really turning around for him. And for his family."

"Trucking's a good job."

Debbie shook her head, and her dark mane of hair swirled a bit. "No, it wasn't that. Apparently he was coming into some money from somewhere. I thought he was giving me a snow job so I'd go out with him. The Listons have never had two dimes."

"I know."

"So I didn't believe him. I figured he was trying to make himself sound important, you know?"

"I know."

"But maybe he wasn't lying." Debbie sighed. "I mean, look at this wake. You can't do this when you're broke. So maybe he got that money he was talking about."

"I hope so."

"Me, too." Debbie's smile was rather sad. "Well, I paid my respects, so I've got to get going. You need to poke your head up more often, Haley. It's been too long."

A couple more of her girlfriends stopped to chat with her, too, and a couple of guys who'd once wanted to date her but were now happily married to others of her friends.

Life seemed to have moved on during her mother's illness and left her a little behind. But that was okay. She was going to catch up. She was *already* catching up by going to school, setting her sights on her LPN and then her RN. After that, she'd have time to catch up in any other way she wanted.

When things quieted a bit, she made her way over to offer her condolences to Mr. and Mrs. Liston. She didn't know them well. Just as she hadn't known Ray well. It occurred to her for the first time that the Listons might have kept to themselves simply because they were so poor. Look at the way Ray had been treated and ignored in school. Maybe the same had happened to his parents. Maybe they'd never quite fit in larger social circles around here. The thought saddened her.

She avoided looking into the open casket as she approached Ray's parents. They appeared pinched and exhausted, almost worn to the bone by life. Dressed in their Sunday finest, which still looked outdated and thread-bare, they seemed overwhelmed by the number of people who had showed up.

Haley offered her hand to Mrs. Liston. "I'm so sorry about Ray. He came into the truck stop that night, just before…well, I was glad to see he had such a good job."

Mrs. Liston nodded. Mr. Liston, however, said, "He was a good boy, no matter what anyone thought."

"He was," Haley agreed. He'd never caused any trouble in school, and whatever scrape he'd gotten into right after graduation, she'd never learned the details.

"The cops don't think he was good," Mr. Liston said. "You saw him right before?"

Haley hesitated, wondering what he was seeking. "Yes, I did."

"They kept asking did he do drugs. My boy didn't do no drugs. Not ever."

"I believe you," Haley said quickly, although she had no way to know anything about what Ray might have done. "He seemed just fine right before his accident."

"You tell them cops that?"

"I did," she assured him. "I promise. He was just fine."

That seemed to ease Mr. Liston's mind a bit. She gave Mrs. Liston a brief hug then moved away, determined to get out of here.

Enough, she thought, her eyes starting to prickle un-wontedly. The smell of flowers, the peculiar odor of this funeral home, was starting to get to her. The last time… no, she didn't want to think about the last time, when she'd been the one standing there in Mrs. Liston's place, accepting condolences from kind people, few of whom would ever understand, not really, how much her mother's death hurt, or what a relief it was after all that suffering.

Of course, she heard all the platitudes, and they were all true, but none of them could possibly ease the pain and confusion. Not one.

She had become motherless at twenty-three, after a descent into hell that had lasted more than five years. Inside she'd felt hollowed out, except for the grief. No platitude for that.

She was almost at the door when she heard her name. "Haley."

She froze a moment, then turned reluctantly. Buck Devlin stood there, clad in a tan work shirt and jeans. He'd have looked out of place among all the locals dressed in their Sunday best if it hadn't been for the few remaining truckers.

"Buck," she said cautiously.

"I wanted to apologize. Can you give me a minute? Just a minute out front. Plenty of people, so you don't have to be scared."

He looked earnest enough, but that wasn't what grabbed her. *Scared?* She didn't like that. Maybe she had felt a momentary fear the night before, but she wasn't feeling it now. She wasn't a naturally scared sort of person, and it irritated her that he might think she was.

"Sure. Just a few minutes, though."

Outside, they stepped off the sidewalk a few paces so they wouldn't block the people who were coming and going. Dusk was just settling over the world.

She just looked at him, waiting, reluctant to give him an inch.

"I'm sorry I made you uneasy," he said. "So maybe I should explain a few things."

"That might help."

"For starters, I'm not exactly on vacation."

She folded her arms tightly beneath her breasts, her guard slamming into place. "So you're a liar?"

"No." He sighed and ran his fingers through his dark hair, cut high and tight, almost military style. "I'm on vacation in one sense. Legitimately. That's how my company has me listed right now."

"So what's the not exactly part?"

"My company also asked me to look into what happened to Ray and what might have been going on in your parking lot that night. We're having problems with shipments."

She looked at him, her jaw dropping. "I'm supposed to believe that? You're a truck driver, Buck Devlin. Why would they ask you?"

He glanced over his shoulder. "Could you hold it down? I don't want the whole world to know."

"That you're a storyteller? Got any more tall tales for me?"

"It's not a tall tale. Yes, I'm a driver now. But before that, I was a military cop. That's why the company asked me to look into this. They don't want to bring the feds in because it could kill business."

"Prove it," she said shortly. What kind of idiot did he take her for? Angry about being lied to, she stormed toward her car. Damn, he wasn't even a *good* liar.

"Haley."

She didn't stop. Not that it made any difference. He was beside her before she reached her car.

"Just listen," he said. "Please."

"I may be a small-town girl, but I'm not stupid. I think I've heard enough."

He caught her arm, and when she tried to pull free, he didn't let go. That made her even madder. "I'll scream."

"Dammit, Haley, just let me finish. My company's

been having problems with our shipments. You saw something happening with Ray's truck that night. You recognized him in the diner. You talked to him. Less than an hour later he's dead. If Ray's death wasn't an accident, then you're the proverbial loose end."

That froze her. Her ears buzzed and the world seemed to rock beneath her. Haley leaned against her car, waiting for it to settle down again. What the hell was going on?

"I'm sorry," he said. "But there's no easy way to tell you. Is there some place we can talk where you'll feel safe but half the town won't hear me?"

She might have laughed if she wasn't still feeling so shaken. Anger had turned to shock in an instant, and her brain was having trouble making the adjustment. "Around here? Anybody who wants a private conversation here has it at home." And that was the truth.

He let go of her arm. "Are you okay?"

"I will be. I always am." She knew that for a fact. Still leaning against her car, she closed her eyes and tried to take it all in. What if he wasn't lying? And what if what she had seen, or thought she had seen, had something to do with Ray's death? How many people knew? Two cops. Claire and Hasty. And that other driver she had never seen before, the one who had come in for coffee with Ray. The one who, now that she thought about it, had probably been driving the other truck when the cargo had been transferred. God!

She opened her eyes and saw Buck watching her with evident concern.

"I'm sure," he said, "you don't want to come to the La-Z-Rest with me. I'm equally certain you don't want me to know where you live. So where else will you feel safe while we talk?"

Haley nodded as her mind stopped reeling. The whole

town was going to be talking if she and Buck stood here any longer. "Do you know where the college campus is?"

"Yeah. I walked around some today."

"I'll see you there in fifteen minutes." She didn't offer him a ride. That would make people talk, too. But over on the college campus there were people who weren't local. A stranger wouldn't stick out and tongues wouldn't start wagging. "There are some benches in the center of the quad." And there'd still be plenty of students and faculty around at this hour, even if it was summer.

"Fifteen minutes," he agreed.

She drove off, glancing at him in her rearview mirror, and wondering what the heck she had just gotten into.

Buck had spent the day wandering. A need to know the physical territory was ingrained in him. He'd hit a surplus shop and found a decent pair of lace-up boots he could run in, and added some extra jeans and some shirts that would fit in around here, although he didn't go for anything approaching the perennially popular Western look. A ball cap suited him better than a cowboy hat, and he wasn't putting anything on his feet that might keep him from moving fast.

He could have run to the campus. In fact, he would have liked to run, it would have felt good, but he figured it would draw attention. A brisk walk would have to do, and he still arrived at the quad on campus before Haley.

He sat there on the bench, wondering if she would even show, or if he'd find himself talking to a couple of cops, explaining why he was harassing a nice local girl.

He wondered about it, but he didn't worry about it. He didn't worry about much, and he was fairly sure that even a superficial background check would reassure the cops. The stuff they'd never see, the stuff so deeply classified it would never see the light of day, was another story. But nobody could get at that.

So he waited, pondering how best to gain Haley's trust after having given her plenty of reason to think he was either crazy or a con man. He could see it from her point of view. Seeing things from other people's points of view was one of his gifts—and one of his curses.

She was right to be dubious, and he sure as hell hadn't given her a thing to reassure her. Wild story from a stranger. Great start.

But she showed up. He heard the car door slam and turned his head in time to see her coming his way.

She was still wearing the simple black dress she had worn at the funeral home and he couldn't resist giving her the once-over. Trim figure, shapely calves, delicate ankles. Even so modestly dressed she wouldn't ever fail to catch a man's attention. Much to his surprise, she carried two large cups of takeout coffee and when she reached him, she handed him one.

"Okay," she said as she sat on the bench beside him. A group of young men and women emerged from a building and started walking across the far side of the quad from them. Not long after, a smaller group appeared.

"I'm waiting," she reminded him.

"Somebody know you're here?"

"Of course."

"With me?"

"Yes."

He sighed. "I hope you trust whoever it is."

"More than I trust you right now."

"Just tell me you didn't tell them the whole story."

"Of course not! Sheesh, Buck, I don't believe it myself yet. It sounds like something out of a movie."

"I'll give you that." He put his coffee on the ground

beside his feet and pulled out his wallet. Opening it, he flipped out his military ID and his commercial driver's license. "The ID doesn't say much, but maybe it'll help."

She peered at the two laminated cards in the dim light from a nearby pole. "How can you still be military and drive a truck?"

"Ex-military. I have privileges because I was medically discharged. That card means I can use base facilities, like the exchange and the hospital."

"What happened?"

"That's a long story for another time. There's a more pressing matter."

Slowly she handed the cards back to him, but her eyes were on his face. "Buxton Devlin," she said slowly. "It looks real, I guess. But Buxton?"

."My mother's maiden name. She died having me and my dad named me for her. I guess he figured Mary wouldn't work."

Humor sparkled briefly across her face. "I guess it wouldn't."

"Anyway, Buxton became Buck real fast. My dad shortened it when I first started talking and couldn't get the whole thing out right. Good thing, too, since I was a military brat. It was easier navigating childhood as Buck."

"That probably would have been true almost anywhere." She paused, waiting. Okay, his name appeared to be real, but what else could she be sure of? A little childhood story hardly added up to a huge heap of truth.

He shoved his wallet into his jeans pocket and picked up his coffee. "This is hard."

"Why?"

"Because I'm not used to having to prove my credentials. I either worked solo, or with a group of other

MPs. Either way, I had a badge. Explaining this to someone who doesn't have any background…" He paused, then shrugged. "I'll try. Ask questions. I'll answer what I know."

"Okay." She was agreeable to that. Her eyes followed another group walking toward the little student union, hardly more than a coffee shop, but a great place to gather.

"Before I left Seattle on my last run, my boss asked me to keep my ear to the ground. It seems some shipments are getting messed up and they can't figure out how or why." He stopped. "Maybe I need to backtrack."

She just nodded and waited.

"We're pretty careful about what goes on our trucks. Drivers are supposed to be extra careful, because when we sign for a load, we're responsible for it until it reaches the next terminal or destination for off-load. You get that?"

"Perfectly." It seemed sensible to her.

"Okay. Well, everything that comes into the terminal for shipping is in crates or containers. Those are all labeled. Everything has a bar code. So we scan those labels every time we move anything around. When my truck gets loaded, I stand there, count crates, and every crate is scanned while it's being loaded. I have a manifest of what they said they were going to load, to compare to the scan of everything that goes on my truck. It covers my butt, and covers the company. So when I pull out of the terminal, I know my manifest matches exactly what's on the truck."

She nodded. "Makes sense."

"It does. And it works. Or it did until about four months ago. Then something started to go wrong. My boss said they couldn't find anything wrong at the terminal. No mismatched scans or anything. But somehow, by the time trucks arrived in Denver, the cargoes had changed. Some crates arrived late and on different trucks. And it's getting more frequent."

Suddenly she understood. "What I saw in the lot!"

"Maybe. Bill, my boss, figured something had to be happening along the road, and he asked me to keep an eye out because I used to be an MP."

"Why not just call the authorities?"

"Because we'd have a federal investigation. Inter-state commerce and all that. The head honchos are afraid they'd shut us down by opening and searching every crate going in and out of our Seattle terminal. It would kill business. So he doesn't want to do that if we can solve the problem ourselves. I guess he figures that if I can nail something down, we can put the authorities on the right track without sacrificing all our business."

She sipped coffee, noting that her hand had started to shake a little. It matched the uneasy fluttering in her stomach. "It just got bigger, didn't it? Ray, I mean."

"I'm seriously wondering about that. I could drive that stretch of road blindfolded. No reason for a truck to roll. Or for a driver to be dead."

She had to put her coffee down as her heart started to climb into her throat. "What do you want from me?"

"I want two things. The first is to keep an eye on you, because you might have seen the very kind of cargo switch I was supposed to be looking out for. A few people already know what you saw. I'm worried about you. That's why I told you not to say any more about it. Maybe word won't get around, but I can't be sure."

"What else?" Her voice sounded a little thin even to her.

"Give me cover. People are going to start wondering why I'm hanging around. Like you said, this isn't a dream vacation spot. So let me hang around, doing the lovesick-puppy thing. I'll ask you out. You can keep saying no. I'll look like a fool, but not in a way that arouses any suspicion. In the meantime…"

She turned to face him. "Yes? In the meantime what?"

"Well, you can let me know if you hear or see anything. Just me. I'm going to keep a pretty close eye on that truck stop, but there are other things. For example, the Liston family got an anonymous donation for that fancy funeral."

Haley gasped. "I wondered. Oh, man, I wondered. They've never had any money, and I know how much I had to cut back on my own mother's funeral last year. I looked at that… Do you know how much it costs to have a two-night wake? Or a coffin like that?"

"Thousands."

"More than a few thousand. How did you find out they got a donation?"

"I heard somebody talking."

"Well, I heard somebody talking, too. Apparently Ray had been telling at least one person that he was about to come into some money."

"Money." He almost spat the word. "Well, that would tend to confirm it."

"Confirm what?"

"Where there's a lot of money, there's a lot of danger. Money and power are the two biggest corruptors, and when either gets involved, lives don't seem to matter. I just wonder why they contributed to the funeral. Can't be much conscience in somebody who would kill to keep a secret."

"But folks around here do stuff like that. People would have chipped in so the Listons could bury Ray. They would have." She remembered the offers she had received to help pay for her mother's expenses. Offers she had been able to turn down because she had just enough. "Maybe that's all it was, folks chipping in."

"Maybe. But then you have Ray talking about coming into money."

She didn't like the way this was making her feel. She looked around at the familiar quad, in darkness now, and realized her world had shifted hugely. Would she ever see her friendly little town in quite the same way again? She suddenly experienced the most childish urge to close her eyes, as if that would make it go away. Like hiding under the bedcovers when you thought a monster was in the closet. How much protection did refusing to see give you? Zip, she thought unhappily.

One of her neighbors might be involved in something so ugly he was willing to kill. She shuddered. "I don't want any part of this."

"I don't think you get the choice anymore. You saw something. If the wrong person knows…"

She didn't need him to finish the thought. Another shiver ran through her and she leaned over to throw her coffee into the trash can at the end of the bench. Then she wrapped her arms tightly around herself and looked out at the alien world she had just landed in. If the wrong person knew. She had no idea who the wrong person might be. The Listons, who had asked her if she'd told the police that Ray had seemed fine? Claire or Hasty, who had heard what she told Micah and Sarah when they came in to ask questions? No. She couldn't believe any of them could mean her any harm.

"Haley…" All of sudden, strong arms wrapped around her, hauling her close. She should have resisted, but that embrace felt so good, and those arms felt so strong and

protective. It had been way, way too long since anyone
had hugged her, and her throat tightened as she realized
how much she had missed that kind of comfort. So much,
evidently, that it felt good even from a stranger.

"I won't let anything happen to you," he murmured.
"That much I can swear. Not one bad thing is going to
happen to you."

"You can't promise that," she said weakly into his
shoulder. "Nobody can." Life had certainly taught her
that lesson the hard way.

"I can. It used to be my job. Nobody's going to hurt
you. They'll have to get through me first."

"Why? Why do you care?"

"Because I do. Some things I just care about. You're
at the top of my list right now. Besides," he added in an
evident attempt to lighten the moment, "I've had my eye
on you for months. You're a temptation, woman."

A feeble laugh escaped her. "Is that supposed to make
me feel better?"

He moved her back so that his dark eyes stared straight
into hers. "It should. It's been a long time since I had any
desire to camp on a woman's doorstep."

The words left her speechless. She could see he meant
them by the look in his eyes, and sexual heat began to
drizzle through her until it pooled achingly between her
thighs. Rationally she knew her reaction was foolish, but
rationality had nothing to do with it. She'd been noticing this man for months, even daydreaming about him
in ways she hadn't daydreamed about anyone since high
school. Every time she saw him, she felt that same pull,
that same desire for something to happen between them.

Now something was happening, and it was not at all
what she'd imagined. Almost unconsciously, she clamped
her thighs together, wishing she wasn't abruptly aware

that every breath she took made her shirt slide over nipples that were suddenly sensitive even through her bra. She made herself look away from him, trying to get her grounding. Trying to think sensibly. Trying to regain her self-control.

As soon as she looked away, his arms dropped from her. The loss of his touch was almost enough to draw an incautious protest from her. She bit it back. There were more important things. This man had just told her she might be in danger. She couldn't afford to lose sight of that.

"This is hard to take in," she said after a minute.

"It's not the usual way of looking at things," he admitted. "And I could be wrong about you being in any danger. God willing, I am. I just don't want to risk it."

That was reasonable, she supposed. She tried to shake off the feeling that the deepening shadows around her might hold a threat. God, she wasn't used to thinking this way. Life had dealt her its blows right out in the open.

And now here she was, putting in place the first building blocks of a future, and some guy came virtually out of nowhere to tell her that she might wind up like Ray? All because she had glimpsed something in the truck-stop parking lot?

Deal! Her brain almost barked the order at her, and she stiffened. If she could say nothing else about herself, if there was one thing she knew about herself for certain, it was that she dealt with life's curveballs. All of them.

She sat up straighter, drew a breath and thought, *All right. This is how it is.* Now what was she to do about it?

There was one thing she knew instantly, of course. "Well, you've successfully made me afraid to go home alone."

"I'm sorry. Like I said, I'm not sure you're at risk. But

equally, I can't be sure you're not. You saw something that nobody was supposed to see. You saw the driver of the other truck, right?"

"Yes. He came in for coffee, too."

"And you saw the transfer of cargo."

"I *think* I did. It's not easy to see that parking lot clearly from inside the restaurant at night."

"But you mentioned it. Others may have mentioned it after they heard what you told the police. Regardless, if I was that other driver, I'd be feeling a bit edgy. You could identify him. Maybe you could describe his truck. He might lie low and wait, but then again, killing Ray seems awfully stupid to me. If you want a quiet operation, you don't draw attention to it by murder."

She looked straight at him. "Do you think Ray was killed because of *me?*" The thought made her heart quail.

"Actually, no. I suspect Ray had irritated them in some other way. Maybe by talking about coming into some money. Something made them think he was a liability. But again, that's my guess. I'm not even going to be sure of that until I see the accident reports."

"How will you do that?"

"I'm going to talk to the cops in a few days."

He couldn't have said anything more likely to make her believe he was exactly what he said he was. "Why would they talk to you?"

"Because I'm here on behalf of my company. And they're going to do a background check on me and find out I used to be a cop just like them. They'll talk."

She nodded, believing it. Cops were a tight bunch.

"As for your apartment…if you don't mind me knowing where you live, I'll go home with you and check it out. Then I'll leave and you can rest comfortably."

She sat quietly, common sense battling with more

primitive needs. She liked this man. She liked his attention, but what did she really know about him? She'd seen couple of IDs, but she had no way of knowing if they were real.

For all she knew, this was flimflam, and she didn't have any means of checking it out. So...did she want him to know where she lived? Heck, the way he had glommed on to her might put him squarely on the side of the wrongdoers. If there *were* any wrongdoers. She couldn't even know that for certain.

All she knew was that he seemed determined to frighten her and then set himself up as her savior. When she thought of it that way, her internal alerts started to go off.

"No, thanks," she said, standing. "Don't follow me."

There were other ways of dealing with all of this, but none of them involved inviting Buck Devlin any further into her life. As for going home alone, she did that every night, and she'd never been afraid until this man had suggested it.

All of a sudden she didn't like him.

Turning on her heel, she walked to the car, leaving him sitting on the bench behind her. Something smelled fishy, and when things smelled fishy it was best to stay away.

Chapter 3

Buck watched Haley walk away, feeling something between frustration and genuine concern. He couldn't blame her for her response. It *did* sound like something out of as movie, and something for which he was willing to bet life in this town hadn't prepared her.

On the other hand, his life experience had taught him to be suspicious by nature. If things didn't fit, if things weren't orderly, then something was going on. Sometimes it wasn't a big deal. All too frequently it had been. And noticing those out-of-kilter things had often been his biggest guide to solving a crime.

He'd come on this trip expecting to find out absolutely nothing at all. He'd figured it would be a while before he learned something about what was happening with those shipments, if he heard anything at all. Instead it had practically landed in his lap because of an observant waitress. Follow that with a dead driver who'd been seen doing something squirrelly with another truck, and his internal klaxon had become deafening.

But how did he explain that to someone else? Especially someone like Haley, who had no idea that long-haul trucks shouldn't be trading loads in a truck stop in Nowhere, Wyoming, or that a driver might be killed because of it. Who wouldn't even begin to understand the dimensions of shipments disappearing and reappearing.

It was an alien world to her.

Then, of course, he must seem like the next best thing to a drifter to her. Rootless, wandering, a total unknown who had just approached her with the wildest story imaginable. She was just being smart, by her lights.

Maybe she was right. Maybe nothing threatened her at all. Maybe he looked like a bigger threat than having half seen something through the window of the diner.

He'd certainly come on pretty strong and from somewhere out in the stratosphere, given the world she knew.

He sighed and rose, heading back to the motel. So, okay. He couldn't ignore his instincts. He couldn't be sure that Haley was at risk, but he couldn't be sure that she wasn't. That didn't leave him any really good options, except to do his best to keep an eye on her from a distance without worrying her.

In the meantime, he had to wait a few days before he went to the local cops to get the result of their accident investigation. He wanted autopsy results. He wanted toxicology results. Those took time.

For now he just had to remain on alert for anything that seemed odd.

Like a very expensive funeral, paid for by an anonymous donor, for a guy who'd been bragging that he was about to come into some money.

As he was walking along quiet, darkening streets, he

thought about that funeral. A large donation struck him as a bit obvious for someone who wanted a quiet operation.

But maybe it had bought some silence. Maybe the Listons were up to their necks in this.

If they were, he had to find out.

He realized as he strode the quiet, tree-lined streets that he'd resumed more than the mantle of his old job; he'd resumed its habits. As if he'd never let go of them, his vigilance heightened, his eyes scouring every shadow and cranny, his ears listening for anything unusual.

Tension ran along his nerve endings, more out of habit than real necessity at this point. No one other than his bosses had any idea why he was hanging out here, and to the casual observer it must appear he had his eye on Haley.

Well, hell, he did. Not that that was going anywhere, but he was an ordinary man and like any other guy he couldn't avoid being attracted to a woman like her. He'd seen enough other truckers noticing her in the same way.

He wondered if he should have just kept his mouth shut, left Haley out of his suspicions, made himself a bit obnoxious by seeming to be interested in her without telling her why. It would have been an easy enough role to play.

But he didn't want to scare her by acting like a stalker, although maybe that's what he had done anyway.

Losing his touch, he thought. Or maybe it was one he'd never really had. Dealing with soldiers was a whole different ball game, requiring a very different approach. His touch with women hadn't won him any high marks, either.

As he neared the motel, though, he knew the game was about to change, for good or ill. There was a squad car parked near his unit, lights off, motor off, and occupied by a large deputy.

He took care to make some noise, make his approach overt. He'd never taken kindly himself to someone coming upon him without warning.

As he neared the car, the big deputy he'd seen the night before last climbed out. "Got a minute?" the big man asked as Buck neared.

"Sure. Want to come inside or talk out here?"

"Inside. A little privacy is a good thing."

"That seems to be a major concern around here." Buck pulled out his key and threw the door open, flipping on the lights. He was careful to step inside, keeping his hands in the open, then stand away from any possible weapon and wait.

The deputy looked around, taking in the duffel, the freshly made bed, the absence of any other personal belongings.

Then he regarded Buck from head to foot, as if measuring him. Buck returned the look. Some things were second nature. The deputy might have a few pounds on him, and an inch or two in height, but at thirty-four he had at least a couple of decades on the deputy. He noted, though, that the man hadn't felt the need to unsnap the holster on the nine-millimeter pistol hanging from his utility belt. For the moment, this was a friendly visit.

The big man stuck out his head. "Micah Parish."

Buck shook it. "Buck Devlin."

"Mind if I sit?"

"Help yourself." Since there was only one chair, Parish took it and Buck settled on the edge of the bed.

"We're a friendly town, Mr. Devlin," Parish said.

"I get that feeling."

"Not many folks around. We kinda keep an eye on each other."

Buck figured he knew where this was leading, but he didn't try to head it off. Let the man have his say.

"Someone said you seemed to be having a bit of a disagreement with Haley Martin outside the funeral home."

"It probably looked that way."

Micah's eyebrow lifted. "So what way was it?"

"I was trying to explain something to her."

"Is that what she would tell me?"

"I honestly don't know what she would tell you at this point. I'm fairly certain she thinks I'm a nut or a liar right now."

One corner of Micah's mouth hitched up, but it wasn't with humor. "Would she be right?"

"By her lights."

Micah's mouth tightened into a straight line. "Quit fencing with me unless you want to be escorted out of town in the next hour."

Buck hesitated. It went against the grain to let anybody in on his investigations before he was ready, but he decided to let the cat out and see where it went.

"Wallet," he said, so Micah wouldn't think he was reaching for a weapon, then dug into his pocket. He drew out both his IDs and turned them over.

Micah scanned them. "So you're a truck driver and disabled vet. Neither one is necessarily a recommendation."

"No. But maybe Army Third Military Police Group, Tenth Battalion will help."

Micah's brow furrowed, his dark eyes searching Buck's face. "Tenth Battalion. Criminal investigation division. I know what you guys do. The only question is what you're doing here. This card says you're medically retired."

"I am. My boss asked me to look into something for him. My misfortune to be the only former MP he has working for him."

Micah tapped the two laminated cards against his knee. "Mind if I keep these for a few hours? I want to run a background."

"Help yourself."

Micah slipped the IDs into his breast pocket. "Tell me what you think is going on in my town and just how Haley fits in. That girl's had enough trouble in her life. You bringing her more?"

"Actually, I'm suffering from a white-knight complex. I'm hoping to keep her from getting into more trouble."

"That's not helpful, Mr. Devlin. Is there some reason you don't want to talk to me?"

"How about that I don't know who is involved?"

Micah stiffened at that. "Maybe you should come to the office with me. I think our sheriff might want to talk to you, too."

Buck rose to his feet. "Let's go. I'd like to meet your sheriff. Then maybe you two can tell me enough about yourselves that I know I can trust *you*."

Micah's frown deepened. "You'll ride in the cage," he said flatly.

"Fine by me. I'd rather look like a criminal than your cohort right now."

Micah wasn't exactly gentle as he put Buck in the back of his vehicle. Which was fine by Buck.

If anybody was paying attention, and they might be since his hanging out here was apparently suspicious enough to garner legal attention, they'd think he was in trouble.

Right then, that's just how he wanted it.

Miles away, in a living room that looked ancient in every way, Mr. and Mrs. Liston sat in their usual chairs, hands linked, still wearing their best clothes. Mrs. Liston was crying quietly, but her husband looked almost empty.

Across from them sat their eldest son, Jim. He had arrived only a few hours ago from Los Angeles. Until just a few months ago, he'd pretty much disappeared from their lives, much as Ray had, and they couldn't understand it. But at least he was coming home again. For the past half year or so they'd seen him every few weeks. In a way they were grateful to him, because he'd helped Ray find that trucking job.

But now Ray was dead.

"I'm so sorry," he said yet again. He sat there looking fine in his expensive clothes, and the corners of his mouth drooped.

"We're all sorry, son," Mrs. Liston finally said. "You know your brother was a good boy."

"I know. We kept in touch, obviously. But you say the cops are asking about drugs?"

Both the elder Listons nodded.

"It was just a terrible accident," Jim said soothingly. "Ray hadn't been driving that long. I'm sure that's what they'll find out."

Mr. Liston spoke. "He didn't do no drugs. I know that much. And that Martin girl said the same thing."

"What Martin girl?"

"Haley Martin. Works at the truck stop. She saw Ray just before…she said he was fine. Just fine. She don't believe it was no drugs, either."

"I'm sure it wasn't," Jim said firmly. "I'm positive. Ray wouldn't do that."

"No," Mr. Liston agreed. "No. Not my boy."

Mrs. Liston wiped away her tears. "I'm gonna go get in my nightclothes. Then I'll make us all some Ovaltine." It had always been her soothing solution to everything. No one disagreed with her. Her husband went with her to change clothes.

Jim sat where he was, then as soon as he heard them reach their bedroom, he stepped outside and pulled out his cell phone. The signal was almost nonexistent, but he got through. The call was brief; he said very little.

But he did mention Haley Martin.

The sheriff's office was located in a storefront on a corner across the street from the courthouse square, a bit of eastern charm transplanted to the West. Inside, the dispatcher's desk was surrounded by other desks apparently for use by deputies. Each desk boasted a relatively new computer, all of which looked out of place on desks that were at least thirty years old, maybe older. Wooden floors creaked with every step.

A young deputy sat at the dispatcher's desk, sipping coffee and looking bored behind a console that would have done a big-city operation proud.

Micah pointed Buck to a chair next to one of the desks. "Wait there." Then he crossed to the dispatcher.

"Get Gage in here. I need him. Then run these IDs." He pulled out Buck's IDs and tossed them on the dispatcher's desk. "I want everything you can find, and then you're going to forget all of this unless I say otherwise."

Evidently, Buck thought with mild amusement, gossip could be a problem in this office, too.

"Who made the coffee?" Micah asked.

"I did," answered the young deputy, whose name tag said he was Rankin. "It's not lethal."

Micah glanced at Buck. "Coffee?"

"Black, please." Evidently they hadn't gotten past being courteous, always a good sign.

Micah brought two mugs over to the desk, handing one to Buck. "Getting decent coffee around here is a trial. Our day dispatcher, Velma, turns it into battery acid. Nobody has the heart to tell her to stop making it."

"I'm used to stuff you can stand a spoon in."

"Then you might like Velma's brew."

Silence fell. A call had been put out, but then the radio grew quiet. The only sound was Rankin tapping busily away, looking into Buck's background.

"Do you really need a night shift around here?" Buck asked eventually. Not that he was opposed to silence, but a little friendly conversation seemed in order. He wanted these guys to cooperate, if possible, but at the very least not to get into his way. Unless they turned out to be part of the problem.

"We have roadhouses," Micah said, as if that explained it all. It probably did. "You must have broken up a few drunken brawls in your day."

"Plenty."

"Cowboys coming in off the range are pretty much like soldiers on a pass. These days, cowboys aren't often on the range."

"Times are bad everywhere."

Micah nodded. "Not getting any better, either. Too many folks trying to drown their sorrows."

The sheriff arrived in about fifteen minutes. A man who appeared to be somewhere in his late fifties, with a burn-scarred face and visible limp, entered the office wearing a light jacket, jeans and his badge clipped to his belt.

He paused, looked at Buck. "What's up?"

"Well, that's what I'm trying to find out," Micah said. "Got a complaint from someone that this guy seemed to be bothering Haley Martin. According to him he wasn't bothering her."

"Have you talked to Haley?"

"Not until I figure out what's going on here. Rankin's pulling his background right now."

"And you needed me for?"

"Well, I thought you and me together in a quiet office might get a little further. I get the feeling there's something we need to know."

There were a couple of ways to take that, but Buck decided to take it favorably until he had reason to think otherwise.

That was when Rankin looked up. "Holy cow," he said.

"What?" the sheriff asked.

"This guy's for real. I mean, really real."

"Would you like to explain that?"

"You want the list of medals or the job description?"

The sheriff took a printout from Rankin and led the way to an office in the back. Buck followed with his coffee, waiting to see how this played out. Every muscle in his body was coiled and ready. He'd seen corruption in local law enforcement before, and trust wasn't his strong suit.

For now, though, everything seemed on the up-and-up. The sheriff's office was small. The nameplate on his desk, identifying him as Gage Dalton, Sheriff, looked as if it had taken more than one tumble to the floor. A computer filled one corner of the desk and a stack of papers the other.

Gage sat behind it, and Micah and Buck took up the two chairs facing it, while Gage scanned the printout. A moment later he handed Buck's IDs back to him.

"Okay," he said. "You're former CID. Plenty of commendations. Plenty of blanks, too."

Buck said nothing.

"Being former DEA myself, I know about those blanks. They don't worry me much. So maybe you'd like to explain to Micah and me why someone would think you're harassing Haley Martin and what you're doing hanging around in my town."

Buck hesitated a moment longer, glancing toward Micah.

"SF," Micah said, referring to Special Forces. "Retired."

"I wanted to scope things out a bit more before I came to you," Buck said frankly. "I don't know much about what's going on right now, but something is, and I wanted to have some feel for who might be involved before I go shooting off my mouth."

"It looks like the time for that is past," Gage said bluntly. "You're the stranger here, and you just got some unwanted attention. We can make your life easy or hard. Your choice."

"I'm worried about Haley," Buck said. "Among other things."

"Why would you be worrying about somebody you hardly know?"

"Good question. I asked myself that same thing. It remains, I'm worried anyway. Old instincts die hard."

"So explain," Gage said.

Buck explained. He gave them his boss Bill's name, he told them about the shipment problem, he pointed out that Haley had seen something unusual in the parking lot, that Ray shouldn't be dead, and that he was seriously concerned that something was happening here that could endanger her if someone thought she knew too much.

"You could have just told us to keep an eye on her," Micah pointed out.

"Sure. And then everyone would know the cops smelled something wrong and I might never find out what's happening with those shipments."

"Are you sure you're not just dragging her in deeper?"

"Nobody knows I'm investigating except my bosses. Everyone would think I was just hanging around because of Haley. At least that was the plan. A lot of guys would hang around because of her."

"So she's your cover."

"Yes. And I tried to reassure her about it, but that didn't seem to work. Which I can understand. But I tried. I didn't want her to think I was *actually* stalking her."

"Backfire," Micah remarked.

"Clearly," Buck agreed.

Gage drummed his fingers on the desktop. "Apart from this being totally unconventional, was your master plan to follow Haley around until you figure something out?"

"Well, I need an excuse to hang around until the next irregularity occurs. Then I'll follow the second truck to see where it's going. If I can. At the very least, I have to confirm that shipments are being switched here. That's my official task. What happens after that…" He shrugged. "Let's just say I might want to know where the other truck is going."

At that Gage leaned forward. "If you find out, you're going to let us know. Right? You're not going to take the law into your own hands. Not here."

"I'm not allowed to anymore. I get it. But as everyone keeps pointing out to me, this is a small, tight-knit community. How many people around here don't know every single one of your deputies by sight?"

Gage and Micah exchanged looks.

"He's got a point," Micah remarked.

"He damn well does." Gage leaned back, grimacing faintly. "I'll agree on one point, Mr. Devlin—"

"Buck."

"Buck. Okay. I'm Gage. I agree with you on one thing. This seems like an awful lot of trouble to go to unless something illicit is being shipped in some of those containers. Illicit and worth considerable money. There's no point in it otherwise. And maybe you're right about Ray talking a little too much about coming into some money. Around here that would get attention."

"So did his anonymously-paid-for funeral."

Gage disagreed. "That doesn't fit with the rest of the story."

"Unless the Listons are in on this somehow."

"It's possible," Gage said after brief reflection. "That family has been dirt poor forever. They might be willing to do almost anything to make ends meet." Then he shook his head. "Only one problem. In all their lives, they've never done one thing wrong."

"Except for that scrape Ray got in right after he graduated," Micah said.

"Alcohol and tough words don't mix well," Gage remarked. "I've seen worse sins in my day. He paid for it."

From Buck's perspective, it was interesting to hear how well these lawmen knew the people of this area. He'd almost never had that advantage in the army. "So," he asked slowly, "who might be up to something?"

"That's the question, isn't it?" Gage regarded him thoughtfully. "All right. When can I call your boss?"

Buck looked at his watch. "Right now if you want. He's on until midnight Pacific time. Ask for Bill Grayson." He recited the phone number and Gage scribbled it down.

Gage called, waited a few minutes, then started speaking to Bill. From Buck's perspective, it was interesting.

"Your employee didn't have much choice, Mr. Grayson. Strangers around here get a lot of attention. We're a small town. We wanted to know why a truck driver was hanging around. This isn't exactly a vacation destination. He's sitting in my office right now. Yes. No, we're not getting directly involved in what he's doing. It might create more problems. Yes. I'll tell him."

Gage hung up. "That's one upset man."

"He wants this quiet so the company doesn't lose business. It hardly looks good for a trucking company to keep messing up its manifests."

"Doesn't look good at all." Gage sighed. "Okay, you're legit. I see two problems here. First, you stick out like a sore thumb. Second, you're right, if *we* start doing anything different, half the county will be wondering what's going on within a day or two. So I'm going to give you free rein. Within the law, that is. As for Haley..."

Buck waited while Gage frowned. "Why couldn't you have picked someone else?"

"Like I said, it's Haley I'm worried about. Micah knows she reported that something was going on in that parking lot that night. So two deputies and at least two other people know what she thought she saw—the guy everyone calls Hasty, and the other waitress. I gather folks around here talk about nearly everything."

"The downside of a small town," Gage remarked. "If you want to know what you're doing, ask a neighbor."

That surprised a laugh from Buck. "That bad?"

"Damn near. On the other hand, nosiness doesn't keep people from hiding things they want to hide. It just makes them a damn sight more cautious." He looked at Micah. "If Buck here is right, these folks are willing to kill."

"We won't know that until the reports are back."

"No, but can we afford to take the chance? So I guess we'd better let Haley know Buck is okay. She can decide how much she wants to trust him or help him." Then his gaze returned to Buck, as strong as laser beams. "You be careful of that girl, hear? She's strong, but there's a part of her that's fragile. No hanky-panky with her. No leading her on. You're here for a few days or weeks, and I don't want to see any broken hearts."

"That's not on my agenda. At all."

Gage continued to study him. "Why do I get the feeling you like to give people a hard time?"

"I've heard that before." And damned if he was going to apologize for it.

"I bet you have." A lopsided smile appeared on Gage's scarred face. "You know you're at a disadvantage. Being an outsider, nobody around here is going to tell you much."

"I'm used to that."

"I'll bet," said Micah. He looked at Gage. "If you think a stranger investigating around here is going to be tough, watch an MP looking into a unit of Rangers. You'd think they all became instantly deaf, dumb and blind."

At that Gage cracked a laugh. "Okay. I'll call Haley and tell her you check out. But that's all I'm going to tell her. I want her to sleep easy. Other than that, it's all her decision. If I hear you pushed her even a little, you're on your way out."

Buck could live with that. He just hoped he hadn't tipped his hand to the wrong people. Given the way these cops seemed to know about every little thing around here, he had to wonder how they could be unaware of whatever was happening at the truck stop.

It didn't leave him feeling easy at all as he walked back to the motel.

Haley didn't exactly feel nervous when she got home. Buck hadn't tried to follow her, and she was still torn between believing him and thinking he was some kind of nut. What he said made a certain sense, and in her heart of hearts she found it hard to believe that Ray had rolled his truck on that stretch of road unless something major had happened. Then there was that shadowy exchange in the parking lot, which might or might not be weird. What did she know about the trucking business, after all? Maybe it had been a delivery for some place near here. That struck her as far more likely than that someone was doing something wrong.

But then there was Buck's story of mixed-up shipments. That sounded even stranger, but she had to admit it had an element of plausibility to it. The things he'd said about money...

She sighed after she finished brushing her teeth, then climbed into sweats for sleeping. Summer nights sometimes turned cool around here, and this one was cooling a lot. She didn't want to turn on the heat because she needed to save money.

Padding around in slipper socks, she went to get her nightly glass of milk. She didn't care for it warm, so despite the night's chill she drank it cold.

Well, if she had anything to be grateful for, it was that Buck hadn't dumped his story on her earlier in the day. At least she had finished studying for the exam tomorrow morning. She looked at her nutrition books, piled on her cheap little desk beside a lamp, and decided enough was enough. She needed to get some sleep, needed to calm her mind down.

She paused to look at a framed photo of her mother, one taken before illness had robbed her beauty, and found herself thinking about the costs of funerals. How *had* the Listons afforded all of that? Even if the entire county had chipped in a dollar per family, it wouldn't have covered that coffin.

There she went again, pondering matters that had no answers. It occurred to her to be sorry she had ever talked to Buck Devlin at all. Before he had entered her life, things had seemed so generally uncomplicated. At least since her mother's passing. She needed some calm and stability after those long years of riding the cancer roller coaster with her mother. She *wanted* her life to be calm and even dull. For a while.

She knew life had been bound to knock her out of her quiet little pond at some point. She might be young in some respects, but she figured she was pretty old in others. Old enough to know that smooth sailing was the exception rather than the rule.

Sitting in her mother's old armchair, she sipped her milk and tried to absorb all her conflicting feelings about Buck Devlin. At some point, she realized she wanted to believe him, but was afraid to.

Interesting. She wanted to believe there was some illegal activity going on in the parking lot at Hasty's and that Buck was seriously investigating it? That she might be in danger because she had glimpsed something she could barely make out through a window that had acted more like a mirror?

That Ray had been murdered?

That wasn't a world she wanted to live in. But much

of her life had been a world she hadn't wanted, and that was probably true for most people.

She sighed, finished her milk and headed to the kitchen to rinse the glass, wondering if her attraction to Buck Devlin wasn't screwing up her thinking. Claire's warning drifted back to her. Yeah, he was a rolling stone, here today and gone tomorrow. That alone should make her wary.

Then the phone rang. It startled her because she wasn't used to having late-night calls. There'd been a time when such calls meant that her mother had taken a bad turn in the hospital.

It was over now, but the dread of late-night phone calls remained. Her heart started hammering as she reached for the receiver as if it were a poisonous snake.

"Hello?"

"Haley, this is Gage Dalton."

That made her stomach lurch. Immediately her mind started scrambling for ideas of what might have gone wrong to make the sheriff call her at such an hour.

"I just wanted you to know," he said, "we had a complaint tonight that a truck driver, Buck Devlin, was harassing you at the funeral home."

Haley felt her stomach sink. She hadn't wanted this, no matter what. He might be what he said he was, or he might be a nut, but he hadn't hurt her. He hadn't even scared her enough to get the police involved. "Not really," she managed to say.

"I'm not saying he did. I'm just letting you know we had a report so we checked into him."

She caught her breath. "And?"

"He's exactly what he says he is and is doing exactly what he told you he's doing. I'll leave it to you to decide whether to get involved with him. But I don't think you need to fear him."

That slight emphasis on *him* left her wondering if Gage thought she had something else to fear, but if he had, wouldn't he have said so?

All of a sudden she didn't want to be alone. All of a sudden, despite the milk, she felt wide awake. Great. That was going to help on her test in the morning.

Regardless, she pulled on a bra under her sweat suit, tugged on her jogging shoes, grabbed her purse and headed for the truck stop.

She needed bright light, the swirl of people around her and some carbs to calm her down. At that moment nothing sounded better than a piece of Hasty's cobbler and a bit of sensible talk with Claire.

As it happened, the place was pretty busy when she arrived. Claire and another waitress, Meg, were busy enough they could have used some help. Haley considered clocking in and digging a spare uniform out of her locker, but Hasty stopped her.

"You're supposed to be resting, what with that test tomorrow and the play the next two nights. What in the world are you doing here?"

"I was called by your cobbler."

He unleashed one of his rolling laughs and promptly dished her up a serving big enough for two. "Coffee?"

"Milk, please."

She would have settled at the counter except that a table near the window emptied. She headed straight for it and closed her eyes for a few moments as she savored the first mouthful of peach perfection.

She opened her eyes again and studied the lot. The window really did act almost like a mirror. She could choose either to see what was going on around her in the restaurant, or to pick out the shadowy movements in the lot. And they *were* shadowy, until headlights came on.

So how could she be sure of what she had seen the other night? Staring out there now, she decided she really couldn't have seen anything, that her mind had probably manufactured the whole impression to explain sounds and shadowy movement. More, nobody except people she trusted knew she might have seen anything.

She really didn't have anything to worry about.

"Hi, hon." Claire slid into a seat across from her and Haley was startled to realize that she had apparently wandered so far away in her thoughts that she hadn't noticed the place emptying out. The revving of engines and the bloom of headlights from the lot announced that the wave was moving on.

"Hi, Claire," Haley answered.

"You're supposed to be tucked in at home, resting for your big day tomorrow. Not taking a busman's holiday here."

"Maybe I'm nervous. All of a sudden I was wide awake," Haley said.

"This is your first play, huh?"

"Yeah. I didn't even do it in high school. It's only a few minutes onstage, but those minutes seem to keep getting bigger."

Claire laughed. "I felt that way about my first wedding. Two lousy words, and I kept wondering if I'd be able to get them out. Maybe I should have listened to the cold feet."

The last two drivers left and Meg cleared the tables. Then she announced she was going out for a smoke. Hasty went with her, which left Claire and Haley alone in the empty restaurant.

"That Devlin guy is back in town," Claire said. She reached for a paper straw, pulled the wrap off it and began to fold it like an accordion. "Says he's on vacation. Does that make sense to you?"

"I saw him," Haley said cautiously.

Claire looked up. "Aha! I thought you might be the reason he was hanging around." There was a glint in her eye.

Haley didn't know how to answer that. It was certainly what Buck had claimed he wanted people to think. "I don't know about that. I saw him at the funeral home."

"Well, I saw the cops come pick him up a little while ago. You better take care, honey. If there's one thing I've learned, it's that if the cops are interested in a guy, a woman shouldn't be."

Haley caught herself before she said the cops had just been checking him out. She didn't want any of that getting around, and while Claire wasn't the worst of gossips around here, neither was she a sphinx about anything.

"I'll keep that in mind," Haley answered, quickly slipping some more cobbler into her mouth.

"You might also keep in mind that he doesn't come in here with other groups of drivers. A lone wolf. Oh," Claire added, "I asked about what you told the cops you saw in the lot the other night. Seems there was a crate that was headed for Gillette and they just put it on a smaller truck here."

Haley's heart quickened with anxiety. This was something she didn't want to get around. "Who did you ask?"

Claire shrugged. "The guy who came in with Ray. He came in earlier, so I asked. Like I thought, it turned out to be no big deal."

Oh, God, this was exactly what Buck had warned her about. The peach in her mouth now tasted like ash. "Did you mention I was the one who saw it?"

Claire shook her head. "I just said one of the girls. Why would I mention you?"

Maybe because she'd been the only other waitress on that night. Maybe because the driver would know that since she'd waited on him. Butterflies flapped unhappily in her stomach. What had possessed Claire?

The bell over the door jingled and Claire looked up. Her eyes widened a shade. "Speak of the devil," she said quietly.

Haley looked around and saw Buck walking in. He nodded to her and Claire and kept on walking, taking a seat much farther down.

Despite all that had happened, she still thought he looked good enough to eat. Having him pass her as if he hardly knew her didn't make her feel any better, either. Had Gage warned him off? If so, she didn't like it. Sometimes folks around here could be overprotective.

"Well, I guess he's clean," Claire remarked. "Nothing outstanding, at least. I've gotta go take care of him. I wonder if Hasty and Meg are smoking a whole pack out there."

Haley watched as Claire strode to Buck's table and pulled her order pad and pencil out. Buck gave his order quietly, then returned his attention to the window that would give him a fractured view of the parking lot.

After what had happened earlier, she could only conclude that he was avoiding her. She couldn't decide whether that was good or bad. Bad if he was right about her possibly being in danger, that was for sure. But under Claire's gaze she could hardly approach the guy.

Then Claire disappeared down the hall to holler out back for Hasty to come in and cook.

At that, Buck looked across the intervening tables at Haley. "She didn't have to disturb his break."

Haley gave him a half smile. "She doesn't get to annoy him often."

"He doesn't seem like the type to annoy easily."

"He's not."

Then another truck rolled into the lot, signaling the advent of another wave of customers. Haley watched the trucks come, only a minute or two apart, until they neatly lined up and sat growling like mythical beasts. Beyond the window the noise level from all those idling engines would be high enough to require a man to shout to be heard.

That drew her up. How had she even heard that clanging from the ramp? It would have had to have been awfully loud, unless Ray had turned off his engine. Some drivers did and some didn't, and she didn't know why. But try as she would, she couldn't remember if Ray's engine had been idling that night. Of course, it would have been only a single engine, not as loud as a bunch of them.

As the place started to fill up, she ignored Claire and Hasty and everyone else, picking up her cobbler and milk and walking down to join Buck at his table.

He watched her with a lifted brow. "To what do I owe this honor?"

"I'm curious."

He waited. She didn't know what to say next, nor could she quite miss the way Claire looked at her when she brought Buck's meal of steak and eggs.

"Somebody doesn't approve," Buck remarked as Claire walked away.

"She's protective of me."

"Maybe with good reason." He picked up his knife and fork. "What are you curious about?"

"Why the sheriff called to say you're okay."

"He checked me out." He sliced into his steak and

forked a piece toward his mouth. Then he paused. "You still don't know anything about me, Haley. Nothing that really matters. So maybe I should just keep you completely out of it."

"I thought I was going to be your cover."

"I can hang around like a lovesick bull without you doing a damn thing except brushing me off. Considering the way this town seems to gossip, that would probably be best for you."

"But what about the danger part?" Haley said. "You were worried I might be in danger."

Buck sighed and put his utensils down. "There is that," he agreed.

"Are you still worried?" She was on the edge of her seat as she awaited his answer. She wanted him to say no, yet she feared she wouldn't quite believe him if he did. Not with Ray dead.

The whole thing revolved around Ray. What he might have done, why he was dead. It could have just been an accident. Of course it could have been. But right now she was finding that awfully hard to believe.

"I don't know enough about what's going on," Buck said finally. "I'm damn near in the dark here. Shipments are turning up on the wrong trucks. You saw something being transferred in that parking lot out there. Ray is dead. Does that mean you're in danger? Possibly. But I can't say for sure. How many people know what you saw? Two sheriff's deputies and your waitress friend and Hasty. And me, of course."

"Right."

"So how many other people know what you saw by now?"

"I don't know." She hesitated, unsure if she should

tell him what Claire had done. "It's not a great topic for gossip."

"So what would be a great topic for gossip around here?"

"Me sitting here talking to you. Well, no, probably not even that."

"Coming over to the motel with me. Me coming to your place."

She nodded, feeling her cheeks heat a little. "Apparently that conversation we had outside the funeral home."

"Yeah." He gave a short, quiet laugh. "The tom-tom went into overtime on that. The thing is, me hanging around with you gives me cover. But I've also gotten the dimensions of this town after my little experience tonight. So if I hang around with you, everybody will talk. And while that might be a nice diversion for me, it might not be so good for you. Quite the opposite."

"It's also not the nineteenth century anymore."

Suddenly his dark eyes sparkled with laughter, and his lips quirked upward. "So you want to have a whirlwind romance for pretend? To hell with what the neighbors say?"

She liked that sparkle in his eyes, the almost devilish look it gave him, with just that hint of danger she'd sensed around him before. "Frankly, I don't give a damn," she said.

And realized that she didn't. Almost before she knew it, something had wakened in her: a thirst for adventure. A thirst to break out of her rut.

"Your call," Buck said finally. "Want me to escort you home?"

She did but she didn't, and the conflicting feelings were enough to call a halt for the night. She might not be concerned about gossip, but what frightened her was that she felt herself wanting this man.

That was the real danger here—the danger of derailment, the danger of disappointment and heartbreak. She had to rein herself in a bit before she'd be ready to handle those feelings.

"No, thanks," she said with a pallid smile. "Tomorrow night after my play. Maybe."

Then she got up and walked out without even busing her own dishes.

Chapter 4

Buck had seen the moment of decision come over Haley's face. He wasn't prepared to question her further. After the way she had stood up to him at the funeral home and then at the campus, he figured she was quite capable of making up her own mind.

Tough but fragile, the sheriff had said. Well, he sure didn't see any fragility in her, except possibly her youth, and twenty-four wasn't exactly a baby. Nor did he know quite how to proceed. It was one thing to investigate criminals. It was another to give the third degree to a nice woman who had just offered to help him.

Still, he spent more time thinking about her than about the play the next evening. He came late, sat in the back and hoped she didn't notice his late arrival.

He'd gotten an email from his boss earlier and had spent hours sorting through the annotated manifests, building himself a little calendar of the operation. One thing was for sure: the altered shipments didn't keep to a regular schedule, although the activity had been increasing.

He showed up for the play just long enough to watch Haley. Not that he could have resisted. That woman was watchable under any circumstances.

As soon as the curtain calls were over and the house lights came up, he headed for the outdoors. The need for space overwhelmed him.

The same space that was going to make this investigation so difficult. A trip to the library to look at maps of the county and the surrounding areas, with the help of the lovely librarian who turned out to be the sheriff's wife, had given him some appreciation for the odds he was up against.

Hell, he should have gotten a rose somewhere. Wasn't that what you were supposed to give an actress after a performance?

The hoppity-skip of his own thoughts amused him. Haley was turning into a major distraction. Maybe he should scuttle his plan to use her as cover and just do it all alone. Except that nagging feeling that she might be at risk wouldn't leave him alone.

He muttered a cuss word.

"Hi."

He turned at the sound of her voice and saw her approach almost shyly. God, she called to him like a siren. Everything about her appealed to him. "You were great," he assured her.

"I was average. I'm no actress. But it was fun."

"How's your face?"

"Claire's advice about petroleum jelly worked. No reaction."

"Well, good."

They stood there awkwardly, two people pulled together without a good reason, unsure how to step forward. Finally he asked, "Can I escort you home?"

She led the way and he could feel eyes on him. Watching, judging. Soon the mouths would be talking. Good for him, but not so much for Haley.

"I heard the sheriff picked you up last night. I wasn't the one who complained about you," she said as she started her car and headed it out of the lot.

"I didn't think you were," he said.

"Why not?"

He shrugged even though she couldn't see it. "You don't seem the type. I thought you handled me pretty well on your own."

"Unless you were a sick creep."

"If you'd thought that, you never would have met me on the campus, and you never would have gone home alone. No, you handled it yourself. Do you always handle things yourself?"

"I try to. There hasn't been a whole lot of choice."

He caught a tone of sadness in her voice, but chose not to pursue it. He didn't want to create a false sense of intimacy, not if he was going to protect her from himself as well as whatever might be going on in this county.

"So you're an MP?"

"Was," he corrected.

"Parking tickets and stuff? Basic cop things?"

"At first. Then I became an investigator and life got more interesting."

"So you were more like a detective?"

He almost laughed at the rapid-fire questions. Now that she'd made up her mind, she wanted the mysteries solved, starting with him. "It was the toughest detective job in the world," he said, deciding to volunteer what he could. "Military units are a little like gangs. They don't squeal on each other. And when one of them is under investigation, the rest get protective. Sometimes dangerously so."

"Oh, wow," she said quietly, turning onto a darker, deserted street overhung by some very old trees.

"Unit cohesion and pride," he said. "It works for us and against us. Mostly *for* us. The more specialized the unit, the more likely they were to give me trouble. These guys develop a total dependency on each other. They have to—it's how they survive. These guys would die for each other, and they'd never squeal. So unlike a regular detective, I usually didn't get very far by asking questions of anyone in a unit. I had to find other ways."

"I can't imagine."

Nor did he have any intention of telling her. "Of course, that wasn't the case in every situation I investigated. I was just good at handling the problems with the harder nuts to crack." Because no matter how tough they were, he had to be tougher, quicker and more alert.

"I need to tell you something," she said as she turned another corner. She was driving so slowly now that a speed walker would have passed them. "Claire told me she saw the other driver who was with Ray that last night. So she asked him why they'd been moving crates."

Buck stiffened. Not good. Very definitely not good. "I hope she didn't mention you."

"She says not."

"How did he react?"

"Simple explanation. There was a crate on Ray's truck that needed to go to Gillette. It sounds reasonable."

"Only to someone who doesn't know how this business works. Cargo doesn't get transferred at truck stops. Not on my line, not on any big line. There's a huge liability for the shipper and the trucking company, so it's all done at terminals where manifests can be checked until it goes out on local delivery trucks, or reaches the final destination."

She fell silent and he didn't say any more. Now he was more worried. Claire had talked to one of the drivers involved and had made him aware the transfer had been observed. Since Buck was certain it was not a legitimate transfer, he now had plenty of reason to worry for Haley and Claire both.

Unless Claire was somehow involved? He had no way of knowing. All he could be sure of was that one way or another, the problems might have just compounded.

His cell phone rang just as Haley was wheeling them into a parking space at a run-down-looking cluster of apartments. He pulled it out of his breast pocket. Bill.

"Devlin," he answered as Haley turned off the engine.

"Ray Liston's truck was just unloaded in Denver. We've definitely got a problem. One crate that should be there was missing, and one that was shipped on a different truck last week was on Liston's truck. Same tally, but different crate."

"I've got a question for you."

"Shoot."

"Is there any way we would have offloaded a shipment for Gillette at a truck stop here?"

"Hell, no. That's a stupid question. I-90 runs through Gillette. You know that. No way in hell short of a blizzard we would have shipped something for Gillette that far south, and it sure wouldn't have come off the truck before Denver if we had."

"I thought so. By any chance do you keep the LoJack info on the trucks?"

"Not until just recently. Hell, Buck, we only activate

it if something big-time happens, like a truck gets hijacked or a driver is really late. We started keeping records a couple of weeks ago, but nothing looked out of line. Trucks pull over all the time for weigh stations, rest stops, food, diesel…. We couldn't see anything."

"I'd like to look at it."

"I'll see what I can do."

"Why haven't you put LoJack on some of the shipments?"

"The shippers are responsible for that, not us. Do you know how expensive that would be?"

He ended the call and stuffed his phone into his pocket. "Let's get you inside."

"Did something bad happen?"

"Not really. Just more of what I've already told you."

Still she sat with her hands on the wheel, and he wondered what was going on in her mind. Finally she said, "You shouldn't have come with me. It's a long walk back to the motel."

"I can jog it in about fifteen minutes, if that. Besides, walking gives me thinking space. Come on, let me see you to your door. Make sure everything is okay."

Her head swiveled and she looked at him. "You think Claire's question might have caused trouble."

"What do *you* think?"

"That I can't believe she even asked the guy. Or for that matter that she remembered him from that night. I was the one who waited on him and Ray, and I'm not sure I could recognize him if I saw him sitting at one of the tables surrounded by other people."

"Face recognition is one of the human mind's greatest talents," he said.

"Then how can so many witnesses be wrong in court?"

"Because we remember a face so well. What we don't

always remember is where we saw it. Then, of course, a little nudging can shift memory. Once you see a face in a lineup, even a photo lineup, it'll always seem familiar to you."

At last she pulled the keys from the ignition. He climbed out quickly so she could lock up, then walked around to do the gentlemanly thing of helping her out. He almost smiled when she ignored his extended hand.

Almost but not quite, because that was the exact moment when it struck him that his attraction to Haley Martin was a little bit more than a passing thing. He wanted her to take his hand. He wanted to reach her door and take her into his arms and find out what that tempting mouth tasted like.

And when her eyes met his then slid quickly away, he saw his desire answered.

A whole lot of instincts rose to the fore then, demanding he forget his investigation for a little while, be the ordinary guy he'd wanted to become when he left the service.

Damn, he wished he weren't such a bulldog. It would be nice right now to tell himself that the investigation wasn't really his problem—he was a driver now, after all, not an MP—and that he could just blow the whole damn thing off.

Except he wasn't built that way. Not even a tiny bit. Being a bulldog about his job had cost him his one and only serious relationship. Hell, that last time they'd called him off in the service, he had disobeyed a direct order and followed his instincts right to the solution of the case. He had been saved by a brass hat who stepped in and pointed out that a medical discharge for the bullet fragment lodged near his spine might be a cleaner, quieter way to handle a guy with an outstanding record.

Since he'd been in a hospital bed and unable to walk, he hadn't been in any condition to object. Probably for the best. But that brought him to the here and now, with a lovely woman he wanted like hell to kiss and maybe make love to, an investigation he'd taken on when he shouldn't have, and a whole lot of obligations and duties goading him in every direction except the one he wanted to follow.

Just focus on the job and on making sure Haley didn't get into any trouble. And try not to be disturbed that Claire had spoken to the driver, possibly putting the entire operation on alert. *That* might make things harder.

Not that they were exactly easy right now. He needed to drive around this county a little more, getting the lay of the areas outside of town, because if there was one thing he was fairly certain of, nobody *in* this town could be running an illegal operation without someone noticing something. That much was clear after his interview with the police.

So wherever those crates were going, it was somewhere considerably more private. He needed to get a rental car, since he'd draw attention bobtailing it in his cab up and down these local roads.

Keeping his mind on the job at hand worked all the way up the creaky wooden stairs to the second floor. It worked until Haley opened her door and he stepped in beside her. It kept him focused as he quickly checked out the one-bedroom efficiency that was scantily furnished with items that belonged to the age range between junk and antiques. He wondered what her story was, and figured he was going to ask one of these days.

Then he faced her, about to say good-night and get his butt back to the motel and the truck stop, the nexus for all he was investigating, and he fell right into those almost violet eyes of hers.

It happened so fast he would never be able to say who moved first or even how they came together. One instant he was falling into a sea of violet, the next she was wrapped in his arms and hers were tight around his waist. Lips met and instantly the night burst into flames.

He had forgotten just how good a woman could feel in his arms. His self-imposed exile for the past two years suddenly seemed stupid to the extreme. He had given this up, and for what? Because he didn't quite trust himself? Because he'd lived in a dark world for so long he was no longer sure he was fit for ordinary society? Because, except for a small group of his fellow MPs, he'd lived as an outsider among a fraternity that all wore the same uniform?

They were probably all good questions, but they blew away for later consideration on a gale of rising desire.

He wanted this woman. His body reacted instantly with a full, throbbing ache so intense he wasn't sure he could contain it. He'd been resisting the yearning since he'd first laid eyes on her, for a million good reasons, but right now he couldn't remember a single one.

Her mouth beneath his was soft and yielding, questing but not really certain, as if this kiss was a new thing. Somehow that penetrated his need, and he forced himself to rein his hunger. Slow. Take it slow. There was no question of her welcome, but her inexperience was equally obvious to him.

It surprised him. He was not used to it. For an instant something in him froze, wondering if he wanted to get into this. But then a little murmur escaped her and one of her hands slipped up to cup his cheek.

It soothed him. It banked the raging fire enough, just enough, to give him back his control. He didn't want to hurt Haley. He didn't want to devalue that gentle touch of her palm against his cheek, a touch that seemed to reach cold places deep inside him.

That gentleness was worth more to him than any passion. He tamed his kiss, caressing her lips with his rather than plundering. Sliding his tongue softly into her mouth to show her the delights he could offer there. To bring her along at her own pace, without overwhelming her.

It was a new experience for him, this freshness and inexperience. He feared damaging her in some way, making her afraid.

So he let her murmurs and the soft pliancy of her body against his guide him. As she grew ever softer against him, he was encouraged.

And increasingly wary. No more than this. Maybe not ever, but certainly not tonight. He didn't want her to feel he had taken advantage of her. Not even a little.

Slowly he lifted his head. A little mew of protest escaped her, but he resisted his own desire to kiss her again.

There were limits to self-control, and he was perilously near the edge of his own. He waited, cradling her, until her eyes fluttered open. Deep violet pools that called to him. Then she smiled.

Relief washed through him. Carefully, allowing his reluctance to be evident, he released her. Then he touched her cheek with his fingertips.

"You're so sweet," he said.

Her smile widened a shade. "You're so hot."

He couldn't help it. He was sure his grin was sappy, but there it was. "I've got to go," he said. "Before the neighbors talk too much."

"I said I didn't care."

"Maybe not right now. You could later." He drew his fingers away. "We just met," he reminded her. "Passion may be a great kick start, but it doesn't guarantee anything you'd be happy about later."

She nodded with clear reluctance. "You're right."

He slipped out just a moment later, then hit a dead run as he headed back to the motel and truck stop. It had grown truly chilly outside, and it was dark beneath the big old trees. His body still hummed with the needs she had evoked in him, and his muscles still felt her in his arms, tucked against him.

There was something about Haley. Something special. It wasn't just violet eyes and a nice figure, or a pretty face. The world was full of lovely women of all shapes, sizes and colorations. He'd never had a type, to judge by his history, and if he had, it certainly hadn't included many blondes.

Thoughts of what he might have done swirled through his brain as he ran. He could have swept her right off her feet, carried her into her bedroom and allowed them both to be washed away on a tide of madness. He would have loved that. But didn't she deserve something more?

Ah, cut it out, he told himself as his booted feet pounded the pavement and pounded away the hunger. He had more important things to think about, a job to do. He twisted his attention back to the shipment problem.

What exactly did he know? Not much, obviously. One driver dead, one load exchange in the parking lot that shouldn't have happened, and Claire.

He focused his attention on Claire, considering her potential involvement. She might have glimpsed the other driver's face when he came in with Ray for coffee. It was equally possible that she had recognized him in the restaurant. She had been there when Haley mentioned the crate transfer to the cops, but the cops had dismissed it as irrelevant.

So the question became why Claire had asked the driver about it. Maybe because she was curious herself? That seemed far more likely than that she was involved in the operation. If she was, she wouldn't have told Haley that she'd spoken to the driver, especially since he had every reason to believe that Haley hadn't mentioned the crates to anyone else.

Why? Just because he'd warned her not to? How often did that work? Maybe she had told Claire about his warning, and Claire had been disturbed enough to question the other driver to put her concerns to rest.

It was possible. He needed to find out.

Either way, if Claire was involved in whatever was going on, it was highly unlikely she'd have mentioned anything about it to Haley. Even a near idiot would see that it was wiser to just let the whole thing drop than bring it up again.

So Claire had probably asked an innocent question out of curiosity, gotten an answer that satisfied her, and now the whole damn operation was on alert because a question had been asked.

Crap. So now he had to wonder if they'd shift loads somewhere else, or if they'd cool their heels until they felt the heat was off.

Not that a single question from a waitress constituted much heat. The perps, whoever they were, certainly wouldn't know about him or why he was here. Whether Haley had ignored his injunction not to mention the crates again, he was sure that not until last night had she known anything about his mission here. He honestly didn't think she would have gossiped about it. After all, she could have called the cops, but hadn't. If she had, they wouldn't have had to ask him what he was doing.

No, they'd have brought him in and started by telling him not to step on their toes.

Unless they were involved, but he didn't get that read on either Parish or Dalton. No way, and he trusted his instincts, especially when they *could* have sent him packing and told him to stop snooping in their county. They hadn't and they'd seen his record. Neither of them seemed to feel the least bit nervous about the situation, other than to tell him to stay inside the law.

Well, he was getting the measure of this town, and either nobody in town knew a damn thing about the shipments, or damn near everybody was involved. For sure, every right hand seemed to know what every left hand was doing around here.

He reached a corner and saw a car coming, so he paused, running in place, waiting for it to pass.

It didn't pass. It pulled up right in front of him and Gage Dalton's face appeared as the window rolled down.

"You sure know how to upset folks," Gage remarked.

"What now?"

"Strangers running hell-for-leather along these streets at a late hour won't go unnoticed. Hop in so everyone can get back to bed."

He rounded the car and climbed into the front passenger seat. It wasn't a patrol car, but a private vehicle, so he asked, "Did I get you out of bed?"

"A nice warm bed with my lovely wife."

"Why didn't someone else come? You're the sheriff, you shouldn't be answering calls like this."

"Just how many people do you want to know what you're up to here? Micah lives miles out. Either I answer or one of my other deputies gets inquisitive. Do me a favor. If you have to run at night, head out of town along the highway."

"That strikes me as a dangerous place to run at night."

Gage glanced his way. "Very true. So I don't recommend it. I don't need to be cleaning up any more bodies. How's Haley?"

He wondered if that was a warning. Okay, so someone had already hit the drums about his visit to her apartment. God, this place had a grapevine. "In the same condition she was when I met her, okay?"

"Okay."

He noted that they didn't head straight for the highway, but took a detour down Main Street. "You bringing me in?"

"Coffee and some friendly talk. I have a report you might want to see. I got it earlier."

"I don't want to seem too chummy with you guys."

"Folks will think I brought you in for more questioning about why you were running like a madman in the middle of the night."

"My profile is getting too high."

"You're kind of adding to it."

Buck couldn't deny that. He guessed he needed some more work on the whole civilian thing.

A different deputy sat at the dispatch desk, a woman of about thirty who looked at once sleepy but alert. She straightened and eyed Buck.

"Nothing important," Gage said. "I just need a talk with this gentleman about how it bothers people to have someone running through our streets at this hour."

The deputy, Waycross by her name badge, smiled faintly and nodded. "It certainly would."

Gage stopped near the desk. "How's the coffee?"

"I don't drink it, so I wouldn't know. Beau made it a couple of hours ago."

"Probably safe then." Gage filled two clean mugs and led the way to his back office.

When they were seated behind a closed door, Gage reached for a folder on the top of the stack on one side of his desk. "Came in this morning. Ray's autopsy. You'll see proximate cause of death is head trauma. He must have rapped the hell out of it when the truck rolled."

Buck flipped the folder open and read the pathologist's summary.

"You'll also note," Gage said, "we don't have toxicology yet. Probably not until some time next week."

Buck looked up. "But?"

"Not exactly a but. More like, I don't believe he rolled that truck accidentally. Not unless he'd really unbalanced his load, and how likely is that?"

"Not very," Buck agreed. "High winds could do it, but as I recall there weren't any."

"My thought. So that still leaves this unexplained. Death didn't involve natural causes. He didn't have a heart attack, or an aneurysm, or anything like that. So." Gage exhaled long and slow, not quite a sigh. "Would a driver with a truck that size wrench the wheel sharply to avoid a deer?"

Buck shook his head. "We'd run over it rather than jackknife."

"Also what I thought, and anyway it wasn't any jackknife. Those wind up rolled across the road, not straight on in a ditch. My hunch is someone drugged him with something."

"What are you trying to tell me, Gage?"

"That I may now have a criminal investigation. We'll find out when the toxicology comes in. But this affects what I have to do. I can hold off investigating for a while, depending on the tox report. If it looks like something he could have taken himself, there's no rush. If not, I can't ignore it. So whether you like it or not, you may have me on top of you."

Buck regarded him thoughtfully. "Do you ever feel claustrophobic?"

The unscarred side of Gage's face lifted in a smile. "All the time when I was undercover. I never much appreciated it when other agents would get too close."

"Exactly. Right now I have cover. How long have I got?"

"As long as I can give you. At least until next week some time. Somebody's not too bright in this operation, Buck. Changing crates in a public lot, maybe killing a driver when he's only ten miles away from the scene."

"They've been getting away with it for four months now."

"Something made them a little more desperate, apparently. The question is what."

"Ray talking about coming into money. At least that's my guess. That would have gotten all over town fast."

"Faster than the speed of light," Gage agreed. "And given this community, it's hard to believe I wouldn't have heard *something* if it was going on inside the town."

"I think you're right. This stuff may be changing trucks here, but it's going somewhere else. Somewhere a whole lot more private."

"There's a lot of ranch and farmland out there. Millions of acres. How are you going to check it out? My guys have enough trouble keeping their eyes on things out there."

"Anybody who wants to hide something is going to make sure you and your deputies don't see it. That leaves me. I can go where you can't, and nobody will think anything about it. So how about a list of all the box trucks registered in the surrounding area?"

"A description would be useful."

"I'll ask Haley about the color. I doubt she can give me any more than that. And one other thing, complicating matters."

"What's that?"

"Claire—you know Claire?"

"Of course. You mean Claire Bertram, the waitress."

"Right. She told Haley last night she'd seen the other driver who came in with Ray the night of the accident. And that she'd asked him what they were doing shifting crates in the parking lot."

Gage gave a low whistle. "Damn."

"Exactly. He said it was a crate intended for Gillette. My boss said no way, anything for Gillette would have gone a different route out of Seattle."

"Of course it would have, that's too far north. Nothing would come through here on its way to Gillette from Seattle. Hell." Gage rubbed his chin. "Life just got harder."

"By a mile," Buck agreed. "So, Sheriff, what made you change your mind about sharing this report with me? You could have told me earlier. You knew where to find me."

"I did," Gage admitted. "But I still had questions about you."

"What answered them?"

"Old contacts in the federal government. You could say I got a deeper background on you."

"So you know I'm a loose cannon."

"In one instance. I also know that a loose cannon may be what I need right now."

Chapter 5

Haley would have enjoyed sleeping in the following morning. Not only was she tired after her final the previous day and the play, but she'd tossed and turned for hours last night, replaying that kiss in her mind.

She had dated a little in high school before her mother grew sick, and she had been kissed before, but she'd never had an experienced kiss like this one.

While it had started hard, he had gentled it quickly, and she had blushed repeatedly when she realized he must have recognized her inexperience. That was kind of embarrassing to her.

But he hadn't stopped. Instead he had taught her that her mouth was a finely tuned instrument that could be played to elicit a hunger that had plunged to her very center. His kiss had exceeded even the exploratory gropings of past boyfriends, and she had thought *they* were the height of excitement. How little she had known.

She had fallen asleep touching her lips with her fingers, smiling and remembering. When the knock came on her door, the first thought that popped into her head as she struggled awake was that kiss.

She wanted to roll over and return to dreamland with the memory of Buck's kiss, but the knock came again. Groaning, she rose, pulled on her robe and slippers and went to answer it.

The chain was in place, so even though there was no peephole, she wasn't worried about opening her door a crack. Not that she'd ever worried about opening her door in Conard City.

Through the crack, she saw Buck Devlin. He smiled and held up a paper bag. "Breakfast."

All of a sudden she didn't mind being wakened early. She slipped the chain off and opened the door the rest of the way.

He stepped in, carrying not only a paper bag but two tall cups of coffee. "I guess I woke you. I'm sorry."

"It's okay. It's high time I was up anyway." Eight o'clock. Right.

He laughed and carried the food to her tiny table with its two chairs. "Nice of you to say so, anyway. What are your plans for the day, other than the play tonight? Are you working?"

"No. Hasty gave me three days off because of the play."

"You *were* good last night, you know."

She felt her cheeks warm. "Thank you. Do we need plates?"

"I tried to bring everything. I didn't want to make any work for you." He motioned her to a seat and then sat across from her, slipping off his jacket and letting it hang over the back of his chair. Today he was dressed in jeans and a white shirt with sleeves rolled up halfway to his elbows.

He pulled large containers out of the bag and gave her a choice of omelets, toast, potatoes, sausage, ham and pastries. She looked at the huge quantity of food and her stomach rumbled.

He laughed. "I'm hungry, too."

"I skipped dinner last night because I was so nervous about the play."

"So dig in. Are you as nervous about tonight?"

"No, not really. Last night I was in a state of near panic. I couldn't remember my lines at all before I walked onto the stage, then there they were, coming out of my mouth."

"That's comforting."

She smiled, tucking her hair behind her ear, then reaching for a plastic fork. "It was," she admitted.

Eating breakfast this way struck her as intimate, sharing from the containers like family, or old friends. It was a nice intimacy, one she had been missing for a long time without realizing it. Too many of the intimacies she had shared with her mother, especially later in her illness, weren't ones she wanted to remember. This was in a different category and she liked it.

"How old are you, Buck?" she asked, hoping to learn something more about him. That seemed like a safe enough place to start.

"Thirty-four. Closer to thirty-five. You?"

"Twenty-four." She hoped that didn't sound too young to him, but she supposed it was impossible to be anything but what she was, a small-town girl with very little experience in anything except caring for an ill mother.

"You grew up here? Do you have any family in the area?"

"I've spent my whole life here. I thought I mentioned that. My only family was my mother, and she died of cancer just a little over a year ago."

"I'm sorry."

She looked up from the ham she was slicing into bite-size pieces. "What about you? You live in Seattle? Your family?"

"I've got a sister who works for the State Department. She's in India right now. Other than that, nobody. And I don't live in Seattle. I don't exactly live anywhere right now, except my truck."

She studied his face, noticing again how every line of it seemed to appeal to her. It was a strong face, with a square jaw and little sun lines around the eyes. No laugh lines. She wondered if he didn't laugh or smile much. "How do you stand that?"

He shrugged. "After years of going where I was told and doing what I was told to do, it feels kind of free. Nothing ties me down."

Those words might as well have come in flashing neon, she thought, lowering her gaze to the food. Rolling stone. No wish to be tied down. She knew the price of losing someone you loved all too intimately. *Do not go there.*

Disappointment swamped her, but she forced it down and kept her guard up.

"So Claire spoke to that driver, huh?"

Her head snapped up and the first words that occurred to her popped out. "You're very single-minded, aren't you?"

One corner of his mouth lifted. "Sometimes to my own detriment. I've been called a bulldog."

"I can see why." He said very little about himself, but kept on coming right back to the mystery he wanted to solve. So much for a casual "getting to know you" conversation over breakfast. Probably safer for her, she thought. "I told you what Claire told me. She recognized the guy and asked him about off-loading the crate or whatever they were doing. And I told you what she said he said."

"Would she have mentioned you?"

"Like I told you, she said she didn't. I've never known her to lie. We didn't talk about it after that night."

"Can you remember anything about the truck?"

She almost put her fork down, feeling as if she was being grilled. She probably was, she thought with a sudden spark of amusement. What did she expect from a former cop who was on a case? Besides, she had agreed to be his cover.

"I couldn't see all that clearly. You've looked out those windows at night, and the trucks were parked at the far end of the lot. Let me think." She closed her eyes, trying to summon as vivid a memory as she could.

"It wasn't new," she said after a moment. "It looked a little dirty. I don't even know if I described it right when I called it a box truck. It was one of those trucks where the cab is separated from the container on back, but it's all one piece."

"I know what you mean."

"What else?" she wondered. "It had one of those stubby noses that don't stick out, kind of like the driver is sitting over the engine. I saw it from the side, but just briefly." She sighed. "It was white, I think. Maybe. I can't be one hundred percent certain, because of the lighting in the parking lot, and it was mostly in the dark. I suppose it could have been a very light yellow?" She paused then shook her head. "I get the feeling it was white."

"How dirty?"

"I seem to recall some mud splash. Not unusual

around here. I didn't see a company name on the side. Overall it didn't look very clean." She shook her head and resumed eating. "Take it from me, there was nothing to make it stand out. If it had looked new, that's something I would have noticed. Basically, it was the kind of truck that we see around here making local deliveries sometimes."

"Thanks. That's very helpful."

She pursed her lips. "I don't see how. Could I have been any vaguer?"

"You limited the models of truck I need to be looking out for. You limited the colors and condition and even age. You even said it looked as if it drove dirt roads. The field just got narrowed."

"Not by much," she said, but smiled. "I don't think I remember anything else, though."

"After breakfast want to take a ride with me?"

Her heart leaped, then reason reasserted, much to her own dismay. "Sorry, but my car is old and I try not to put too many miles on it. I can't afford major repairs right now."

"That's okay. I managed to rent one. It looks like it might be able to do a few hundred miles."

She almost laughed at the description, but then said, "Rented one? Where? Our only car-rental place shut down after the semiconductor plant had the big layoff."

"There's a used-car dealer on the edge of town who was glad of some money."

He was definitely resourceful, she thought. That never would have occurred to her. "Where would we go?"

"I want to take a look at where Ray went off the road. And then I'd like to do some dirt-driving around the county."

She perked up with excitement. "Really? We're going to investigate?"

"Call it recon. I want to know the lay of the land."

An hour later, after she had showered and dressed in jeans and a blue T-shirt with a gold-embossed butterfly on it, they set out in his rental. It was more than a few years old but spotless inside and out—to be expected of a dealership. She glanced at the odometer and saw what he meant: this car had rolled over a hundred thousand miles some time ago.

Buck looked amused when she checked. "Trust me, the guy sells them with a ninety-day warranty. It's got to be good enough to make a few hundred more miles."

She giggled and settled in, fastening her seat belt.

"It also," he remarked, "won't stick out around here like my truck cab would."

"I take it you don't want to be noticed?"

"I've already been noticed entirely too much." He told her about being picked up by Gage the night before. "Imagine, a ticket for speeding on foot."

That made her laugh again. "People notice things around here. It's actually kind of comforting."

"Then I guess you've never gotten out of line in your life."

"I really haven't had the opportunity," she replied truthfully.

"Until me," he remarked in a low voice.

That stopped the conversation until they were ten miles out of town and he spied where Ray's rig had gone off the road. It would have been hard to miss. The roadside grasses hadn't been mowed in a while, and in the ditch running alongside the road they were deeper, though not taller, because the mower swiped it all down to the same level. It was easy to see where they had been flattened.

The road itself was elevated above the surrounding land, most likely, Haley had always believed, to help snow blow off the road surface and make sure water drained away, as well. But that elevation made the ditches to either side pretty deep, and the bank down to them steep.

Buck pulled onto the shoulder and flipped the flashers on before climbing out. She hesitated, then followed him. The road seemed completely deserted right now but that wouldn't last. It usually carried a fair amount of traffic toward Laramie and the interstate.

The imprint of the truck was still visible, although tramping feet and the subsequent recovery of the rig had churned the area quite a bit. Buck pointed to a dark-brown blotch in the grass.

"Diesel," he said. "Burned the grass out. He must have been going at nearly full speed when he went off."

"How can you know that?"

"Those diesel tanks are built to be tough. It would take some force to puncture or rupture one, especially against the ground."

He turned and looked back at the road surface. "No skid marks, and absolutely no damn reason for him to go off this road unless he was totally out of it."

"He seemed fine when I saw him at the truck stop," she insisted. "Wide awake, coherent. Buck, he didn't look remotely sleepy."

"I believe you. Besides, I have his check points. He was only halfway into his eleven-hour shift. He'd stopped to sleep earlier in the day."

"Then…" She didn't want to say it. She knew what Buck suspected, she had known it all along, but somehow standing beside this road at the spot where Ray had died made it all the more real. She nearly shivered.

"Let's go," Buck said abruptly. "If there's anything else I need to know from here, I'm sure I can get it from the sheriff."

They waited in the car while several other vehicles passed, then pulled a U-turn and headed back toward town.

"He eased into that ditch," Buck said. "Going nearly straight ahead. There were lots of outcomes from going off the road, but only one of them would have rolled the truck that way."

There was nothing she could say to that. It made her feel sick in the pit of her stomach to face the unquestionable fact that Ray had probably been murdered. Until this moment, she wasn't sure she had believed it.

"If someone was willing to kill Ray…" She didn't finish the thought.

He reached out and covered her hand, squeezing gently. "Just don't talk about it at all. Act like you've forgotten all about what happened in the parking lot. That's the safest thing to do. And I'll keep an eye on you."

"You and what army?" she asked, knowing that he couldn't be with her every minute. It was impossible. But the touch of his hand was somehow comforting, and equally electric. She fought the urge to turn her hand over and clasp his tightly. *Distance,* she reminded herself. *Keep a safe distance.*

But she didn't withdraw from his touch.

He didn't take them all the way back into town, turning instead onto a northbound county road. They drove a few miles and then he pulled over at an access gate, the kind ranchers and farmers had so they could use the roads to get to outlying areas of their land. He pulled onto the level bit of ground leading to the gate, a mixture of grass and dirt, and parked.

"What are we doing?" Haley asked.

"Recon. I want you to think for me, since you know the people and the area, and then we're going to explore some dirt roads."

"What do you want to know?"

He waved to the wide-open spaces that seemed to go on forever except to the west, where they bumped into the mountains. "There's nothing out here."

"Except for fences, there doesn't seem to be."

"But people live out here."

"Well, of course." She frowned at him. "The ranchers, the hired hands, there are even some small properties here and there near the roads."

"Anyone you can think of who seems to be doing better than ordinary, just recently? Places where you might be able to conceal some box trucks? Off dirt roads?"

"Everybody has a barn," she remarked. "Sheesh, Buck, these are impossible questions. We have a couple of ranchers who've been doing well enough since I can remember. We've got plenty of others who are scraping by. The only sudden wealth I've seen anywhere was at Ray's funeral."

"Where do the Listons live? In town?"

She bit her lip, suddenly a little nervous. "No. They have a small homestead, just barely enough to get by on. And I do mean barely. They eat what they raise, they wear clothes from church donations—can you imagine how hard that was for Ray?"

"I can. Go on."

"Any cash they have comes from selling whatever extra they grow. At least a couple times a week in the summer, they'll come into town and set up a little farm stand along with some other people and sell produce and eggs. They raise hogs and chickens mainly, all corn fed, from their own crop. In the autumn when I was kid, and the hogs were all nice and fat, my dad used to buy a side from them and fill the freezer. A lot of other people did, too, I seem to remember. Pork, bacon and cured hams. Apparently it was just enough to get by on."

"Any kids other than Ray?"

"One, an older boy. He left town just before I went to high school. I barely remember him."

"So they're on their own and getting older and living a hardscrabble life."

"That's not a crime."

"No, but it might make someone easy prey for a get-rich scheme. And they may not even know what's going on. How do we get there?"

She hesitated, then finally said, "I don't like this, Buck. They've never had a lick of trouble with the law, except for that time that Ray got into a fight. They're good people."

"I didn't say they weren't. I just need to check it out." He turned in his seat, resting his forearm over the steering wheel so he could look straight at her. "I've got very little to go on here, Haley. The only thread is the Listons. They might have nothing to do with this, but I have to check it out. Maybe Ray was the only one involved. Or maybe he got his parents into something they barely understand or know about. I'm not *accusing* them."

After a minute of internal warfare, she finally nodded. "Okay. Give me the map. It's been a while and I need to refresh my memory."

He pulled it from the visor over his head and passed it to her. She studied it, then said in a quiet voice, "It's amazing how well I remember it all."

"What do you mean?"

"My mom used to love Sunday drives. We drove all over the county time and again, and then when she got too sick to drive anymore, I used to take her out. She said the wide-open spaces, the fresh air, did her a world of good."

He clasped her shoulder, saying nothing, just offering silent comfort. She was glad he didn't say anything, because that memory had brought a huge lump to her throat.

She forced herself to focus on the way to the Liston place, and when she felt it was safe to speak again, she started giving him directions.

No, she didn't like this at all, but she had to admit he was right. Unless something landed in his lap, he had to start with the Listons.

A dirt-and-gravel road was their last turn to the Liston homestead.

"Well," Buck remarked, "this is the right kind of road to spray a truck with mud."

"Do you have any idea how many roads there are like this in this county? Or how many driveways to ranches are simply graded dirt?"

"Don't smash my illusions."

Haley laughed in spite of herself. She was quite confident this was a wild-goose chase anyway. She just couldn't imagine that after all these years the Listons would suddenly decide to break the law. If they were that type, they'd surely have done it decades ago.

The farmstead appeared in the distance. All the necessary buildings were there, from the small two-story house to the barn and the smoking shed. The outlying fence wasn't in the best of conditions, but nearer to the buildings it improved. Hogs and goats began to dot the landscape, and the large chicken coop appeared a long distance behind the barn. An expansive field of corn was turning golden behind the buildings. In front of it sat a rusty tractor and implements that looked as if they had been salvaged from the dust bowl. The whole place looked sad and neglected. Most people would have passed it without a second glance.

"See?" she asked Buck. "They have nothing."

"They have a barn," he remarked.

"Everyone does!"

"But who would be most likely to rent it out?"

That silenced her. As they got close to the house, though, Buck nearly jammed on the brakes. "Do you see what I see?"

She could hardly miss the brand-spanking-new silver sports car parked in front of the house. It looked so out of place that it was jarring. "Maybe Jim came home," she said finally, her mouth dry. "He's Ray's older brother."

"He must have been successful."

"Maybe he's the one who sent money for the funeral. I mean, if he owns a car like that…"

"Then why wouldn't they have said so, instead of claiming it was an anonymous donation?"

"Maybe Jim didn't want them to feel bad."

"Maybe."

They were just approaching the rutted drive when Haley suddenly said, "Turn in."

"What? And set off alarms?"

"I have a perfect excuse to drop in. I'll find out if the car is Jim's. Just turn in."

He seemed to hesitate, but then he gave a sharp turn to the wheel and they bounced their way along the deeply rutted drive. Haley noticed the ruts, although she said nothing about them right then, but it remained there wasn't a farmer or a rancher out here who couldn't grade his own drive. It was a necessity unless you could afford to hire the job out.

"When did it last rain?" Buck asked.

So his thoughts were following the same path. "We've had some heavy rain this year. Maybe ten days ago?" Plenty of time to grade this mess.

He pulled up near the silver sports car and muttered something about eighty to a hundred grand. Haley was a bit stunned. Who spent that kind of money on a car?

"I'll wait out here," he said. "They don't know me from Adam. Just be careful what you say."

"I'm not an idiot," she said sharply. "I'm just a neighbor stopping by to see if they need anything."

"Forty-five minutes out of town is a little more than dropping in."

He was right, and nervousness started to twist her stomach and dry her mouth. She looked again at that car and hoped like hell Jim had come home and that he'd found a successful career wherever he'd gone.

Her palms had grown damp and wanted to slip on the door handle. She tightened her grip and climbed out.

"Five minutes," he said. "Or I'm coming in."

The way he said that led her to believe that he felt he could take on half an army and win. She wondered if that was true.

She steadied as she walked to the door, climbing weathered and uneven steps, crossing a porch with planks that were warped and splintering. When she reached the wooden door, she knocked.

A minute later, the yellowing sheer curtain twitched as someone looked out and then the door opened, revealing Mrs. Liston.

"Haley! What are you doing here?"

"I was out on a drive with a friend and I just wanted

to stop by and see how you were doing. To ask if you needed anything."

"We're fine, just fine. Come in."

"I can't stay," Haley said as she crossed the threshold into a ragged-looking parlor. "My friend is waiting." Then she gave Mrs. Liston a hug and looked around. Mr. Liston sat in an armchair that boasted duct tape over worn fabric. Another man sat on an ancient couch covered with horsehair. He resembled Ray, only neater, cleaner and better fed.

"Jim?" she said, managing to sound surprised.

He smiled at her. "Sure enough," he said easily. "I wish I could have gotten here in time for the funeral."

"Well, it's nice to see you again. Life treating you well?"

"Well enough. I do pretty good selling cars down L.A. way."

She smiled and crossed the room to shake his hand. "It's good to see you again. It seems like forever. That's some car you have out there."

He laughed, dragging his gaze appreciatively over her. She didn't like that look, as if he was mentally stripping her. It made her skin want to crawl.

"I wish it were mine," Jim said. "I get to drive some of the dealer models. Maybe someday."

She turned her attention to Mr. Liston and went to bend over him and give him a light hug. "How are you doing?" she asked.

"About as well as can be expected," he said, a bit angrily. "Losing a son ain't easy."

"No, it's not. I'm so sorry about Ray." She hesitated, noting that she hadn't been offered a seat or a beverage, both common forms of local hospitality. But maybe it was because they were grieving.

"Well," she said, just as it seemed the silence was about to grow too long, "I just thought I'd check in and see if I could help somehow. I guess with Jim here to look after you, you certainly don't need me. You take care."

No one suggested she stay, but she could understand that, too. Fifteen seconds later she had been ushered out the door and was headed back to the car and Buck.

She climbed in. He didn't say a word, simply turned them around and headed away from the house. When the farmstead began to disappear behind them, he finally asked, "Well?"

"I was right. Jim is home. That's his car."

Buck gave a low whistle. "He's doing damn good for himself. You think he'd help the family out."

"It's not his car. He says he works for a dealer who lets him drive demos."

Buck didn't say anything for a couple of minutes and she wished she knew what he was thinking. Finally she asked, "Buck?"

"Think about it, Haley. If you were a dealer, would you let one of your salespeople drive a car that expensive up to the wilds of Wyoming? And unless you owned that car, would you want to risk the dings that you could get on a gravel road? It could cost you your job."

"Oh." She twisted her fingers together, considering it and realizing he was probably right. "It doesn't add up, does it?"

"No, but I'm glad you thought it did. At least you didn't do or say something to make them think otherwise. Anything else?"

"Not really, except I didn't feel welcome. There's no crime in that. The Listons are grieving, and anyway, I'm practically a stranger. I guess I was expecting too much."

"They might just be grieving," he agreed.

She replayed the entire encounter in her mind and realized that there was one other thing that had made her feel unwelcome: neither man had risen to greet her. In these parts, men still stood when a woman entered a room like that. They definitely hadn't wanted her there, and had done nothing to extend her visit. But that certainly wasn't evidence that any of them were up to something wrong.

"You really think he owns that car?" she asked, running over everything one more time, seeking something she might have missed.

"Well, if he doesn't own it, then he lied about where he was taking it."

"That's possible." Then another thought struck her. "He might be lying to his parents. If he's making that kind of money, you're right, he should be doing something for them. Maybe he hasn't done one blessed thing and is hiding his success."

"It's possible. He wouldn't be the only person that selfish."

They wandered some more of the gravel-and-dirt back roads, but nothing seemed to catch Buck's eye, or if it did he said nothing about it. She got the feeling he was building a mental map, but its meaning to her was opaque. Must be a military thing.

He broke the silence finally with a question. "Does Claire live in town?"

"She used to, but a couple of years ago she married Murdock Bertram. He's got a sheep ranch near here."

"How are they doing?"

She could, if she let herself, resent the way he seemed to be suspicious of nearly everyone. Given how little he knew about the area and what he was trying to figure out, though, she supposed she could excuse him.

"All right, I guess. Better than some. Claire sometimes

talks about quitting her job but she always comes back to her policy, never trust a man."

He chuckled at that. "Bad experiences?"

"This is marriage number three. She says she's never again going to be dependent on anyone."

"Makes sense. Do you feel the same way?"

"I do about being independent."

He nodded. "Smart." Then, "So where exactly is Claire's place?"

So she guided him to it, even though it meant going back the way they had come. The Liston and Bertram houses were only about ten miles apart. Most of the road to the Bertram place was paved, but like on so many other ranches, the road up to the house and outbuildings was not. Buck pulled in at the gate and turned the car around.

From this distance, the Bertram ranch looked to be doing okay. White clapboard gleamed in the sun, and sheep grazed the pastures as far as the eye could see. Green lawn graced the front of the place, well tended and unusual in these parts where most ranchers had more important things to do than tend an acre of useless grass. A relatively new steel barn dominated a small rise not too far from the house.

"They're definitely doing okay," he remarked.

"Wool prices haven't dropped as much as other things, I hear," Haley explained. "And Murdock has started to raise alpacas, too. Claire was complaining how expensive those animals are, but I guess their wool is worth it."

"Must be."

He scanned the area, and she thought a little wryly that he was probably disappointed that he didn't see a white box truck in plain view.

Then he put the car in gear again and headed them back toward town. "Let me buy you lunch," he said. "And please don't suggest the truck stop. You spend enough time there. I did notice, though, that there aren't a lot of restaurants."

"There's the City Diner."

"So basically it's a choice of the same or the same?"

She laughed. "Pretty much. Unless you want to get a sandwich or some fried chicken at one of the bars."

"Still more of the same."

They found parking near enough to the diner. As it was Saturday, the streets were fairly busy with pedestrians, most of them people Haley knew by sight and often by name. They smiled and nodded as they passed, and only a few looked askance at Buck.

Maude, the diner's owner, was nowhere in sight, and they were served by her daughter, who might have been a clone, every bit as stocky and graceless as her mother.

"Don't see you here much," she remarked to Haley as she slapped menus on the table.

"Hasty feeds me at work. Is Maude okay?"

The woman nodded. "Just claimed she needed a day off. After all these years, she wanted a day off. Imagine that."

Buck was clearly fighting to hide a smile as the woman stomped to the next table. "Service with grace?" he said quietly.

"Not here." Haley battled her own twitching lips. "The food makes up for it, though."

Because the place was packed for lunch, they were treated to only the minimum of service and no conversation. Voices around them created a buzz just loud enough to have a private conversation, a rarity in here.

Haley ordered a chef's salad that proved to be big enough for three, and Buck took her recommendation on the steak sandwich.

"So what now?" she asked him.

He shrugged. "I'm thinking. So tell me more about yourself. You mentioned your mother, but what about your dad?"

"He died in a hunting accident when I was sixteen."

He faced softened. "I'm sorry. So that leaves just you?"

"Yeah." She looked down at her salad. "It's something I try not to think about too often."

"Understandably. So now you're in college."

"I want to be a nurse. I figure I'll start with my LPN, save some money and then go for my RN eventually."

"That's a long-term plan."

She looked curiously at him. "Don't you have one?"

"Not right now. I've been running in the short term. I look a day or two down the road and no further."

"Why?" she asked baldly.

He set his sandwich down, reached for his napkin and wiped his mouth. He didn't say anything for a few minutes. Then he said something so painfully honest it tore at her heart.

"Have you ever been so disturbed by something that you felt everything you thought you were, everything you ever believed in, had just been thrown into a shredder and you had to figure out how to put it back together again?"

She caught her breath. "What happened, Buck?"

He just shook his head. "Maybe another time. Certainly not here."

She had to respect that, but the ache that filled her at his description was hard to ignore. It also worried her. There was sympathy and then there was sympathy. Was she feeling more for Buck than she should?

Then she wondered how she would know. For five of the past six years, she'd thought of little but her mother. For the past year, she'd refused to deal with anything except her grief and school. She certainly didn't have some kind of emotional barometer built from experience to gauge what she should be feeling and what was a little too much.

Buck had come from a darker world. Intellectually she recognized that, but having watched him in operation, she almost felt sorry for him. Suspicious of the Listons, who had never done a single thing wrong? And now, she gathered, suspicious of Claire as well, a woman whose only crime had been to question a truck driver.

But the more she thought about Claire asking that driver, the more anxious she got herself. Why in the world would Claire have done that, especially when the police had considered it unimportant and Haley hadn't mentioned it again?

Then there was Jim Liston showing up in that ridiculously expensive car. She had to agree with Buck that it was unlikely he would have been permitted to drive a demo like that all the way up here. But if he made that kind of money, why wasn't he helping his family? Why had the Listons stood there at a fancy wake wearing threadbare Sunday clothes?

Nothing was adding up, she realized. According to Buck, something had to be going on that wasn't aboveboard.

But what?

After lunch he took her directly home, remarking that she needed to get some rest before the play. He did ask where in town he could find a warmer jacket, and that put her on alert.

"Buck?"

"Yes?"

"You're not going to prowl on any of those ranches, are you?"

"Why would I do that?"

He had just pulled up in front of her complex and was reaching to take the key out of the ignition.

"Just don't," she said. "Don't even think of it. Out there it takes as long as a half hour for a deputy to respond to a call, so people pretty much look after themselves. A prowler could get shot."

He gave her a half smile. "I have no intention of getting shot. Been there, done that. No desire to repeat the experience."

Her breath caught in her throat. "You've been shot?" she whispered. "When? How?"

"Again, a story for another time. No, I'm just going to wander around town a bit today, get some clothes."

"Go to Freitag's," she said automatically. Why didn't she believe him?

He came around to help her from the car, and this time she let him. Once again he walked her to her apartment, but he didn't come in. He leaned forward and brushed the lightest of kisses on her cheek. Then he followed the touch with his fingertips, heightening her awareness of him instantly to an almost painful longing.

"I'll see you later," he said. "*Before* the play."

She watched him disappear down the stairs, then closed the door. "He wouldn't go out there in broad daylight," she said to the empty room. "He's not crazy."

At least she hoped he wasn't. Because right now it occurred to her she didn't know a damn thing about Buck Devlin, except Gage said he checked out, and that he was a former MP.

That wasn't a whole lot of information, and he seemed determined to avoid any subject that could really reveal anything about him. Although, in all fairness, he didn't exactly know much about her, either.

What's more, he'd been quite blunt about using her for cover. She needed to keep that in mind before she wasted any more worry on Buck Devlin.

If only his lightest touch didn't make her body sing.

Chapter 6

A trip to the local gun shop proved illuminating to Buck. He'd had no idea how easy it would be to buy a piece, even though he was just passing through. Apart from the requisite shotguns and hunting rifles, there were plenty of semiautomatic jobs, both pistols and long guns.

"People around here like shooting for fun?" he asked the proprietor, who had introduced himself as Rick. "Hobbyists?"

"Some. Mostly there's a lot of varmints. Wolves, bears, coyotes, cougars. A man's got to protect his livestock."

"I couldn't agree more." And if a man wanted to, apparently he could have an arsenal to rival an army's.

Rick pressed him to take a look at some, but Buck already knew them all intimately. Their look, their feel, their reliability, even how to strip them down and put them back together. Knowing weapons had once been part of his job. "Sorry, I can't," he told Rick. "Not allowed to have a firearm in a truck."

"Really? That's purely stupid."

Buck nodded agreement, moving down to a case of knives. "Now these I can have."

There was the usual assortment of what Buck thought of as vanity knives—they looked mean but weren't all that useful if really needed. Then there was an assortment of hunting knives. He hovered over them for a while, then moved on to find what he really wanted: a modified Filipino barong by a manufacturer he trusted. Hefting it, he felt it settle into his hand like an old friend. "I'll take this."

"Anything else?"

"I'd like to look at a folding knife. Some of the places I spend the night are pretty dark and deserted. I'd feel better with something in my pocket."

He departed a short while later with the knives and sheaths in a bag, but he was far from done. Next he headed to the hardware store. Obvious weapons could be a liability. But other things…

He pulled out his cell and called Gage Dalton. Ten minutes later, Gage called back and agreed to do him a favor.

Too bad, he thought, that it felt so good to be back in the saddle.

Buck piled the last of his purchases into the trunk of the rental. Freitag's even had a whole section devoted to the kind of clothing he wanted: heavy-duty and dark.

They also had plenty of camo, which amused him, because the animals these folks would be hunting wouldn't be fooled by it. They depended on their sense of smell more than their eyes, unlike human predators.

Nor did he want any of it himself. When you infiltrated at night, you went dark. He needed to start keeping a closer eye on that parking lot in case another exchange was made. The question was when. Did he want to risk missing a cargo exchange? They'd been getting closer together, to judge by the information he'd gotten from Bill, but it wasn't anything like regular. The shortest time frame so far had been ten days, and that had been the last one. Would they speed up their business or slow it down until they were sure the heat over Ray was off?

Good question, and he couldn't answer it.

Whoever they were, they seemed to be an interesting mix. Some elements of caution mixed with others of confidence, like exchanging crates in the truck-stop parking lot. He had a mental map of the road going in both directions, though, and he figured he could understand why they would have chosen to make a switch in the parking lot.

How many people would readily recognize that was wrong? Only truckers. So wait until you were the only two trucks around, and most casual observers would think it was normal. Do it out somewhere on the road, like a deserted turnout or a rest stop, and then it would look squirrelly to almost anyone.

So it made sense to choose the truck stop. However, since Claire had asked the other driver about it, the people involved might now be on high alert. Or they could have believed the explanation had satisfied Claire. Damned if he knew which way they'd flop. The important thing was that they didn't guess why *he* was hanging around.

Which he supposed meant he should take Haley to the truck stop for a late dinner after her play, making it look like he was pursuing her. In a way he hated to do that to her, because he was sure a lot of looks, winks and nudges might happen.

Usually he didn't have a Haley to consider when he

was doing something like this. Often in his career he'd been a solo missile, and those times when he hadn't been alone he'd worked with people who had the same training and experience. Haley was a whole different matter.

He was honestly worried about her.

Damn, he had to figure this out before Gage started looking into it. Because sure as hell, that toxicology was going to come back positive for something. He hadn't been certain until he looked at the wreck site earlier, but he was convinced now. And Haley was about the only person who could testify that Ray hadn't been under the influence at the truck stop. A dangerous witness.

At this point Buck would be willing to bet a month's pay that whatever had been running through Ray's blood was enough to kill him, because nobody with half a brain would trust an accident to do that.

It was pure luck that Ray had hit his head hard enough to be fatal. If that word went out, maybe these guys would relax.

This group was no bunch of masterminds. They'd had an idea that could work for a while, but sooner or later someone was going to put two and two together. So all along, they'd been racing against a clock they couldn't see: the clock of when the cargo switches would add up enough to get attention. That was actually stupid, unless they honestly believed that the Seattle terminal would hold such a noisy investigation that they'd get warned.

Or unless they had eyes and ears in the terminal.

He pulled in to park next to Haley's car and sat drumming his fingers on the wheel. At some point, he thought, an operation became so big it would fail through its own weight—too many people knew, and thus too many people could make a mistake.

So assume he was shipping contraband. He wouldn't want to use the same shipper every time because that would become too obvious when the shipments were switched. Would he really want to be paying someone at the terminal to keep an eye on these random shipments? No. It would have meant trusting yet another person and leaving another money trail.

It was possible, of course, but given what Bill had told him, Buck figured the likeliest way this was playing out was the simplest: offer someone at the shipper's warehouse a bit of money to stick something small in a crate. No questions, no explanations, just shove it in along with the packing material on a certain date and send us the shipping info.

Then came the question of how you could ensure the shipment would go out on the right truck for the exchange.

The lightbulb went on then. Those trucks didn't depart at random. He needed to get back and take a look at the list of trucks and drivers Bill had emailed him. Somewhere in there would have to be a clue. He must have just missed it on his first time through, when he'd been so busy looking at dates.

All of a sudden he was impatient to get back to the motel. But he'd promised Haley he'd see her before her play.

Well, he'd already parked at her place, and if he wanted to keep up the appearance of being interested in her, nothing would look stupider than leaving before he'd even gone inside.

Sighing at his own impatience, because patience was essential and impatience could be deadly, he climbed out and headed inside.

* * *

Haley had just finished blow-drying her hair but had not put it up yet when Buck arrived. He took one look at her and smiled.

"You should wear your hair down more often. It suits you."

"It also gets in the way," she said lightly, flipping it back over her shoulders.

She felt awkward, though, as she invited him in. Was she wrong to trust Buck just because Gage Dalton said he checked out?

Because, really, how much could Gage actually know about Buck, other than whether he had a police record? Certainly nothing about the kind of man he was. Not even whether Buck was involved in these cargo switches he was supposedly investigating.

Where had that thought come from?

Troubled, she turned away as Buck entered and closed the door behind him. She wasn't a suspicious person by nature and now she was suspicious of everyone.

"Did I come at a bad time?" Buck asked quietly.

She rounded on him, disturbed by the changes in herself, but having no one else to share them with.

"How do I know I can trust you?" she demanded. "I saw one little thing in a parking lot. Barely. Yet the next thing I know you're telling me to keep quiet. That I might be in danger. And like some naive kid, I'm taking it all at your word. You haven't given me one scintilla of proof that I could be in danger! What if you're the one who is up to no good?"

He stood by the door, expressionless, hands at his sides. When at last he decided she was finished, he spoke. "You're right. I'm asking a whole lot of you. And I haven't told you enough."

"What more is there?"

"Ray was murdered."

She gasped. "You can't know that."

"But I do. I talked to the sheriff yesterday. Ray was killed by a severe blow to his head when that truck went off the road. But the only way he could have driven that truck off the road the way he did was if he was unconscious. How did that happen? The sheriff is waiting for the toxicology, but he suspects Ray was drugged. Ask him. In the meantime, I can only offer my experience for it. Ray would not have driven off the road in that way if he'd been awake. If he'd taken evasive action of some kind, there'd have been skid marks from the brakes. He'd probably have jerked the wheel and jackknifed. He did neither."

She stood there feeling oddly numb and sorely troubled, as if the burst of anger and suspicion had fled, leaving near emptiness in its wake.

"As for you," he continued, "when I started, my primary focus was on using you as an excuse for me to be here. That's changed, because it's inescapable that you are the one person who was a witness."

"What did I witness? Some boxes being moved between trucks? That's nothing, especially when I can't really be sure."

"And it would have remained nothing except for Ray. You are the only person who can testify that Ray was alert just a few minutes before. If drugs of some kind turn up in the toxicology, you're going to be the one person who can say they were introduced *after* he left the restaurant. You and you alone."

"I'm not proof!"

"Your word that he was fine when he talked to you is enough. It raises the question of what could have happened to him so fast. And it leaves only one likely answer. Without you to say he was fine, lots of explanations could occur and the whole time frame changes."

The words fell into her heart like stones, because they made sense. Just as it had made sense to her when he had said that people wouldn't be going to all the trouble to switch cargo unless big money was involved. And big money, even she knew, probably meant something criminal. Probably drugs.

"But why should I trust you and not people I've known for years? Like Claire and the Listons."

"They might not be involved in anything at all. I just need to check them out, because the Listons came into some money, because their son drove up here in a car only millionaires own. That's enough reason to check. And it's likely enough I won't find anything."

"But Claire? You're suspicious of her, too."

He shrugged. "Not exactly. I just find it odd that she questioned that driver. Why would she do that?"

"To put my mind at rest."

"Did she think you were worrying about that cargo being switched? Did you give her any reason to think you believed it to be a big deal?"

Her heart sank even more. "No," she said finally. "I mentioned it to Micah and Sarah, and then you. Nobody else."

He shrugged. "Maybe she was just curious after you mentioned it. But part of investigating is removing possibilities from the table. It's what I do."

"Which brings me back to you," she pointed out. "What do I know about you, really? Not much."

"No, you don't," he agreed. "The best thing I can offer is to talk to your sheriff. He checked me out, and he even talked to my boss."

After a moment, another question burst out of her. "Who do *you* trust?"

"Right now I can't trust anyone even remotely associated with this mess. Not even the guy who sent me out to investigate."

"Lovely world you live in."

And yet it amazed her just how much she didn't want him to leave, this stranger who had turned her world on end, changing it from a friendly place to one that held shadowy threats.

She dropped into her desk chair and wrapped her arms tightly around herself. Her stomach churned on the edge of nausea as she tried once again to battle her way through a familiar world that had turned into dangerous quicksand.

"Claire called little while ago," she said finally, hearing an odd dullness in her voice. "She seems awfully worried about me."

"So I'm a potential threat?"

"In her mind." She hesitated. "She also seems certain you must have an ulterior motive for staying here, and it's not me. Or at least she kept asking."

From the corner of her eye, she saw him stiffen. Then he said, almost lightly, "That's not very flattering to you."

That penetrated her muddled state enough to draw a small laugh from her. "Maybe not. But maybe her concern is genuine. If you were any other trucker, she'd be right. But you're not just any other trucker."

"According to me, at any rate."

"There is that. There's also the fact that Gage called me to tell me I didn't need to worry about you. So either you're the best con artist this side of D.C. or he thinks you're exactly what you say you are."

"You trust Gage?"

"Of course I do. You don't know him, but I've known him most of my life. He's kept this county clean. Everyone has great respect for him."

He came closer, finally sitting on the armchair she should have offered and hadn't.

She continued, sensing he was listening intently. "What's bothering me is that now I don't entirely trust Claire. In fact, I don't really trust anybody. I've never felt this way before."

"I'm sorry." The apology sounded genuine.

"You've made me realize that in some ways I've been living in a cocoon where most people don't do really bad things. I can agree that Ray might have been murdered, and that the cargo transfer was anything but routine. I'm having trouble believing I'm in danger, though."

"Maybe you're not. I can't swear to that one way or the other, but I also can't afford to act as if you aren't. One man is already dead."

She nodded. "I get it, Buck. I do. But what's bugging me is that I'm asking questions I wouldn't have asked a week ago. That's what I hate."

"I wish I could say I understand that, but the truth is I've been so damn suspicious for so many years I wear it like my own skin."

"That's sad."

"It wasn't in the world I used to live in. It even saved my life more than once."

She stared at him. "Then how do you know you can trust *me?*"

"Because you mentioned the cargo exchange to the police. You wouldn't have done that if you'd spiked Ray's coffee."

She gasped then. "Oh, God!"

"What?"

"I just thought. I wasn't the one who poured the coffee for Ray and the other guy. Claire was getting some for a couple of customers, and she just filled their cups at the same time and put them on the counter."

Buck grew very still. "It's opportunity, but it's not proof. The other driver could have had something to do with that."

She couldn't disagree. "They went over to the condiment bar. But why would she have questioned that driver if she was involved?"

Buck's expression turned grim. "Maybe she didn't. How would you know?" Then he said something that truly chilled her. "I think they're worried about both you and me."

Chapter 7

Well, didn't that blow everything all to hell, Buck thought after he left Haley at the college for her play and returned to the La-Z-Rest, from where he could watch the comings and goings in the parking lot. The best thing he could do for Haley would be to disappear.

But how could he keep watch on the lot and Haley if he pretended to leave? If the tox screen showed poisoning, she would become an important witness. They must realize that.

He sat drumming his fingers, scanning the info Bill had sent him for any connection among the drivers who'd had mixed-up shipments. This was a great nest from which to observe, but if everyone knew he was there, and the bad guys suspected his purpose, it would do him no damn good.

But his major worry was Haley. If Claire was involved,

that signified real trouble. Especially if Buck's presence had aroused suspicion among the gang.

When he thought about the Listons, though, he knew it had to involve more than the brother, if Jim was involved at all.

Step back, he told himself. While he was perfectly capable of living on the sly in the countryside around here, it would make his job more difficult. What was more, it would prevent him from keeping a decent eye on Haley, and his sense of foreboding about that had increased a hundredfold since she told him about Claire's call today. It bothered him even more to have learned that Claire had had the opportunity to drug Ray's coffee.

Claire, with her husband's well-to-do sheep ranch, with its recently acquired and very expensive alpacas.

Then there was Jim Liston, showing up at his parents' run-down farm in a car so expensive it could probably pay to spruce the place up for them. How would that make them feel? Or were they part of it?

Of course, narrowing in on this small handful was a danger. There were thousands of people in this county, and any one of them could be involved.

But he couldn't help but notice that two nails were sticking up higher than the rest: the Listons and Claire.

He decided he needed to do two things: the first was make it look like he had absolutely nothing on his mind but Haley. That wouldn't be hard, if she was willing to play along. The woman was enthralling and sexy enough to get his motor humming with a mere glance.

Then he had to make a night recon of those two homesteads to see what he could find. Because until he eliminated the Listons and Claire, they were going to sit right at the top of his radar, rightly or wrongly. He *had* to find out.

As soon as he checked out those two places, he decided he should get rid of the rental car. If people thought he'd be traveling in his truck cab, they'd think he'd be too damn obvious to be up to anything. And they'd be right, of course.

Scanning the email in front of him and the list he'd been making, he tried to see some kind of pattern. He almost had the feeling that some information was missing, but that was probably just a blind spot on his part.

He hated to think he might have disrupted the pattern, that his mere presence might have endangered Haley when he wanted to protect her.

Thinking of Haley dragged his gaze back to the parking lot, and all the patience he'd learned during his years as an MP deserted him. He found himself willing a switch to take place, willing that box truck to show up and do something suspicious.

That was when the phone rang, making life even more complicated. It was Bill.

"The honchos want you to come back."

"What for? They were all hot enough to send me out here."

"You're asking me to explain them? From what one of them said, you've probably gotten all the information you're going to get, and given that none of our shippers has yet complained about a later arrival, we don't really have to worry yet. Plus, I talked to the sheriff out there and he said Liston's death was purely accidental. Whatever's going on, they don't think it's big enough for you to plant yourself out there. They're paying you to drive."

"I'm staying," Buck said flatly.

"You can't. They want you off it."

"Consider me off it."

"Then why won't you come back?"

"There's a woman."

"Tell me you're not lying."

"There's a woman," Buck repeated. "I want another week of my vacation, or you can fire me."

Bill fell silent for a minute. "A woman."

"Seriously."

Then Bill gave a laugh. "Women will do that. But I can tell them that absolutely and positively you're not working this anymore? Because part of what was bugging them was paying you for driving when you're not."

"Cheap bastards," Buck said. "No, I was getting ready to back out. I haven't learned a damn thing. It's like hunting a needle in haystack and I don't have a metal detector. Something bigger is going to have to happen to figure this one out. In the meantime, there's a lady and you just freed me up to spend all my time with her."

"Fine by me," Bill said. "Just make sure I don't hear otherwise."

"You won't." He'd make damn sure of that.

When he hung up, he revised his estimation of whether someone in the Seattle terminal was involved. The question now was who.

Haley stayed for the cast-and-crew party, but only for a little while. She was tired, and somehow the bonhomie of the people she had worked with over the past two months just rasped on her. Serious things were going on, things that might involve people she knew. Things that involved a murder.

Tonight, for the very first time, she noticed how dark the parking lot was. Oh, there were pole lights, but they left dark spaces between them and the parking lot, full of cars, provided plenty of easy hiding places.

She stopped, never having noticed that before, and

felt her stomach flutter. God, she couldn't allow this to continue. She could not, would not, live in fear of things that had been familiar and safe forever.

Setting her chin, she began to stride in the direction of her car. She was halfway there when she caught sight of a shadowy figure standing near it. She froze and considered running back inside.

"Haley?"

Buck's voice. Relief washed through her. He started walking toward her, moving in and out of the dim puddles of light.

"Sorry, I guess I frightened you."

She couldn't deny it, but she didn't want to admit it, either. "I didn't expect you to be here."

"I know, you said you'd be late because of the party."

"Then why did you come?"

"I was thinking about trying to gate-crash to give you these." He held out a bundle and she almost gasped as she saw a dozen yellow roses wrapped in florist's green paper. "Oh, Buck!"

"It seemed like the right thing to do for an actress."

She held them close and drew in a fragrant breath of their beautiful scent. "They're wonderful! Thank you so much." No one had ever given her roses before, and her throat tightened a bit at the gesture. She reminded herself that he'd just done it because she had finished a play, and for no other reason.

"Well, since you're out early," he said, "how about I take you for a late dinner?"

"At the truck stop?" As if there was any other place.

"Better than a bar at this time of night," he pointed out reasonably.

There was no way she could argue with that, but suddenly the roses didn't seem quite so beautiful. Of course he wanted to go to the truck stop. To keep watch. Her heart sank, and she scolded herself. She knew why he was here. Why did she seem to keep hoping it was something more?

Part of her wanted to claim tiredness and just be done with it for the night, but another part of her quickened a bit. What if they saw a transfer? Hadn't she already decided that she wanted to break out of her rut?

"Sure," she said.

The diner was busy enough when they arrived, but not too busy, and they couldn't get seats by a window. Not that it mattered, Haley thought. If there was going to be a cargo transfer of any kind tonight, it was unlikely to happen when there were so many people around.

Buck spoke when they were seated. She noted that he had chosen to face the window. "I'm sorry I can't recommend the broiled lobster or the beef tournedos," he said with a charming wink. "I think you already know this menu pretty well."

"Another time for lobster," she smiled back, as if they were any normal dating couple.

"Did you manage to eat before the performance?"

"Not a thing. I got nervous again."

"But don't you know just about everybody who was there? Wouldn't that make it easier?"

"Actually, I think it made it harder. If they were all strangers I'd never see again, I doubt I'd have been half as nervous."

He laughed, and the sound drew the attention of other diners. Haley looked down as she realized how many guys were looking their way, and wondered if this was going to make life harder for her after Buck left. Until now, the excuse of never seeing a customer outside of work had worked pretty well.

But Hasty would keep an eye on things. In fact, she no sooner had the thought than Hasty appeared at their table.

"Hi," he said, measuring Buck and then looking dubiously at Haley. She almost wanted to sink, wondering what he thought of her. But the whole town had been gabbing, as near as she could tell, so this couldn't possibly surprise him.

"Hi, Hasty," she said, hoping she looked relaxed.

Buck stuck out his hand. "Buck Devlin," he said.

Hasty wiped his hand on the towel at his waist and shook Buck's hand. "I know who you are." But then Hasty seemed to catch himself, and he smiled in a friendly manner. "Be good to our Haley, hear?"

It sounded nice, but the intention was clear. Haley felt her cheeks heat. Did everyone in this county think she needed a protector? She wasn't exactly a kid anymore.

"Funny," Buck said amiably, "I got the same message from the sheriff."

At that Hasty laughed. "Okay, okay. I'm not trying to play the heavy. Just don't like to see my girls go someplace they might regret."

With that Hasty strolled away, pausing to talk to a few other people before returning behind the counter. Meg came up to take their orders and Haley chose something light so it wouldn't keep her awake. Buck, she noticed, ordered as if he were about to run a marathon.

"This is so embarrassing," she said after Meg walked away.

"Why? I think it's nice you have so many people concerned about you. That should make you feel good."

"But they're acting like I don't have an ounce of sense."

"No, they're acting like a wolf has just walked into a sheep pen. You've told me yourself this place isn't like the big, bad world beyond. I come from out there in that big, bad world. Their concerns are reasonable."

"Are they? Do I have a reason to be concerned?"

"I hope not," he said after a moment. "Dammit."

"What?"

"Oh, I'm so out of practice talking to a woman it's not funny."

"Why?"

"Bad experience a number of years ago. I pretty much limited myself after that."

"Honestly? You're afraid?" The thought astonished her. He didn't seem like he was afraid of much.

"Self-protective," he corrected. "Not afraid. I just don't see getting involved like that again until I get to know someone really well. I jumped before I looked last time."

"Oh." Well, there was little chance he was going to get to know *her* well. Her stomach sank, so she forced herself to sip her soda and pretend everything was fine.

"Look," he said after a moment, leaning toward her and lowering his voice, "I hope you don't have a reason to be concerned. The last thing I want is for you to be hurt in any way. But the truth of the matter is I want you like hell. I keep on wanting you. I tell myself to ignore it, to squash it, that there's no way it could be good for either of us, and I keep right on fantasizing about you and wanting to touch you in every way possible."

She couldn't have imagined a less romantic place for such a declaration, and she had to fight not to look around to see if he'd been overheard despite how quietly he was talking. She could feel her cheeks flaming as brightly as if she were having another allergic reaction.

"Told you I've forgotten how."

She swallowed hard and shook her head the tiniest bit. "Actually," she said, and cleared her throat when her voice came out funny, "actually, that's the nicest thing a guy's ever said to me."

"Really?" He sat back looking amazed. "Is everybody around here blind?"

She felt her flush deepen. How in the world could she respond to that?

"You don't have to answer that." He reached across the table and covered her hand with his almost tentatively, as if he expected Hasty to suddenly arrive with a cleaver. "There are some things you need to know about me."

Her heart climbed into her throat. This couldn't possibly be good, especially following right after what he had said about wanting her. That had lifted her high instantly, and now she was sure she was about to crash.

"I don't always walk the line," he said. "That's part of the reason I'm sitting with you right now."

Her heart thudded heavily. "What do you mean?"

"I get in trouble. Well, I got into trouble. I was working on a case, the order came down to drop it, and I didn't drop it. I pursued it and found out why some people had tried to call me off. It's not good to embarrass generals."

She gasped. "No!"

"Yes. In this case, the perp was a prominent man's son. In the process of going after him, I got shot."

"Oh, Buck, no!"

"Yes. I can't give you the details. Believe me, they're so highly classified now I could spend a long time in jail for telling you. So let's just leave it at that. A very important man stood to be embarrassed and have his future wrecked because of something his son had gotten involved with. So I had to be shut down. I was. Firmly. I took a bullet that bruised my spine and paralyzed me for a while, and then I was swiftly discharged for medical reasons. Part of the bullet is still lodged in there. It

won't cause any problems, but it was a good excuse to
usher me out. And I got the message. Don't mess with
the big dogs."

"That's not right!"

"Doesn't matter. I'd become a loose cannon. I'd disobeyed a direct order. If it hadn't been too messy, I'd
probably have been court-martialed. The quietest way
to deal with me was medical retirement. Of course, if I'd
been in any condition, I might have been stupid enough
to fight it. The order was unlawful because it obstructed
an investigation. I could have made a case, but it probably wouldn't have gotten very far. Most people are more
concerned with their careers than I was."

"But that's awful! If the son did something wrong, he
should have gone to jail."

He shrugged one shoulder, gently stroking the back
of her hand with his fingertips. Delightful shocks ran
through her entire body. "They dealt with him another
way. I'm pretty sure he got the message, too. Jail isn't
the only answer for some things. My mistake for not accepting it."

"How can you call that a mistake?"

"I'm a little older and much wiser now. In some situ-
ations, some people are almost untouchable. And what's
more important? Putting someone in jail, or just stopping
them from whatever illegal thing they're doing? Sometimes the latter is the best answer. There's also another
way to look at it."

"What's that?"

"Why ruin a good man's career because of something
his son did?"

She looked down at his hand on hers and pondered.
"A lot of people get hurt by what their kids do."

"Of course. But the military officer corps is a very

tight-knit elite, and appearance counts for a lot. More so than in most civilian positions. Hell, a divorce can end your hopes of rising high. Imagine what having a criminal for a son could do? So this guy was important, he was on his way to the top, he was widely liked and supported, and everything would have come crashing down because of his son's failure. I get it. They were fast-tracking him for a lot of good reasons, and they didn't want him knocked off the track."

He leaned back, taking his hand from hers. Meg served them their dinners, his steak and eggs, hers a fluffy omelet with mushrooms and green peppers. Haley looked down at her plate but barely saw the food.

"Anyway," Buck went on when they were alone again, "at the point when they called me off, I wasn't sure who I was dealing with. I just knew I was close to solving the case. I didn't care what they said, I was going to finish it. That's what I was paid to do. What's more, I've got more that a little bulldog in me, and I wasn't about to give up my bone. I wanted the answers."

"And that's the thanks you got for being a good cop?"

"They *did* thank me. They could have crushed my career, put me behind a desk pushing papers, and I'd never have seen another promotion. Instead they gave me a Meritorious Service medal, a promotion, a full medical disability and retirement."

She studied his face, which revealed little. "How does that make you feel?"

"Glad I'm not the one in jail." He shook his head. "The point I'm trying to make here is that when I take the bit between my teeth, I don't quit. Stubborn might as well be my middle name. Plus, I hate unsolved puzzles. So I walked into a thicket in defiance of orders, rightly or wrongly, and I came out better than I had a right to expect in the circumstances. Does it chap me? Hell, yeah. But some things you just have to accept."

Haley knew all about accepting things. She'd had a lot to accept herself. "It just doesn't seem right," she said finally.

He smiled crookedly. "Fairness, right and wrong—they're things we impose on the world. Life isn't inherently fair. I think you know that."

"I do," she said reluctantly, thinking of how life had treated her mother. Picking up her fork, she started on her omelet before it turned cold. "So is that why you decided to start driving? To get away from all that?"

"Maybe in part. I like being on the road. It's mostly peaceful."

"Until lately," she said a little tartly.

"Obviously."

Conversation trailed off as they ate, giving Haley the opportunity to think over what he'd told her. She decided that he'd probably been more upset by what had happened than he was letting on. Of course, he'd had to make peace with it afterward, but at the time it must have seemed like a terrible betrayal.

"How much more school do you have?" he asked eventually.

"That depends. First I'm getting my LPN, so I'll spend most of the coming year working at the hospital, being trained on the job, so to speak. There'll still be some classroom stuff, but mostly it'll be hands-on. I'm looking forward to that."

"And then?"

"I plan to work for a few years and save some money, then go for my RN. Well, actually, I'm thinking about a bachelor of science in nursing."

"Will that take long?"

"Two or three years, depending on me, mostly. And where I decide to go."

"So you can't do that here?"

She shook her head. "This is just a junior college."

He smiled. "Big plans."

"I've had a lot of time to dream them up."

"Where do you want to wind up eventually? What kind of nursing? A big hospital?"

His questions provided the perfect opportunity to forget about everything else and focus on something that didn't leave her unsettled. She was only too happy to talk about the specialties she was thinking about down the road, and her indecision about whether she wanted a big hospital or a small community hospital. She warmed to her topic so much that she was startled to realize they were finished eating.

"Wow, I ran on!"

"I enjoyed it. It made a nice change from my obsession."

His obsession being whatever was happening with those shipments. The reminder caused a tiny trickle of ice to run down her spine.

"What are you going to do?" she asked him.

"Not here."

So she let it go for now, passing on dessert because it was so late. She didn't feel particularly eager to go back to her apartment, but there was nowhere else to go.

Worse yet, he said goodbye to her in the parking lot. Just a quick hug and a peck on the cheek, nothing meaningful, and certainly nothing to be misinterpreted. Then he said good-night and started walking toward the highway and the motel.

Unhappily, she started her car, eased out of her parking place and headed out of the lot. She hadn't driven very far down the highway, moving slowly because she was so reluctant to go home, when Buck was suddenly there, trotting alongside her car and tapping on the window.

She stopped and he slid in quickly, shoving a duffel onto the floorboards.

"Go," he said.

"What was that all about?"

"Unless someone was paying awfully close attention, they think I'm back in my motel room."

"That's important why?"

"Because from there I could see the entire truck-stop parking lot."

And his rental car was parked out there, she realized. It was a great bit of misdirection. But to what end?

"I'm thinking about getting rid of my rental in the morning," he remarked as they drove.

She almost didn't hear him because she was busy wondering why he was coming with her. Everything that interested him was at the truck stop. All of a sudden her head was buzzing with questions.

"Buck?"

"Yes?"

"Why didn't you drive to the college?"

"I like walking and it isn't all that far."

"It's going to be a long walk back from my place."

"I like walking."

"What aren't you telling me?"

"About what?"

She reached the traffic light in the center of town. At this time of night it blinked red in all directions. She stopped and looked. "You just said you're thinking of getting rid of your rental, right? Why?"

"Because it makes it look too easy for me to get around."

"What?"

"I'm sorry, I'm confusing you."

"Just slightly."

"It's really simple. If everyone thinks the only thing I have to drive is my truck cab, they'll be looking out for that."

"Oh. Will you need my car?"

"Not tonight."

They turned onto a quiet street two blocks from her apartment.

"Let me out here," he said.

She braked and gaped at him. "Buck, what in the world?"

"I have to meet someone. I'll see you in the morning."

He leaned over, pecked her cheek again in an almost brotherly fashion that annoyed her, then climbed out with his duffel. "Morning," he repeated, then slammed the door.

She stared after him as he walked down the street, then accelerated toward her apartment. She had lost her mind, she decided. Completely and totally. She had given her trust to a man she didn't know, one who was now acting suspiciously enough that if she had two brain cells left she'd be wondering if he was involved in this mess.

What she never expected when she pulled up at her apartment was to see a car in a usually empty slot nearby. She could see a shadowy figure inside it.

Her mouth turned dry and she hesitated. Maybe she shouldn't get out. Maybe she should just go somewhere else for the night. Like the sheriff's office, or some friend's. Not that she felt comfortable about calling any of them out of the blue for a bed, especially when she wouldn't be able to explain it.

But as she sat there, motor running, trying to make

up her mind whether there was any reason to be afraid, the car's door opened and a woman climbed out. A split second later she recognized Deputy Sarah Ironheart despite the civvies.

Sarah came up to the driver's side and bent down, waiting for Haley to roll down her window.

"Hi, Haley. I just wanted to tell you how great you were in the play."

As if, Haley thought. Her hands tightened on the steering wheel. "Is something wrong, Sarah?"

Sarah's smile became gentler. "Not a thing. I just thought we could have a glass of milk or something, gab for a couple of minutes. Do you mind?"

Something was definitely wrong, Haley thought. Her every instinct kicked into high gear and her heart found a faster rhythm. Damn, she was getting sick of not knowing anything and being nervous about everything as a result.

She climbed out of the car, bringing Buck's roses with her, and walked into the building with Sarah. Sarah Ironheart was much older, married and the mother of two. They didn't move in the same circles at all, and there was absolutely no reason Sarah should have gone out of her way to come talk to Haley about the play.

Something was going on, all right. She just had to find out what it was. She hoped Sarah would at least tell her when they got inside.

She didn't say much as they climbed the stairs. Sarah did all the talking, about the play, about her kids. Once they were inside the apartment, though, everything changed.

Sarah made no bones about checking out the two rooms. "Everything look okay to you?" she asked Haley.

Haley glanced around. "Yes. Now will you tell me what's going on? Did something happen?"

"Not that I know of. I just know Gage asked me earlier to be here when you got home tonight and check things out. Consider them checked. He also asked me to make it look like a normal social visit. I hope it looked that way."

"To everybody but me." Haley dropped the roses by the sink, then retreated to her desk chair. "So you don't know anything about what's going on?"

"Whatever it is, no. I get that Gage asked me to do something and he doesn't ask lightly, so I figure somebody's giving you some trouble. That trucker guy?"

"I don't think so." Haley hesitated. "Gage checked him out and called to tell me he was okay. I think...well, they may be working together."

Both of Sarah's dark eyebrows rose. Her Native heritage had kept her beautiful well into her forties. "That would explain a lot."

"How so?"

"Gage and Micah have been putting their heads together more than usual. There's something not right about that truck accident, but we're not investigating it yet as anything but an accident. I can tell you, though, it doesn't look like an ordinary accident to any of us. So I'm wondering why we haven't gone into full-scale investigation mode."

"Oh." Haley didn't know what to say to that. If Gage didn't want Sarah to know, assuming Gage knew everything, then it wasn't her place to talk.

"Then we ran a random registration check on a certain type of truck, but nobody said why. White or pale yellow box truck, I believe."

Haley bit her lip.

"You don't have to tell me," Sarah said philosophically. "It'll come out in good time. Just weird."

"Are there a lot of those trucks around here?"

"A few. I didn't get the count." Sarah suddenly laughed. "Cloak-and-dagger stuff. I haven't seen that in a while. How deep into it are you?"

"Everyone's trying to keep me out of it, pretty much, whatever it is."

"Welcome to the club. Well, apparently that's why I'm here. And you're stuck with me."

Haley felt her eyes widen. "You're my bodyguard?"

"I'm something."

"But don't you have to get home?"

"Sweetie, despite the clothes, I'm on duty. And frankly, I'd rather spend my time sitting here than driving the roads. You don't have to stay up on my account. Go to bed, read, anything you feel like. I'm just here until my shift is over."

Chapter 8

"Don't tell me what you're planning," Gage said to Buck as they drove out of town and into the countryside. "I'd hate to have to stop you."

"I won't."

"But if it involves trespass, let me warn you. If you wind up dead, there won't be much of an investigation. Folks protect their property."

"I don't intend to wind up anything."

"No one ever does," Gage said philosophically.

Buck almost laughed. "I'm just a guy going for a walk."

"Right. I've got a deputy with Haley like you asked. How worried are you about her?"

"Worried enough that I don't want her to be alone. She saw the driver of the box truck. She can testify that Ray was perfectly alert a few minutes before he died, which pretty much limits the time and opportunity frame for him to have been drugged. She saw the cargo exchange. And I've got two more pieces of information."

"What would they be?"

"That Claire Bertram poured the coffee Ray drank, and that Claire also talked to the other driver and asked him why the hell they were shifting cargo in the lot."

Gage swore. "She tell Haley that?"

"Yup."

"Thin leads, but I've been there before. Twist around, will you? You'll feel a sheepskin on the back floorboards. You might need it."

Buck came up with a patch of sheepskin, wool still attached. The wool felt oily with lanolin. "What's this?"

"Let's just say if you happen to wander among sheep, you should smell like them if you don't want to disturb them. Friend of mine gave that to me earlier. Should you happen to lose your way, rub it on yourself."

"What about hogs?"

"Can't do anything about hogs except warn you they can be mean. You don't want to startle them."

"Well, I won't be getting close."

"Not as far as I know, anyway," Gage agreed. "We ran registrations on the truck description you gave us. Nine of 'em in the county, most owned by local businesses in town. That doesn't mean a damn thing, though. It could be from out of county."

"It wouldn't surprise me if it was. But it's got to have a base here in order to meet with the trucks at the truck stop in a timely fashion. Truckers are regular enough, but not that regular. You don't want to spend an hour or two hanging around waiting for one to arrive if you don't want a lot of people to notice you."

"True." Gage tapped his fingers on the steering wheel. "Nothing from trip logs to help you?"

"Not yet."

"Hell. But why the parking lot? It's kind of an obvious place."

"But most casual viewers wouldn't know it's wrong for the cargo transfers to happen there. It would take another trucker, and even then it might be dismissed as some shipment having gone the wrong direction. You try that at some turnout along the highway in the middle of nowhere, and *any* passerby is going to notice."

Gage nodded. "I sure would. I think most folks would."

"The problem I'm having is keeping an eye on everything. Like tonight. I can't watch Haley, so I'm grateful to you for that, but if there was a cargo exchange going on right now, I'd miss it."

"You need some help."

"Haley goes back to work tomorrow night."

"But there's tonight." Gage sighed and reached for a radio on the dashboard. He held it to his mouth and keyed it. "Nine-ninety-nine to base."

"Base here, Sheriff."

"Tell Beau to meet me at the truck stop for pie."

"Any reason?"

"No reason. Just tell him I'm meeting him for pie. I can't sleep and I'm keeping Emma awake." He keyed the radio off and slipped it back onto the dashboard. "Nobody will pull a switch with a patrol car sitting there. Better?" he asked.

"Thanks."

"We're on the same side, you know. Loosen up a bit and let us help when we can."

"If I had more information, that would be a whole lot easier." Buck hesitated. "I got a call from my boss. He pulled me off the case. I told him I hadn't learned anything and I was going to stay another week because I'd met someone."

Gage gave a low whistle. "Think he's involved?"

"I wish I knew. It sounds crazy as hell to send me to investigate, then back off. I smell someone covering a backside."

"Maybe not Bill," Gage said presently. "Somebody had to have reported the discrepancies. Would it have gone through him?"

"Or one of the other shipping supervisors. At this point I'm really flailing in the dark, but it's likelier I'll find the end of the thread out here than back there."

"Maybe so. I take it by what we're doing right now that you're not quitting. Okay. If he calls us again, I'll stick with the story that you told us you were pulling out and I'll tell him we have nothing to investigate other than an accident. Or something to that effect."

"Thanks."

Gage dropped him at a crossroads seemingly in the middle of nowhere. Buck started to climb out, but Gage stopped him with a question. "How much of a country boy are you?"

"Depends. If you mean what do I know about farming or ranching, I know squat. I was an army brat."

"Then let me warn you. Folks sleep lightly. Any sign of distress from their livestock wakes them. They have to constantly worry about predators."

"Thanks for the warning."

"Another warning. Murdock Bertram has at least one hired hand I know of, and he doesn't sleep in the house. There's a bunkhouse out back, a few hundred yards from the barn. Of course, since you'll be staying on the roads and shoulders, you don't have to worry."

"Exactly," said Buck, keeping up the pretense. He understood perfectly the need to protect Gage from having to lie on a report or under oath. The man had gone far enough out on the limb by bringing him out here.

"I'll see you where we agreed at first light. You don't have a whole lot of time. I hope you walk fast."

The large knife was already tucked on his belt. The folding knife was tucked in his boot, but after he pulled on his black clothing, he'd tucked it into his pocket so it wouldn't irritate his ankle. He tugged on a ski mask, rolling it up to serve as a stocking hat for the time being. Before the sound of Gage's motor had completely faded away, he was running, not walking, toward the Liston homestead.

Gage's remark about time had been an understatement, but he knew how far and how fast he could run.

Quick in, quick out. He just needed to check a couple of barns.

The night was as dark as any he'd ever seen. Starlight didn't help much when it had nothing to reflect off, no snow or metal. The ground seemed to soak it up the same way rain soaked up headlights.

He made good time to the Liston place, though. The expensive sports car was still parked out front, seeming almost to glow compared to everything around it. Not a single light gleamed from anywhere. He wished he could get inside that house, meet Jim Liston and get a measure of the man.

That wouldn't help him look inside the barn, though. Those crates that were changing hands had to be somewhere reasonably nearby. The truck could maybe be in another county right now, but there was too much risk in transporting the crates too far. An accident could blow the whole thing, and a damaged crate would raise huge questions. He figured they were taking them just far enough to hide them until the next exchange, at a place that provided sufficient privacy to pull something out of them and make them look like they hadn't been tampered with at all.

A place like a barn.

He glanced at his watch, the glowing dial assuring him he'd made good time. Reaching into one of the many useful pockets of his new black hunting jacket, he pulled out a cheap nightscope that he'd had for years.

A scan of the farmstead told him everything was quiet. The hogs had settled for the night in a large pen that wasn't too close to the barn. At least he hoped it wasn't too close. How the hell would he know at what point those pigs might decide he was a threat?

He'd almost have preferred to have a unit of Rangers camped out there. Evading human detection was relatively easy and something he had been trained to do. Animals were a whole other game. For all he knew, they might be better than the highest-tech security perimeter.

He decided the best approach was directly up the rutted dirt drive. The grasses were browning either from lack of sufficient water or from the approach of autumn. Either way, they'd make noise, crackling at every step. At least his clothing didn't rustle. Thank God for the passion for hunting around here.

He kept to the side of the drive where the clay was less rutted, and stepped as lightly and quickly as he could, freezing when he heard stirring from the pigs in the pen. Mostly they seemed to be huddled in deep sleep.

At last he made it to the well-packed front yard, where the sports car and an older vehicle were parked. From there he turned and light-footed it to the barn.

Pulling out a small penlight, he hooded it with his

hand and began to edge around the barn, taking care not to trip on any obstacle as he approached each window and tried to peer inside.

Screwed, he thought instantly. If the window had ever been washed any time since the barn had been erected, he couldn't tell. It was so covered in dust and grime that all it did was diffuse his flashlight, seeming to light up the glass like a beacon. He switched the light off immediately and leaned as close as he could, trying to peer inside. If any light penetrated the interior, he couldn't tell. It was as dark as a tomb. He tried to open the window, but it refused to budge.

Hell. Moving carefully, he went window to window, only to find the same thing. Around back he found a small door, but it was firmly padlocked. For a minute he toyed with breaking in, then decided against it. He didn't want anyone to know someone had been here, and he didn't want to disturb those damn pigs by making the wrong noise.

Then he found a place where the boards had warped enough to give him an opening. Pressing both the flashlight and his eye to the gap, he was able to see something of the interior. Dark shapes everywhere, some of them clearly equipment, but on the far side of the barn he saw a big, rectangular block. It was as black as the night outside, shrouded in what appeared to be a tarp.

But it was the right size, as big as most of the crates he transported.

His heart accelerated a little, even though that glimpse wasn't enough to confirm anything. What he knew now, though, was that he needed to get closer to what was going on at the Liston place.

He glanced at his watch again. Time to move on to the Bertram place. No time to waste.

He took a step and his foot hit something that clanged. As quiet as this place was in the dead of night, it sounded as loud as a gunshot to him. He flattened himself immediately on the ground in the darkest shadow he could find, switching off his penlight.

Barely had he hit the ground when the pigs reacted. God, he'd never guessed they could squeal that loudly. Squeal, yes, but at that volume?

Thank God he wasn't easily visible from the house, but it was entirely possible that if Liston came out because the pigs were acting up he might look far afield for a wolf or a cougar.

The side door of the house slammed open, and he recognized the figure of the elder Liston stepping outside, accompanied by the unmistakable silhouette of a shotgun. Then a high-power flashlight switched on, flooding the night with brilliance as it wandered toward the pigs' pen.

He heard the old man muttering as he clomped down his side steps and headed toward the pigs. Buck pulled his ski mask down swiftly and closed his eyes to protect his dark adaptation, then pressed his face to the ground. His ears would have to be his sentinels, and the old man sure wasn't making any effort to be quiet.

The footsteps trailed away from the barn toward the pigs. Good.

Then a young voice called out, "Dad? Everything okay?" Jim.

"Dang pigs took a fright. Don't see nothing. Maybe one of them hogs was gettin' randy."

Jim laughed. "Wouldn't be the first time. You want me to check around?"

Buck stiffened.

A long silence answered the question, and Buck realized the hogs were beginning to settle again.

"Nah," said Mr. Liston. "They're quietening. Wouldn't be if'n it was some wolf or cougar."

A few more minutes dragged by endlessly, then Buck heard the heavy steps heading back toward the house. The door slammed closed again. Buck risked his eyes and looked up. There was still some dim golden light pouring from the window beside the side door. And some from a room upstairs.

Counting the minutes on an internal clock and getting more restive as each one passed, Buck waited. A glance at his watch told him he was now going to cut it very close. He didn't like the idea that he might not be able to check out the Bertram place tonight.

But at least he'd been able to put the Listons on his list of possibilities, higher than they'd been before. This place didn't look as if it made enough money to afford much that would come in a full-size shipping crate.

Even so, he wasn't sure it was one of the crates he was looking for. Lying there, he tried to tamp his impatience by figuring out how he would insert himself into the Liston situation. He would have to come up with a believable reason.

The last of the lights went out. Peace fell over the world again. Aware that he had no time to spare, he backed up and rounded the barn on the side away from the house, taking care not to make any noise louder than wind rustling in dry grass.

As he came around front, though, he noticed the wheel ruts leading into and out of the wide barn doors. Wide enough to accommodate a box truck. Those ruts seemed deeper than they should be for a regular car, and the elder Liston clearly left his tractor outdoors. At least at this time of year.

No way to know how old those ruts were. From what little he'd been able to see inside, though, there was no big machinery in the barn that could have carved them. He tucked the thought away, looked toward the house one more time, then began to slip away down the driveway, half expecting to hear a door behind him open and a voice yell out at him. His neck crawled.

The night remained quiet.

As soon as he reached the road, however, he took off at a dead run for the Bertram place. As he ran, his body settled into comfortable rhythms from years of practice, and his mind cut loose the way it always did.

That was when it occurred to him he might have done this exactly backward.

He should have driven out here in his rental, instead of worrying about creating the impression he was still at the motel.

After all, he thought, giving himself a mental kick, he'd wound up with at least one sheriff watching the lot for him tonight. Who the hell cared where people thought he was?

The perps, he reminded himself. The perps. If they had the least suspicion why he was hanging around, he didn't want them to know he was running a night recon.

It still made sense, but as the minutes and finally the miles ticked away, he started to think he might have gotten rusty.

The idea didn't agree with him at all.

Buck made it to the Bertram place, but he'd damn near run a marathon tonight and his body was feeling it. He hadn't hit the wall yet, but it was damn close. He pulled out an energy bar and crouched beside the road, looking toward the Bertram place.

As the sugar began to hit his system, his irritability began to diminish. Okay, so he might have gone at this whole illegal-shipment issue from another angle, except for Ray's death and Haley's peripheral involvement. But he still would have looked into it because of that damn itch of his, the one that wouldn't let him stay uninvolved.

Without murder, it became a crime of property, and those didn't concern him nearly as much. With a murder, though, the stakes had gone through the roof. Anyone willing to kill in cold blood once would do it again. Haley had stumbled into it, and until he was sure she was safe, he couldn't walk it back.

Then there was the woman presumably sleeping in that house up there. Claire. He pulled out his nightscope and surveyed the area. Her involvement had raised some serious question marks in his mind. She hadn't been the one who had just happened to see the transfer, but considering that the cops had thought it was unimportant, and Haley said she hadn't mentioned it again, what had possessed Claire to ask the man who had driven the other truck?

The thought that wouldn't leave him alone was that she hadn't asked anyone at all, but was simply trying to deflect any possibility that Haley continued to think about it or mention it.

If that was the case, Claire had made a serious misjudgment. On the other hand, by doing so, she may have removed Haley from the sights of the bad guys. Maybe.

Ray, after all, had gotten himself into trouble by talking to enough people about how he was coming into some money that it seemed to be common knowledge. Haley hadn't said squat to anyone but him after she spoke to the cops.

She had to be low on their threat radar. Had to be. Except for Claire. If Claire had asked the guy out of curiosity, she'd raised the threat level to Haley and to herself. If she'd been trying to deflect, well then, Haley might be safer. But if she'd felt it necessary to deflect Haley, then…

He stopped. The truth was he didn't know what was going on in anyone's mind. All he knew was that one guy was dead and somehow associated with some illegal activity. At this point he was fairly certain drugs were being smuggled. There were easier ways to smuggle other things.

And now there was this new wrinkle with Bill. Either Bill or someone higher up was involved, but either way, the bad guys probably knew Buck had been investigating. Now that he'd had his chain yanked and been told to leave it alone, it remained to be seen if the folks involved believed he was backing off. Now he had to redouble his effort to appear to be chasing Haley. He wondered how she was going to feel about *that*.

He looked at his watch, more concerned now with the timer he'd set. It was getting close to first light, and he didn't have long now. He was even willing to bet that Claire's husband or at least the hired hand got up with the sun.

Hurry.

He reached out and stroked the grass, glad to find it dry. No dew in which to leave footprints that would appear as bright as neon for hours.

Unlike the Listons, the Bertrams had a front lawn of neatly shorn and green grass, and he was able to run up the drive beside the gravel. At least the grass muted the sound of his feet. He wasted no time, taking the risk of rousing the sheep to frightened bleats simply because he had to find out what was in that barn. With any luck, the windows weren't clouded with years of grime.

The drive branched off, leading away from the house to the barn. Everything looked very well maintained. He might have thought these people needed no money at all, except for Claire's complaint about the price of alpacas. You could spend a lot on alpacas, as he'd discovered from web surfing earlier, but you didn't have to. It all depended on what you wanted from them, and they seemed to be pretty good investments in terms of wool. Breeding champions with the finest wool was where it could get expensive.

But the expense question remained. The guy had plenty of sheep. Why move to alpacas when the start-up costs had to be so high, whichever way you were going? Breeding stock and all that. Types of wool varying the price. It all sounded a lot more complicated than simply raising what you already had.

And expensive enough for the wife to complain about it.

So maybe the sheep weren't doing as well as everyone thought? Maybe the Bertrams were looking for a better way to make money?

He slowed down as he approached the barn, pulled out his nightscope and surveyed the entire area. Sheep huddled in pens, not very close, actually. When he'd driven past the first time he hadn't seen the bunkhouse out back of the barn. It was dark as the night itself, indicating the hired hand wasn't up yet.

A look back at the house assured him everyone there was still sleeping.

He pulled the wool out of his backpack and rubbed it on himself the way Gage had told him. If the sheep caught a whiff of him, maybe they'd ignore it.

The breeze hardly stirred at this hour, as if the night held its breath. The hours before dawn were often the stillest of the night.

Everything was locked up tight, but he expected that. He wasn't sure why people in this place that Haley thought was so quiet and safe would even lock their doors, let alone their barns, but maybe Conard County wasn't as safe as she believed. Or as crime-free.

The windows were cleaner, too. He was able to use the flashlight judiciously and get a bit of a look around. Until the beam fell on an alpaca in a stall. Huge eyes opened and blinked at him. He shut off the light at once, trying to maintain a memory of everything he'd seen.

No truck, that was for sure. Not that that meant anything, really. What he'd seen were neat rows of stalls, some of them occupied by alpacas, some empty. Why would they be indoors overnight, when the sheep weren't? Because they were worth too much to risk a predator attack?

Something to look into. There had to be a way he could find out just what Bertram was spending on that stock and what he intended to do with it. Breeding for championship wool raised it to a whole new category, he supposed. He wondered if Gage could recommend someone he could talk to about it.

These thoughts ran through his head at top speed, and he was just turning away from the barn when the alpaca let out a loud, squealing screech. That didn't sound like a happy cry.

Buck scanned the area, judged his exit option, and vaulted a nearby fence to take off over an expanse of lawn, lifting his feet so as not to scuff the grass.

Hell and damnation, he hated livestock.

Chapter 9

"How'd it go?" Gage asked as he picked Buck up at the crossroads. "You look like hell, man."

"Who expects a roadside ditch full of grass to be that muddy?"

Gage gave a smothered laugh. "Runoff from irrigation. I've driven past here four times. I was starting to wonder."

Buck had pulled off his jacket and stuffed it in his bag, but the front of his pants still had the remnants of nearly dried mud on them. "What do you know about alpacas?"

"Not much. Why?"

"I need to know why a sheep rancher would want to get into alpacas and how much it might cost. Anyone I can talk to who is discreet?"

"I know a guy. He raises sheep."

"Won't gossip?"

Gage shook his head. "In a previous life he was an intelligence operative."

"You seem to have a lot of formers around here."

"It's the peace and quiet."

Buck wondered about that. So far he hadn't seen a whole lot of that.

"So did you see something at the Bertram place?" Gage asked.

Buck shook his head. "Some alpacas."

"Then?"

"I took off like hell. No, I'm wondering because Claire Bertram complained about the expense to Haley. If the guy's in over his head financially, that could be relevant. If he's not, that's relevant, too. The process of elimination."

"I see where you're going. What about the Listons?"

"Something in their barn is covered with a tarp, and it's about the right size and shape for a shipping crate."

Gage fell silent, drumming his fingers on the steering wheel. "Could be anything," he said finally.

"Could be," Buck agreed. "I need another favor."

"That depends."

"Of course. If possible I need you to let it get around that it appears Ray was killed in an ordinary accident. True, so far as you know at this point. If you wait for the tox screen, that might change."

"You trying to put folks at ease?"

"That's the idea."

"I don't lie to people around here, a result of *my* former life. I'll have to think about that one."

"Let's just forget it." Buck hadn't really expected him to agree, but it was worth a shot.

"Care to share the rest of your plans now?"

"I'd like to get to know Jim Liston. If he's involved

and someone at the terminal let him know I was looking into this mess, that could be a huge mistake."

"Let me run a check on him first. I might even arrange to pay a courtesy call myself on the family. Give me your bare-bones estimate on how many people might be involved."

"Well, someone has to be getting contraband to the various shippers. Then someone at the shipper has to be paid off to put the stuff in one of the shipping containers. Then you need various drivers who want some extra money to pull a crate switch in the middle of nowhere. On this end…well, you need a driver. You need a place to store the crate. So somebody around here is, at the very least, getting a payoff for allowing the use of a building for temporary storage. Then you've got whoever is running the show. My thought is the smaller the ring, the better, but I figure you're going to need at least a half-dozen people involved one way or another."

"So not very big."

"Big would make it harder. Of course that leaves out people at the ultimate destination, and people who provided the contraband to begin with. But that's not within my scope."

"Nor mine."

"But if we can roll up the middle—and I think this is the middle—we should be able to get the ends."

"I'm inclined to agree this is the middle," Gage said. "Or at least one of the middles. I haven't noticed anything around here to suggest this town is an endpoint for contraband of any kind. Which I'm thinking is most likely drugs of some kind."

"That's my guess. I don't know what else would be worth this amount of effort."

"We have some drugs around. Who doesn't? But I

would have noticed if there was any increase in usage. It wouldn't pay to sell them here, anyway. Not that many people, and few have any real money."

Buck nodded his agreement. "I presume nothing happened at the truck stop last night?"

"Beau and I spent most of the night there. Nada."

"Well, if they haven't been completely scared off, something should happen again soon."

"Do you think they'd be scared off?"

"Not if there's good money in it. If someone in Seattle is keeping them informed, Bill pulling me off this might make them feel good enough to get started again. We can only wait and see. One thing for sure, nobody involved in this knows that I can't be turned off like a windup doll."

Gage remained quiet for another mile, then asked, "Why would it be unreasonable to question one of the drivers who had a mixed-up shipment? What if one of them talked?"

"It's unlikely they'll talk because it would cost them their jobs. Then there's the question of whether they even know who paid them to make the exchange."

"Makes sense. So the middle it is. Unless something else happens, anyway."

"That's the way it's looking."

Gage glanced at him. "How do we do this part? I sure as hell can't drop you off at your motel at this hour looking like that."

"Leave me outside of town. I'll jog back in like I'm out for a morning run. I could have fallen anywhere."

"Your bag would give you away. Leave it in my car. I'll get it to you later somehow."

Haley was starting to worry. Sarah had driven off around dawn, making some joking remarks in the hallway and parking lot about how a cup of tea had turned into a pajama party. Haley surmised that had been cover if anyone overheard or had noticed that Sarah had been with her all night.

But there was no one around as the sun crept over the horizon. It was Sunday morning, too early for the town to be stirring much. Out on the ranches it was probably different, but in town people tended to wake late, have a lazy breakfast and not poke their noses out until it was time to start going to church.

She was starting to worry about Buck, though. He'd gone running off into the night with nothing but a promise that he'd see her this morning. Where had he been going? What if he'd gotten into trouble?

What if that bullet fragment lodged near his spine had moved? He said it wouldn't cause him any trouble, but how could anyone guarantee that?

She told herself to stop inventing reasons to be anxious, but the anxiety wouldn't leave her alone. She didn't know enough about anything, really, and the big voids left a whole lot of room to worry.

Back in her apartment, her eyes burning from lack of sleep, she told herself to catch a nap. She had to go to work tonight, and without sleep that would be nearly impossible.

But just as she was trying to find a comfortable spot in bed and punch her pillow into some kind of shape— it had decided to feel like a rock for some reason—there was a knock at her door. Instantly she knew it was Buck.

She jumped up eagerly and went to answer, and seeing him sent the first feeling of calm through her that she had felt all night.

"You're okay!"

"Shh." He smiled and stepped inside, but she noted

how exhausted he looked. Even more exhausted than she felt.

"What have you been doing?"

"Checking some things out. I need some sleep. See you later?"

She hesitated, then said rather boldly, "Just crash here. That's what I was about to do. I've been up most of the night chatting with a deputy because I was worried about you. The bed's big enough for both of us to get some sleep."

When had she become so brash? She didn't know, and as she watched him hesitate, she felt her heart start to sink.

Then he surprised her. "Thanks. You under the covers, me on top."

At once her spirits soared. Ridiculous, she tried to tell herself as she headed toward the bedroom. Buck didn't follow immediately, but she heard running water in the kitchen and assumed he was getting a drink. That gave her time to slip off her robe and climb under the covers. She squeezed as close to the edge of the queen-size bed as she could, to give him ample room, and closed her eyes as if sleep had already claimed her.

Her own boldness embarrassed her, and she wondered if he thought she had been suggesting something more. His insistence that he would be on top of the covers suggested he might have. Or maybe he had meant it to reassure her?

Either one was possible, and nervousness accelerated her heart. She caught and held her breath as she heard him enter the bedroom. Why? What was she expecting?

She felt his weight as he settled on the edge of the bed, heard the sounds of his boots dropping to the floor, then listened to springs creak as he stretched out. The covers tugged a little, but not much.

"Sleep well," he said quietly.

He didn't touch her. Not even the merest brush. Apparently he was far on his side of the bed, too.

Another time it might have been funny. Instead she fell asleep with a single tear rolling out of her eye and onto the pillow, wondering what in the world was wrong with her.

When at last she opened her eyes, she could tell by the light that the afternoon was waning. She had turned over in her sleep, and Buck lay on his side, breathing quietly, his arm thrown casually over her waist.

Wow. It felt so good, even though he was soundly asleep and unaware of doing it. Maybe she was just too hungry for human touch since she had lost her mother, but the weight of his arm felt so good. It answered some need deep inside her and filled her with warmth.

She tried not to move a muscle, and blinked the sleep from her eyes so that she could study him.

Always before she had seen him either reserved or animated, but never utterly relaxed as he was now. Sleep softened his face in an appealing way and she noticed again how attractive he was. He didn't have the kind of appeal an actor might. His was very different. She supposed a lot of people might think he looked almost ordinary, but he never had to her. She'd always thought he was a hunk.

She wished she had the right to reach out and stroke his tousled dark hair, or trace the line of his cheek and jaw. Stubble darkened his chin and cheeks right now, and she wished she could feel how prickly it was.

Her fingers itched to learn him in a way her eyes never could.

His scent reached her, too. He smelled a little musky and maybe a little sweaty, as if he'd engaged in some heavy exercise before coming here. It was a pleasant smell, though, and appealing. As appealing as his face.

The warm weight of his arm across her waist soon had her thinking about touching more than his face and hair. It was a little embarrassing to realize that at her age she had almost no experience with the male body. Those gropings in dark corners a few times at school, while they had been exciting, had not been very good, for the most part. And her boyfriends had done most of the groping, rather awkwardly and sometimes painfully in their eagerness.

Buck was more experienced, and it occurred to her that judging by that one kiss he had given her, he was probably a lot more skilled at making a woman feel good.

What would it be like to learn his angles and planes, the taut curves of his muscles? What would it be like as he learned hers?

Her cheeks heated, but her mind refused to give in to embarrassment. The nice thing about the mind was that it was private, so as anticipatory tingles started between her legs and in her breasts, she just let them happen. He would never know, and it had been so long since she'd given in to even the merest of physical desires. Well, other than Buck's kiss, which had been so arousing.

She wanted another of those kisses, and so much more. She ought to feel shy about it, but as the pulsing began between her legs, shyness was the least of the things she felt.

So what if she'd never been naked with a man before? Suddenly that seemed like the most delightful thing in the world. She tried to imagine what it would be like for their naked bodies to press together, whether he would feel hot and smooth, or if it would be different. What turned a man on? She had only one idea, one she wasn't sure she could even do.

But he would have to touch her in the same ways, and she melted a little imagining it. What would it be like to have his huge, warm hands on her bare breasts? Or his mouth? And what about between her legs? No one had ever touched her there before, and she couldn't imagine what it would be like. Or what it would be like to be filled by him.

So much she didn't know, and so much she suddenly wanted to know.

"Hi," he said without opening his eyes.

She almost squirmed with discomfort, then reminded herself that he could not possibly know where her thoughts had wandered.

"You smell positively delicious," he said. "You have the most enticing, womanly scents."

What did he mean?

"I ought to shower. I must smell like I came from the gym."

"You smell fine," she blurted. "I was just thinking that."

His eyes opened drowsily. "Not as good as you. Are you aware the body sends out sexual scents?"

Oh, my God, she thought, wanting to sink right through the bed and then through the floor. Her throat locked up and she couldn't say anything.

"I didn't think so." A drowsy laugh escaped him. "You may not know it, but you smell like a woman ready for love."

She could stand it no longer. She pulled the blanket up over her head. Moments later, his fingers tugged it gently away. She couldn't help but meet his gaze, and found his dark, warm eyes had moved closer.

"Don't be embarrassed," he said quietly. "If you knew these things, you'd probably realize I'm giving off the same scents."

Two things struck her. First, he knew she didn't know all that much, which was a little awkward at her age, and second, he was essentially saying he felt the same way.

She couldn't decide which to focus on.

He settled the question by rising a little and leaning over her until their mouths met.

"There is no greater aphrodisiac," he murmured against her lips, "than the scent of arousal."

His lips began to sip at hers, gently encouraging response. It didn't take long. She tugged her arms free of the blanket and wrapped them around his neck, trying to hold him closer.

He responded at once, tightening his arm around her waist, leaning himself into her so that for the first time she could really feel the strength and hardness of his muscles. His mouth remained gentle, however, as he deepened his kiss, claiming her tongue with his as if it were his own.

She'd never experienced a kiss like this, as if he knew every sensitive nerve ending in her mouth and how to stroke them so that sensations exploded throughout her entire body. At first little rivulets, they turned into rivers of need, awakening her everywhere.

Expectancy began to pour through her, an almost hushed yet demanding hunger to learn more of what she was capable of feeling. The protection of blankets rapidly became a hindrance she longed to get rid of.

Yet he refused to hurry, even as she felt her body arch toward him in an ancient signal of passion.

"Easy," he whispered, dropping another light kiss on her mouth, then traveling gently over her cheeks, chin and throat. "There's no rush."

No rush? Hunger was rapidly turning to heat, and heat to fire, as if the pent-up years of her inexperience were igniting all at once.

But he would not be hurried. Each brush of his lips caused another shiver to run through her, driving away the rest of the world, driving everything away except her awareness of this man.

God, she didn't want to wait. She wanted to *know*. But he proved a master torturer, refusing to give in to her need, taking his own good time about every little thing.

It seemed almost forever before his mouth moved lower, to the open throat of her nightdress. There he found more exquisitely sensitive skin, and her focus zeroed in on her breasts, only a little lower. They began to ache fiercely, and swell with demands of their own.

It grew increasingly harder to catch her breath. Her hands clenched at his shoulders, her fingers dug in, but he resisted the plea.

Pulling aside the neck of her nightgown, he bathed her collarbones in little nips and kisses, and when he pulled his mouth away, she felt the chilly wake. The contrast between the heat of his mouth and the cool dampness it left behind only heightened her senses more.

Then she nearly froze. His hand had slipped beneath the blankets and was tugging up the hem of her nightgown. Oh, man, that drove her even crazier. Helpfully, she lifted her hips so he could pull it higher, then felt almost disappointed when his hand didn't linger.

Regardless, she responded to the movements, first of the nightshirt moving upward, then to the blankets above. Helplessly she arched, seeking stronger sensations.

But still he denied her. The shirt crept upward, his fingers barely brushing her exposed skin, but they might as well have been brushes of fire.

Then, almost startling her, he pulled her nightdress over her head and tossed it away. The blankets covered her modesty, although she was long past caring about it. Something primal overrode her every inhibition.

One of his big, warm hands at last closed over her breast, squeezing it. The sensation rocketing through her made her clamp her legs together, not out of a need to protect herself, but out of a need for pressure, more pressure in places still unexplored.

He kneaded her breast, each gentle squeeze making every nerve ending more sensitive. The world ceased to exist except for his touches and the cells in her body that cried out for the next step on this journey.

Hardly aware of what she was doing, consumed by the fire he stoked in her, she grabbed the back of his head, demanding.

He obliged, closing his hot mouth over her nipple, sucking hard on it, lapping it with his tongue at the same time. A groan rose from her depths and escaped her as she arched into him, pleading.

"Easy," he muttered again, but she was in no mood for easy. She might have no idea where this train was going, but she didn't want it to stop. She wanted it to speed up. Had she ever guessed she could feel like this, she was sure she wouldn't have waited so long.

The covers pulled down, and she opened her heavy-lidded eyes to see him looking at her breasts. For an instant, just an instant, she started to pull her hands away to cover them, an instinctive response.

He shook his head and caught her hands, smiling first into her eyes and then down at her breasts again. "You're perfect," he whispered. "Just perfect. Look at yourself, if you can. I wouldn't change a thing."

Excited and blushing all at once, she lowered her gaze, then watched transfixed as he began to brush his thumb over first one nipple than the other. They were hard now, bright as cherries, and sensitive beyond description. The sight of him touching her added to her pleasure, and she kept watching as he lowered his head again and sucked first one and then the other breast, lifting his head from time to time to flick his tongue over a nipple.

Each and every sensation arrowed straight to her center, making her throb more and more, until the ache of need almost hurt.

Then, taking her by surprise, he took her hands and placed one on each breast. "Pleasure yourself," he said. "Whatever feels good. I have other things to give you."

Shyness almost stopped her, coming out of nowhere to nearly frighten her out of passion's haze, but he guided her himself, making her thumbs brush her nipples until she forgot to be shy because it felt so good.

Then he trailed his mouth lower, across her midriff, causing muscles deep within her to quiver. She could hear herself panting now, caught on a drawn bow of desire, wondering if he would ever let the arrow fly.

The covers moved lower with his head until he had sprinkled kisses across every bit of her abdomen. Until he had licked her hot skin and left a trail of coolness behind. Then he reached the point just above the apex of her thighs and she froze in anticipation.

A groan escaped her as his fingers parted her and stroked ever so lightly.

She caught her breath, almost unable to breathe as she waited, knowing there was more and so incredibly impatient to experience it.

His finger slipped between her folds and stroked almost gently. At once her thighs clamped around his hand, trying to hold him closer. That didn't stop him. Those knowing fingers parted her, opening her, and one actually dived into her innermost depths. The sensation was electric. She arched and groaned and cried his name.

Then he found that nub of nerves. The first touch was almost painful in its intensity, but he didn't stop. Instead he continued to rub it while one of his fingers moved in and out of her. Then he straightened a bit and brought his mouth back to her breast, sucking deep and hard.

She felt herself climbing, climbing, almost afraid she wouldn't be able to make the pinnacle, that everything would suddenly collapse on her.

But she made it. The moment, when it arrived, felt like an explosion throughout her body, and her mind went utterly blank as completion, painful and exquisite all at once, silenced it.

Buck watched her crest and land, his gaze drinking in every inch of her beautiful body, his own aching so hard he thought it would bust.

God, she was gorgeous. Sexy. And so new to this. He managed to smile faintly, tried to congratulate himself on a nearly inhuman amount of self-control, then pulled the blanket back over her.

Propping his head on his hand, he laid his other arm across her waist and waited for the tremors to ease.

Finally she sighed, and he looked into violet pools.

"Wow," she whispered.

He grinned. "Yeah."

"But you…" A faint frown marred her brow.

"Shh," he said, dropping a quick kiss on her lips. "I

don't have any way to protect you. There'll be another time, if you want."

"I want," she admitted. Then she crawled into his heart by the simple expedient of turning into him and hugging him.

The absolute trust she had showed him reached places he'd been keeping on ice for a long time. He tried to resist it, but it was too late. He cared what happened to this woman, if nothing else.

He held her close, knowing time was limited one way or another. He had to get back to his job eventually. He had to try to solve a crime, or at least part of it, in the little time he had. And he had to do something to keep her safe until this matter was closed.

Sometimes he just wished the world could go away.

It never did, though. All too soon she sighed. "I have to get ready to go to work."

"I know." He squeezed her, one last bear hug, and reluctantly let go. "I'm going back to my motel if I can get out of here unseen. I'll see you later when I come in for dinner."

It wasn't much of a promise, he thought, but it was the only one he could give her.

She saw the other truck driver that night, the one who had come in with Ray.

A warm glow had followed Haley all the way to work and stayed with her through the early hours. She was certain it must show on her face, but no one seemed to act any differently.

Then she saw the stocky, balding driver who had come in with Ray, and she recognized him. Her heart slammed, but she kept on working her tables, pretending she hadn't noticed him.

He didn't go to the counter for coffee, but instead took a table. She scanned the parking lot as quickly as she could through windows that didn't cooperate, but saw no box truck.

"I've got him," Claire said to her.

"Thanks." Haley's arms were full with a tray from a table of four she had just cleared. Even though her legs felt suddenly weak, she managed to walk past the other driver without even looking at him and to the back room, where she stacked the dishes for the dishwasher.

She had just emerged, thinking she'd slip into the ladies' room and call Buck to tell him the other driver was here, when her name was called.

"Haley!"

She knew the voice instantly. Reluctantly she turned and saw Jim Liston standing at the counter.

"Hi, Jim," she said, hoping he couldn't hear the nerves in her voice. Did he have something to do with that other driver? She glanced that direction and saw the man was eating a burger. Already. She wondered if she'd be able to phone Buck before he left.

"Got a minute?" Jim asked.

"Just. We're busy. What's up?"

"I heard you were working here. I just wanted to see you." He smiled, a very charming smile. "You've sure grown up nice."

She didn't know how to take that comment and wondered how to respond. Finally she settled on, "Thanks."

"Really," he said, his smile fading. "I also wanted to talk to you about Ray. Can't you find a minute?"

She hesitated. The place *was* busy, but not that busy. Hasty looked up from his grill. "Take a minute," he said. "But just a minute."

On leaden legs she walked around until she faced Jim

beside the counter. "I don't know what I can tell you," she said hesitantly.

"You were the last person to see him alive."

Not quite, she thought, but caution held the words back. "I guess," she said carefully. "But I don't know anything else. I mean, I hadn't seen him since high school, Jim."

He nodded. "Dad and Mom say you said he was okay when he was in here."

"He seemed to be. But what would I know?" She gave a little laugh. "I'm no expert, but he seemed fine. I only talked to him for a minute, if that."

"They're really worried about it because the cops asked them if he did drugs."

"I wouldn't know, but I told the cops he was fine. That's all I said." That and about the crates being moved. Come to think of it, she had already told his parents that Ray had seemed fine, so why would he come in to ask the same question?

"I appreciate it. There's talk, you know."

"I didn't know. I can't imagine why there'd be any talk. It was just a terrible accident."

"Yes, it was," he said firmly. Maybe too firmly.

She managed a nod. "It was awful. Sometimes we'll never know how these things happened."

"No, I guess we won't." He sighed. "It's just crushing them. But I wanted to ask something else. Somebody said you saw something happen in the parking lot beforehand."

"I did?" All of a sudden it was as if she had tunnel vision, and everything in the room except Jim seemed to recede as if she were looking through the wrong end of a telescope.

"Yeah. Someone said you saw cargo being moved from

his truck? Haley, I need to know if something happened. It might be relevant. My little brother is dead."

He seemed utterly sincere. Totally so. She wanted to believe him, but Buck's warnings silenced her. Who had mentioned it to Jim? Claire? Hasty? One of the deputies? She scrambled for a way to answer as she felt the room try to come back to the here and now.

Finally an idea struck her. She pointed to the windows. "Look out there, Jim, and tell me just how much I could see of anything."

He turned and looked. He and Haley and the diners around them were clearer than anything in the lot by far.

"It's like a mirror," he remarked. "But I still heard you saw something." His gaze tracked back to her.

"I *heard* something," she said firmly, gathering all her courage and a newfound ability to lie. "I'm not even sure what it was. I said it sounded like some banging, as if something was being moved."

"Oh." He studied her intently. "I guess somebody misunderstood."

"I guess so. I don't see that it would have anything to do with what happened to Ray anyway. Lots of things could bang out there. Lots of drivers adjust their loads. I'm sorry I can't help, Jim, but I told you everything I know."

He nodded, but still didn't move away. Out of the corner of her vision, she saw the stocky driver stand, throw some bills on the table and head for the door. It took everything she had not to look at him.

"I guess it's just hard to believe that it was just some random accident."

Her eyes snapped back to his. "That's always hard to believe. As hard, I imagine, as it was for me to believe my dad was killed in a hunting accident because he tripped. Or that my mother came down with cancer."

"You're right." He touched her shoulder lightly, then withdrew his hand. "I'm going to be here a little longer. Would you like to have dinner some time?"

"Thanks, but I have a boyfriend."

He lifted a brow. "That trucker guy?"

She managed to feign impatience. "Yes, that trucker guy."

"So he's hanging around because of you?"

"Is that so hard to believe?" Her temper was starting to come to her rescue.

He appeared a little embarrassed. "None of my business," he said. "Well, I can understand why he'd hang around for you."

"For a while anyway," she said, pushing a lock of stray hair back behind her ear. "Look me up if you're still here when he's gone."

"Haley," Hasty said. "Back to work now."

To her vast relief, Jim didn't stay to eat. He said a simple good-night and walked out.

She turned to go to the bathroom, but Hasty jabbed a thumb toward the back door. "We're talking *now*," he said firmly.

"You've got to cook."

Hasty scanned the emptying restaurant. "Claire, I'm going out for a smoke," he called. "Five minutes. Will you handle it?"

"Sure, Hasty. I just need some cobbler. I think I can cut it myself."

Feeling somehow like a child who was about to be scolded, Haley followed Hasty out back. Damn, she hadn't even had an opportunity to call Buck yet, and God only knew what that other driver was doing.

Outside it was chilly. Hasty pulled a crumpled pack of cigarettes from his breast pocket, pulled out a slightly crushed one and lit it.

"Haley." He said her name as if to get her attention.

"What? You told me to take a minute."

"I'm not mad about that. I could see you had to talk to that guy for a minute or two about Ray. I remember Jim Liston."

"Okay. So?"

"I'm worried. You're dating a driver you barely know and then you told Jim to look you up if he was still in town after the Devlin guy leaves. What the hell are you thinking?"

"Maybe I'm not," she admitted glumly. The urge to call Buck right this instant crawled over her nerve endings like insects, making her tense and uneasy.

"That's my point. But what's worrying me now is that you were asked about what you saw in the lot that night. And what's more, I heard Claire talking about it. What the hell did you see?"

"Next to nothing. Like I said, you can hardly see out those windows at night. You know that."

"But you told the cops something different."

Haley's heart began to sink. "I also told them I wasn't sure what I saw. The more I think about it, the more I think I heard some sounds and interpreted them that way."

"Maybe so. But it seems to me too many people are getting interested in that little bit of non-information, if you get my drift."

"I'm not sure I do," Haley insisted, hoping Hasty couldn't see through her. "I'm not sure I saw anything. I heard something that the cops didn't even think was relevant."

Hasty jabbed his cigarette at her. "*Somebody* seems to think it's relevant. I got Claire telling me to let you know they were just shifting a box headed for Gillette if I see you before she does. Why, Haley? Were you worrying about it?"

"Absolutely not. I never mentioned it again after the cops."

"And now I see Jim Liston come in to ask the same question. To my way of thinking that makes it important somehow. Best to watch your step, girl. Something's going on around here."

"But I have no idea of what!" It wasn't true, but Buck's warnings were enough to keep her mouth shut. "I don't even know what happened out there. Everybody else is asking me questions I can't answer."

"And about Ray seeming okay—"

She interrupted him. "He did seem okay. But what do I know? All I could say was what I thought, and it's not my concern anymore."

Hasty frowned, took another drag on his cigarette, then ground it out beneath his heel only half-finished. It joined a scattering of his other butts on the pavement.

"Watch it with that trucker. He's probably a nice enough guy. Most of them are. But that's something else you don't *know*." His frown deepened, then his face softened little. "Haley, I like you. I kinda feel like an uncle toward you. Something's going on and I just want you to be careful. It's almost like I can feel it."

His concern touched her. "Thanks, Hasty. I'll be careful. It would be a whole lot easier if I had any idea what I needed to be careful about, though."

He hesitated, reached for his cigarettes again, then tucked the pack back into his pocket. "I've been running this truck stop for thirty-five years. You get a feeling sometimes. Something ain't right. You need me, you know where to find me."

Chapter 10

It was too late to call Buck. The other driver was long gone, and so was Jim Liston. Another wave of truckers had begun to arrive, so Haley went back to work, her mind buzzing. Jim had questioned her about the crate transfer. Who had told him? And what was bugging Hasty enough to warn her to be careful? Just the fact that she was dating Buck? It hardly seemed like dating, although when she remembered the way he had made love to her that afternoon, maybe it was.

Claire, Jim, the Listons and now Hasty. She desperately wanted to hear what Buck had to say about all of this. Instead she had to focus on orders and trying to joke with the drivers and pretend nothing at all was going on.

Buck at last arrived around midnight, just an hour before her shift ended. He found a table near the window and sat. Haley was busy with another customer, so Claire went over to take his order.

He smiled and chatted with her. She put another omelet in front of him along with a tall takeout coffee, as if he didn't plan to stay long.

Was he going to leave as soon as he finished eating? Haley hoped not, as it would make her feel awful. Hadn't he enjoyed their time together earlier? Maybe he'd given her what she so obviously wanted, but he hadn't wanted her at all.

How embarrassing and how depressing! After that notion occurred to her, it was hard to keep the smile plastered on while she worked.

Regardless, she had to tell him what had happened tonight. But the prospect was now daunting. What if he was just using her for cover, as he'd said?

The thought squeezed her heart with pain, but she could blame no one but herself. He'd been frank about using her. Then she remembered what he had told her here just last night, about how hot he found her. That lifted her spirits a bit and got her through her remaining hour.

At least until she saw him pay Claire and walk out. She glanced at the clock. Ten more minutes. And of course the place was dead, so she couldn't distract herself.

"Why don't you just go," Hasty told her. "Connie comes on in ten minutes, and there's nothing to do right now."

With dragging feet, Haley made her way back to the lockers, threw her apron in the laundry, pulled her purse out of her locker, dug out her keys and headed outside.

A shadow separated from other shadows, and she gasped before she realized it was Buck. Then relief washed through her. Apparently he hadn't decided to ditch her, whatever the reason.

"I need to keep watch on the lot tonight," he said.

"Think there's any way you can get to the motel without being seen?"

"Car," she said, pointing at her vehicle. "If I leave it there, Hasty will call out the cops."

"Hell."

She thought about it for a few seconds. "I can park behind the motel. I'll be back shortly."

She drove her usual way home, but after a few blocks, when she saw no one around, she turned and took a back street. Ten minutes later she pulled up behind the motel, ignoring the fact that she was blocking a loading door. That wouldn't create a problem before morning.

Only then did it occur to her that she was still wearing her pink uniform. Darn it, she should have gone home and changed. If she walked around to Buck's door, and someone glanced across from the truck stop she'd be immediately identifiable. She might as well wear a blazing-neon sign.

Then she remembered the survival kit she always carried in her trunk. Breaking down on a lonely road in the winter around here could be dangerous, and there were still a lot of places where a cell phone didn't work, so a person couldn't call for help. Safety dictated she carry blankets, candles, warm clothing and even some nonperishable food and a can in which to melt snow into water.

Well, she had a blanket back there. It would cover her enough. She climbed out, popped her trunk and pulled out an old quilt that had seen so many generations of use the dark fabric had nearly worn away in places. She closed the trunk, locked her car, then wrapped the blanket around her, covering her head like a hood and making sure it concealed her all the way to the ground.

A little bubble of humor burst in her as she realized how she was skulking. Even a few weeks ago she couldn't have imagined herself doing something like this. Now she was avoiding tails and hiding her identity.

She had to admit it was a little exciting. From a very dull and ordinary life, she'd moved into the pages of a script for a play.

She saw no one at all as she made her way around to the row of rooms that faced the highway. When she reached Buck's door, she knocked lightly.

A few seconds later he opened it, revealing that the room was in darkness, and his eyes widened. "Mata Hari?" he asked.

She giggled. "I think she was a bit more provocative."

He tugged her into the room, closing the door and locking it. "Nobody could be as provocative as you," he said, then kissed her.

It was a hard, hungry kiss, and dissolved some of the doubts that had been troubling her. It was a kiss that said he hadn't been lying when he told her how much he wanted her. The ache in her heart eased, and a different one started to grow, but before it could fully blossom, he tore his mouth from hers and stepped back a couple of inches.

"Work first," he said sternly, but even in the faint light that reached into the room from across the highway and the red neon that lined the motel's eaves, she could see his faint smile was wry, almost crooked. "I've got to watch that lot. You can sleep if you want."

"I don't feel like sleeping. She let the blanket slip from her and dumped it on the foot of the bed. "I'll help watch. Besides, there are some things I need to tell you." In fact, she was surprised the news hadn't just come tumbling out of her mouth, considering how impatient she had been to call him.

His brow lifted. "Now I'm curious. But let me run across the way and get another coffee first. One for you."

"You don't have to. Besides, you already got one. That might look funny."

"If you knew how much coffee I've been buying in that place… No, it won't look funny. Just give me five and I'll be right back. Then we can watch and talk."

Sitting on the end of the bed, Haley had a decent view of the lot, a very different one from what she usually looked at. From here, little was hidden from view, including whether someone drove around behind the restaurant. She could see the gas pumps, which weren't visible from inside the restaurant, and the entire lot. Right now about ten trucks sat over there, parked at an angle, ready to go when their drivers chose. Another was busy fueling under the bright lights of the pump overhang.

Buck emerged with another tall coffee, but he didn't come straight back. He wandered over toward the parked trucks and fell into conversation with someone, probably a driver. From their postures she could see they were being friendly, and she even got the impression they laughed a few times.

It also, she realized, gave him a chance to scan every truck on the lot, including one that might be hidden to- ward the back, if there was one. Certainly she wouldn't have been able to tell from here.

Coffee with an ulterior motive. She laughed to herself and waited, trying to restrain her impatience. Before he crossed the highway again, he'd talked to a couple more drivers briefly. Everything about the way he walked and held himself suggested a man who was having a good time.

But finally she heard the key turn in the lock and he stepped inside with her.

"Coffee," he announced and passed the cup to her.

"Thanks. No odd looks?"

"I told you I buy a lot of coffee there. Besides, Claire was gone. Why would the other two waitresses even notice?"

"Good question," she admitted. "Did you see anything behind the parked trucks?"

He looked at her with evident approval. "You're catching on fast. No, nothing sneaked in back there during a moment of inattention on my part."

"Do you have many moments of inattention?"

"Only when you're around."

That reply zinged straight to her heart and to the core of her womanhood. For a few seconds she felt nearly dizzy with delight. He pulled the table back from the window so that she could set her coffee on it while still sitting on the bed, and turned the one chair just a bit so he could both glance at her and keep watching the lot.

"So what did you have to tell me?" he asked.

"I *so* wanted to call you, but things kept happening. First, the driver who came in to get coffee with Ray that night was in again tonight for a meal."

"Did he say anything?"

She shook her head quickly. "I pretended I didn't even recognize him. I didn't wait on him, and I didn't look at him directly after the first glance."

"Good for you! I think you've got a natural talent for this."

"I also looked outside and couldn't see a box truck, so he must have come some other way."

"But this makes his third appearance at the restaurant. Claire talked to him the other night, and then there's tonight. That must mean he's staying in the area. I wonder where. I doubt it's here, though, because I'm the only person who has stayed more than a night."

"I don't recognize him at all, so he can't be local unless he just moved here."

"That's also good to know. Do you think you could describe him to a sketch artist?"

Haley hesitated. "Maybe. I could try. You said we remember faces better than almost anything."

"It's true."

"I know for sure he's stocky and balding. And he favors white T-shirts, to judge by the two times I actually saw him. Even though it was chilly tonight, I didn't see him put on a jacket."

"But you couldn't tell what vehicle he got into?"

She shook her head. "Sorry. I was in a hurry. I needed to dump off some dishes and then I was going to call you right away, but before I could something else happened."

She almost enjoyed watching him straighten. "There's more?"

"Some, anyway. I dumped my dishes and I was going to go to the ladies' to call you. Except Jim Liston was waiting for me."

"*Waiting* for you? Are you sure?"

"He had to have been. He didn't even buy a coffee."

He gave a low whistle. He glanced back to the parking lot, then said, "Hold that thought. They're pulling out and I want to see if anything is left."

She sipped coffee, restraining herself, watching the lot along with him. One by one the big rigs roared back to life and began to file out of the lot. At this time of night there wasn't a lot of other traffic to slow down their exits. She watched them turn sharply, most of them heading southeast, but a few going the other way. Finally, there were only two semis left. They might be spending the night, or they might be taking a little longer with dinner. It wasn't as if these trucks exactly moved in convoys.

"Okay," Buck said presently. "Jim Liston. Did he say what he wanted?"

"He wanted to ask me about Ray. The same questions. But then he said the thing that really got my attention."

"Which was?"

"He asked me about the exchange I'd seen in the parking lot."

"Hell." Even in the dark she could see that Buck turned as stiff as a board. "How did he hear about that?"

"I don't know, but I couldn't ask him. He said someone had mentioned it. I lied and said I hadn't really seen anything. Just that I'd heard something and that's what it sounded like to me."

"Good thinking." He swore quietly. "That shouldn't be getting around."

"No, it shouldn't. The cops dismissed it as irrelevant. But then Claire goes and asks that other driver about it, and apparently she told Hasty it was just a crate on the wrong truck—"

"Wait," he interrupted. "How did Hasty get into this?"

"I was getting there. Let me finish with Jim. Anyway, he asked me out. I said I was dating. He knew about you—that doesn't mean anything. From what I can tell, the entire county knows I'm seeing you. That's what you wanted, isn't it?"

"Not to this degree."

She shrugged, trying to keep her nervousness in check. Even as she related what had happened, it was beginning to sound even stranger to her than when she'd been going through it. "Anyway, he said if he was still around after you left town, he wanted to have dinner with me. And then he just left."

"Did he ask about me at all?"

"Nope."

"Okay. One question. When did the other driver leave? I need a time frame here."

"He left while I was talking to Jim. Maybe just a minute or so before Jim left."

He nodded. "So they might have been together."

"I don't know. I mean, the other driver had time to get his burger and start eating before Jim showed up."

"But how long does it take Hasty to make a burger on his grill?"

"Not very," she admitted. "Maybe four minutes?"

"So Jim wouldn't have had to wait too long. We don't know they were together, of course, but the timing is fascinating. Now how did Hasty get into all this?"

"That was interesting," she admitted. "No sooner did Jim leave than Hasty told me he wanted to talk with me out back. So we went out and said he was worrying about me. And *he* mentioned the crate transfer. That's when I found out Claire had mentioned it to him and told him to tell me if he saw me first."

"She told him *that?* A very unimportant bit of information, all things considered, especially since you said you hadn't mentioned it again."

"I didn't. I didn't mention it to anyone after Sarah and Micah."

"Hmm. Anything else from Hasty?"

"Yeah, he's worried that Claire mentioned the crate to him and he thinks too many people are questioning me about the same things. In fact, he came right out and told me that I need to watch my step." She paused. "Oh, and he said he's been in this business a long time and could feel that something isn't right."

"He's right about that." Buck had turned away from

the window now and was looking straight at her, the lot forgotten. She wished she could read his expression. "I'm worried about you. I was moderately concerned at the outset, but now I'm getting seriously worried. Attention seems to be focusing on you, and the only reason that could be is that the wrong people know you might have seen that crate transfer."

"But how would they know?"

"It depends on who knows what you said you saw. It depends on which of them are involved. And if you want the God's honest truth, I got fired from the investigative job today. My boss told me to call it off."

"But you're not?"

"Of course not. My radar went off big-time. I'm wondering if someone at the Seattle center is involved, either my direct boss or one of his superiors."

"God, Buck!" A shiver ran through her. "What are you going to do? How can you protect yourself?"

"I'm not so worried about me. I can take care of myself. What worries me is my boss knows about *you*. I told him I was stopping the investigation, that I was staying in town because I met a woman and I'm finishing my vacation."

She didn't know whether to be flattered. Then she decided he was probably still using her for cover, which hurt. "So, okay, I'm your cover for staying here. How does that help anything, especially if you *don't* stop investigating?"

"It means I can keep my eyes on you twenty-four-seven. And at this point I don't care if they're shipping cocaine in those containers, what I'm not going to stand for is something happening to *you*."

Another shiver passed through her. All this time she'd been dismissing the threat to herself as unlikely. Minor.

Remote. But after tonight, after all of it, from Jim to the other driver, to Hasty and to Buck, she couldn't play mental games anymore. Denial would serve her no longer.

Almost as if he sensed the change in her, Buck left his chair and came to sit beside her on the bed. He wrapped his arm tightly around her shoulders and drew her close to his side.

"I'm sorry. It seemed like a bright idea when it started. I'd pretend to date you and nobody would wonder why I was here. I never guessed they'd zero in on you this way."

"Honestly," she said, her voice trembling, "neither did I."

"I *did* feel concern for you." He spoke quietly. "You were certainly in my thoughts when I made the decision to come back here and stay. You'd seen something potentially dangerous, but I thought we could deflect it. I thought if you didn't mention it, and nobody at the restaurant who heard what you saw was involved, it might go away. I wanted to be sure it went away. I couldn't just leave you hanging out here on your own with nobody knowing you might be in danger."

"I appreciate that," she whispered.

"Really? Somehow it's become worse. Either because someone at the restaurant is involved, or because they mentioned what you saw to someone who is involved. Or maybe because of one of my bosses. I don't know. I just know the threat level seems to have gone through the roof. They're focusing in on you."

"How do you know they're not using me to get at you? In terms of threat, you must be a bigger one than I am."

"That depends on how much they know about me and whether they believe I'm following orders to drop it."

She turned her face to him. Her heart had climbed into her throat. "But Buck, I don't know anything. Not really. What could I know that would make me a threat to anyone?"

"That crates were transferred. That you might be able to identify the driver of the box truck, that you might be able to identify the truck itself. The problem is, no matter what you say, they don't know how much you *know*."

"How much does your boss know that I know?"

"That you saw the transfer. I haven't told him anything else. I'd been busy working other angles until he pulled me off."

He sighed and gave her a squeeze. "I'm getting rusty. I feel like I should have seen this coming, that they might focus on you this way."

"But you were already worried about me!"

"I was." He turned his head and his warm breath touched her forehead just before he dropped a kiss there. "I was worried, but not to the degree I am now. I knew there was a potential threat, but I figured the longer you remained silent about what you saw, the more likely the threat was to dry up. Something is keeping it alive."

He paused. "Me, obviously. My brilliant plan for using you for cover backfired. Someone knew that wasn't what was going on. Someone knew and told these guys too much."

Her voice barely reached a whisper. Her mouth had turned dry with a crawling sensation of fear. "Your boss."

"Or someone he talked to up the chain."

"So what now?"

"I have to think. Last night I did some major trespassing."

"Oh, God, Buck, someone could have shot you!"

"I'm still here," he said with a shrug. "Point is, there might be a crate in the Liston barn. I can't be sure because it's under a tarp, but it's the right size and shape.

As for the Bertram place, all I saw was angry alpacas. Claire's been complaining about them?"

"Not alpacas per se, but about the expense of buying them. Murdock has some idea of breeding a line with really fine wool."

"So he's not buying just any old alpacas."

"Evidently not. He's trying to build a championship herd. It's costing a fortune, and according to Claire it might not pay a return for years yet. She's erupted about it once or twice. Fifteen thousand for one animal."

"That's hefty."

"Very."

"So Murdock might need money at least as much as the Listons. Maybe more, depending on whether he went into debt to buy his alpacas."

Haley's fists had clenched, and she could feel her palms had grown damp. But even as some serious fear battered at her, she realized she was feeling a spark of anger, too. "Dang it, Buck, I don't get this. Why do people do stuff like this for money? Why should Ray be dead over money?"

"If I really understood that, I'd probably be one of the bad guys."

The answer left her without a comeback and with a lot of gloomy thoughts.

He sighed and rose, leaving her feeling bereft as he took his arm away. He walked over to the window, standing to one side as he looked across the highway.

"Look," he said quietly. "We don't have to understand why some people will kill over money. It's been my experience that money, especially a lot of money, can make people do things awful things, desperate things."

"Why?" Considering the people she'd known all her

life who might be involved in this, she needed some kind of answers. Any kind.

"Because people who are motivated by money lose their consciences. Hell, Haley, studies have shown it doesn't even take *much* money to affect our basic compassion and kindness."

"That's ugly."

"I agree. But still true. So while you're sitting here trying to figure out your neighbors, just remember, some of them may still not be such bad people. Doing something illegal doesn't necessarily equate to being evil."

That was a different way to look at it. It eased her heart a bit, although not her fear. Okay, so maybe she hadn't really misjudged all the people she knew.

"The thing is," Buck continued, "we don't know *who* the evil party is. Who was responsible for the decision to kill Ray, who carried it out. So until then, we're going to have to assume everyone is evil."

"Great." Her stomach sank. "And here I was feeling just a bit better. So who are we making assumptions about? Claire, Jim, the Listons, maybe Murdock Bertram, the unknown driver, your boss or one of *his* bosses."

"At the least," he agreed, soothing her not at all.

"There could be others?"

"Of course."

She flopped back on the bed, staring up into the dark. "And you used to do this kind of investigating for a living?"

"Yeah."

"My heart goes out to you. I'm going crazy trying to think this through."

"It always feels that way until you know you've picked up the right thread."

"Who's your money on right now?"

"Jim," he said. "And Claire."

At that she popped up. "Jim I could believe, but Claire? Over some alpacas? Murdock has always been reasonably well-off."

"But maybe not well-off enough for Claire. Maybe the alpacas have tightened the budget too much."

"You have an ugly way of thinking," she said bluntly.

"I know. Blame my training."

It didn't make her feel one whit better.

"Don't you dare lay a finger on that girl's head, or any other part of her for that matter," a man's voice said over the phone.

"She might know more than she's letting on. A lot more."

"She doesn't know a damn thing. I talked to her tonight, and I'm telling you, she doesn't know squat. If people would just stop asking her questions, she'd forget it."

"What if she suspects something?"

"What good is a suspicion? Not a damn thing. And the damn questions are probably exactly what's making her suspicious. I don't know what you're up to, I don't want to know, but I've been turning a blind eye for months now, and if you want me to keep on being blind, you leave that girl alone."

"And what about that guy she's dating? He used to be an MP."

"Screw it," said the first man. "You got more to be scared of from the county cops if they find out something happened to Ray that wasn't *accidental,* if you get my meaning."

"You threatening me?"

"With what? I'm saying I don't know what's going on, I don't want to know what's going on, I never have. But if Ray died for some *reason,* the local sheriff ain't gonna overlook it. You gettin' it?"

Silence. Then, "I'm getting it."

The line disconnected.

Jim Liston hung up the phone and turned to find his mother watching him from hollowed eyes. "You said there wouldn't be any trouble, Jimmy."

"There won't be."

"There already has been. My Ray is dead. Are you next?"

He crossed the kitchen and wrapped her in a tight hug. "No, Ma, no. I just have a little business to finish with, then it'll be done." He held her frail body close and stroked her gray hair gently. "It's going to be okay," he promised. "You'll see."

But deep inside he was beginning to wonder. He didn't even want to think about how he'd gotten into this mess, or about what it had cost his brother. All because of a woman with a wandering eye. All because of one man who had gotten him over a barrel.

He closed his eyes, thinking. Okay, so the Devlin guy had been called off. That left the girl.

Despite what he'd just been told, he was worried about how much she might have seen.

And so was Bertram.

Chapter 11

The first gray light of dawn was breaking. Haley had fallen asleep, much to her own surprise, while Buck kept watch. She awoke to the sounds of him murmuring on the phone.

"I'm sending Haley home by herself. Keep an eye out? Thanks."

Haley shoved herself upright, realizing that at some point Buck must have spread the comforter over her. "Sorry I fell asleep."

"I'm glad you did. This only needs one set of eyes."

He crossed to sit beside her and hugged her tight, giving her a kiss that tingled all the way to her toes. "I'm sending you home before enough people wake up to notice. Then I'm hanging out here until I can ditch the rental car. I should be over there in a few hours."

"Are you sure you should leave yourself without wheels?"

"If my boss or whoever talked, I need to get rid of the car. Make it look like I'm following orders. Nobody will worry about me if my only transport is something as big as that truck cab."

Half-awake though she was, she followed his reasoning. It *would* look best. "Who were you talking to?"

"Gage. I want him to keep an eye on you until you're safely home. After last night, I'm not taking any chances."

She smothered a yawn and leaned against his shoulder, taking advantage of the moment. "Okay. But I still don't think Jim would hurt me."

"Maybe not. But I don't think Jim is the only one involved. He might just be one of the peons, following his own orders."

He was right. God, she hated this whole situation! If she could change anything, it would be to get this whole mess out of her hair and find out if Buck was spending time with her because he wanted to, or because he felt he had to.

Being painfully honest about it, though, she knew the only reason they had come together outside the truck stop was because of this mess. Otherwise he might always have been that handsome driver she'd noticed but never got to know.

"Come on," he said. "Before too many people start stirring around town, you've got to get home."

She couldn't argue with that. She hated to leave him, though, and wondered if she was always going to feel somehow cheated by him or by life. Because since he'd brought all this stuff into her days, she'd been feeling more alive than she had in a long time. And that sense of being alive came from being around him. He heightened her senses, made her feel like a woman. It was as if he wakened her from ages of numbing grief.

Concealed in the comforter, she made her way back to her car. Buck stepped out and kept an eye on her until she was driving away from the motel, with the comforter on the seat beside her.

Back at home, she pulled into her parking place and climbed out. The first sliver of sun had begun to peek over the horizon, and turned the world rosy. She hurriedly slipped inside, hoping it was still too early for any of her neighbors to be looking out the window…although she had a second thought about that. How would any of them know she hadn't just worked all night?

Inside her apartment, she looked around, realized she didn't feel sleepy anymore, and so went to make herself some coffee. Someday, she promised herself, she would have enough money to get herself an espresso machine. While she mostly drank regular coffee, over the past few years Hasty had started making lattes and other such drinks, which she loved. Heck, even Maude's diner was moving into that world.

Change came even to Conard County, she thought with amusement.

She climbed straight into a hot shower, then, with a towel wrapped around her head and dressed in jeans and a blue polo shirt, she returned to get her coffee.

The sun had risen higher in the meantime, starting to take the chill off the morning, and casting it in a golden glow. Everything looked so crisp and clean outside that she decided to step out onto her small balcony and enjoy the burgeoning morning. She had a folding chair out there, and lowered herself into it, putting her feet up on the railing. Life could be good. Despite all the crazy things that had happened last night, despite Buck's very evident concern for her—and Hasty's as well—the morning remained perfect, too nice not to enjoy.

From the corner of her eye, she caught a flash of white. Dropping her feet immediately, she leaned forward over the railing, and caught sight of someone darting around the corner of the building.

At once she forgot her coffee and her heart slammed into overdrive. Why would someone dart around the corner that way? And white. A white shirt, barely glimpsed, made her think of one thing and one thing only: the driver who had been with Ray the night he was killed.

Her mouth turned as dry as the Sahara sands and she hurried back inside, locking the door behind her. Was she being watched? By the guy who might have actually caused Ray's death?

She hadn't seen enough to be certain, but she'd seen just enough to frighten her. She tried to talk herself down, reminding herself it could have been any one of her neighbors. Or just someone taking a shortcut to work. Or the handyman...except the handyman wore brown work clothes.

She sat at her little table, put her coffee down and looked at her shaking hands. Was it something? Was it nothing?

She almost reached for her phone to call Buck, then remembered he had to watch the lot and get rid of his rental. He couldn't come flying over here because of something so stupid she couldn't believe she had let it frighten her.

She hadn't seen anything really. Not really. But the fear wouldn't leave her alone. Closing her eyes, she summoned that image again and again, that flash, that dash around the corner.

It could have been anyone.

So why did it make her think of that other driver? Because of a lousy white T-shirt you could buy in a million places?

* * *

Buck hit the used-car lot on the dot of eight. The guy wasn't too eager to take the rental back, since he'd been counting on the income.

"Look," Buck said finally, "I rented it for a week. I'll pay for the whole damn week."

"Then why don't you keep it to use?"

"Gas," Buck said, inventing on the spot. "I've seen all I want to see of the countryside. I just don't need it to go a few blocks. The things I want to do now are all here in town."

The used-car dealer gave him a knowing smile. "Oh, that waitress."

Buck had to quash an urge to punch the guy just for the knowing look on his face, but he knew part of his anger arose from the fact that he'd deliberately set Haley up for this.

If he got through this and put those creeps behind bars, he guessed he was going to have to make up a whole lot to Haley. Find a way to let her restore the reputation he'd obviously tattered.

Little had he guessed how a small town like this operated. From the look on that guy's face, Haley had just entered the ranks of "easy women." Well, he'd take care of that. Later. Somehow.

He almost sighed as he escaped. He had promised Haley to come to her place and he'd need to do that soon.

Because no matter what kind of son of a bitch it made him, she was still his cover. His only cover. Somehow he'd have to make it up to her, he swore to himself he would, but the simple fact was, cover or not, he was getting scared for her.

He didn't care if they figured out he was ignoring his orders. He didn't care if they came after him. But he damn well cared if they came after Haley, and for some reason they seemed to be zeroing in on her.

Why?

The question shouted at him from inside his brain. Why were they closing in on her? Because she'd hung out with him and they knew now that he'd been investigating? Maybe they'd known about him all along?

Had *he* been the one who had put her neck in a noose? The thought made his stomach turn over.

What the hell had he been thinking?

Was he self-deluded? Because he'd been more interested in Haley personally than he wanted to admit? Had he managed to fool himself, and her, right into trouble?

He tried to reach back to those decision-making moments in Denver when he'd made up his mind that someone needed to watch out for Haley. Using her as an excuse to hang around had certainly struck him as innocent enough then. He hadn't imagined how it might complicate things.

He shoved his hands into his pockets as he walked toward the center of town and tried to make a million mental readjustments, like trying to figure out a puzzle that had looked all right until you got to the last couple of pieces and realized they didn't fit at all.

The streets were getting a bit busier. Stores hadn't opened yet, but people were on their way to do just that. A glance down a side street near the sheriff's office told him that the City Diner was already full. He hesitated, then decided to go get some breakfast for him and Haley.

That was when he realized that in the few short days he'd been here, people had started to recognize him. Where before he'd gotten the barest of nods as he passed, now he was getting nods, smiles and greetings of "morning."

Some low profile.

How much of that, he wondered, came from these folks knowing that he was seeing Haley? How much came from the fact that the cops had checked him out and let him go? He'd probably never know.

He just knew he felt entirely too obvious. The last blow came when he walked to the counter in the diner and Maude's daughter, Mavis he thought her nametag said, greeted him by name. "Morning, Buck. What'll it be?"

He thought of all the years he'd managed to pass anonymously in cammies and desert boots by the simple expedient of changing his unit patch so folks wouldn't know he was from the Tenth Battalion. No patch could make him seem irrelevant here.

He ordered enough food for six hungry soldiers, and marched out into the morning sunshine feeling eyes on him like sniper sights. Which was certainly an exaggeration, but it wasn't something he was used to from friendlies.

And most of these people, if not all, qualified as friendlies.

Okay, he thought as he hiked toward Haley's place. The pieces weren't fitting somehow, and yet he had the feeling they were all there. Mentally rearranging them wasn't helping a whole lot yet.

Money. He knew there had to be a lot of money, and in his experience there were two ways to make large sums of money: guns and drugs, and he'd already dismissed guns because they'd leave huge voids in the crates.

Marijuana, too, was space intensive. No, something much smaller with a huge street value. Something like, say, oxycodone, which could sell for as much as two hundred dollars for a single pill, depending on dosage. At that price, you could make a whole lot of money with a very small space, the kind of space that wouldn't leave noticeable gaps in a shipment.

And while you might need a truck to shift crates around, once the pills were removed they'd require relatively little space to transport. You could carry them under a seat in a car, or in a trunk, thousands and thousands of dollars of drugs, in a comparatively tiny space.

The only thing that didn't add up was why they needed the trucks in the first place. With something so small, they could have used cars to begin with.

But trucks offered a huge advantage. They could transport large quantities without worrying about drug-sniffing dogs at a traffic stop. Trucks were pretty much left alone by the cops unless they did something egregious on the road, or skipped a weigh station.

For all he knew, huge amounts of drugs were coming in through the port or over borders, and this was just a protective measure to conceal the distribution lines.

That would make sense. A lot of sense. Another piece of the puzzle clicked into place. And what if the whole deal had started here for some reason and then reached out to Seattle and other points? That would explain a lot, too.

He ruminated on that for a while, trying to figure out how it would work. Someone here needed lots of money. Maybe the opportunity hadn't dropped into their laps, but they'd created it. But how?

He tried to stop himself as he reached Haley's street. Speculation was only good if it gave him some clues to follow. Right now he seemed to be running in circles again.

But the more he thought about it, the more he realized that the whole mess could have begun right here. Maybe this wasn't the middle after all. Maybe this was a center point from which the web stretched out and encompassed something that was already going on.

Definitely possible, but he shoved it to the back burner for a while. He had some more immediate things to worry about, like Haley, like that driver she could identify. He hoped Gage had a way of making a sketch. Or access to Identi-Kit.

He loved to solve problems, but he had to admit there wasn't nearly as much pleasure in it when he had an emotional investment in someone's safety. Namely, Haley's.

He knocked on her door and she opened it with surprising caution, peering around the chain lock the way she had the first time he'd come.

"Haley?" he asked with immediate concern. He didn't like the tightness around her eyes.

She fumbled at the chain lock and let him in, closing the door behind him and locking it. She didn't usually do that.

"What happened?" he demanded as he put the bags of breakfast on the table and turned to take her into his arms.

She came willingly, and he could almost feel her sag against him. "Nothing, really," she said a bit unsteadily. "Or maybe something. God, Buck, I don't know. I was sitting on my balcony having coffee when I saw something."

"What did you see?"

"That's just it! I can't say for sure. I caught the flash of a white T-shirt as someone disappeared around the end of the building. I don't know who it was. It could have been anyone, but it scared me."

"A white T-shirt?" For a second it didn't connect. Then mental images began to tumble around in his head and he got it. "Almost nobody around here runs around in white T-shirts."

"Exactly. Except that driver. He's been wearing one every time I've seen him. But most folks here…" She trailed off, then said firmly, "It could have been anyone."

He tightened his hug, offering the only comfort he could, that of touch. "Try to eat something," he suggested gently. "I need to think. And right now you don't need to be afraid. You're not alone."

He got himself some coffee from the pot and joined her at the little table. She was obediently opening the foam containers in which Mavis had stuffed nearly half of the diner's breakfast offerings, but she didn't immediately start to eat. He couldn't blame her. Who would have thought a white T-shirt could become such a big deal?

"You're sure it was a T-shirt?"

"No collar, short sleeves. And it was chilly out there."

"Idiot."

She looked up, her expression changing, her eyebrows rising. "Idiot?"

"Idiot," he repeated. "I haven't been here that long and even I know how much he must stick out. The first day I was here I bought clothes to fit in. He never even thought of it."

"So you think it was him?" The fear returned to her expression.

"I don't know. Of course we can't be certain, like you said. But it's likely, given the way Jim questioned you last night, and Hasty's warning. If Hasty is concerned… well, I'll bet there isn't much that happens around that truck stop that he hasn't noticed. He may not know what's going on, but he suspects something."

She nodded, her face still pale.

"Eat. Please. You need to keep your energy up, even if you don't feel like it."

At last she started picking at a sweet roll, then as she

ate, her appetite improved. He dug in himself because it was necessary, paying no attention to flavor or the quality. "You've seen White Shirt up close and personal twice now?"

"Yes." She paused with a piece of roll in her hand.

"You said you might be able to help with a sketch."

"I can try. But how do we do that?"

"I'm thinking on it. I don't want to give you a higher profile than I already have."

"You're blaming yourself? Buck, no!"

"Oh, yes. If I hadn't blithely thought I could use dating you as a cover for my activities here, you'd have dropped off the radar pretty fast. Instead, I concoct a stupid plan and it's blowing up. And somebody in Seattle must be involved or I wouldn't have been ordered to stand down. You saw something, I'm investigating, and we're hanging together. I might as well have put a target on your back."

"You couldn't have known!"

"I shouldn't have forgotten that it seldom pays to trust anyone. I learned that freaking lesson the hard way."

She crumbled the roll between her fingers. "But why would they ask you to investigate if they're involved? I don't get it."

"Cover for them. They can say they asked me. The thing is, they assumed I was an ordinary MP. No idea what I'm capable of. They figured I'd come riding back and say I didn't find or hear a thing. Instead I announce, like an idiot, that I'm going rogue on them because a driver is dead and I'm worried about you. Hell!"

He swore almost savagely and jumped up from the table. "I got rustier than I even imagined. I should have considered that the trail might lead right back to the people who sent me. I should have just done what Bill wanted me to, picked up Ray's load and taken it to Denver and let it drop and played dumb."

"That's not like you."

"Obviously not." He shoved his fingers through his short, dark hair. "The only thing I've got going for the two of us right now is they think I'm basically a traffic cop. They think they called me off. God, I wish I'd never mentioned you."

She rose and went to lay a hand on his arm. "Look, like you said, they think they've called you off. You said you were hanging around because you wanted me. If they believe that…"

"But that's the question, isn't it? If they believe that. Do they? I don't know. I know my military records are hard enough to get at. The cops could, but even then their access was limited until Gage called on some friends of his in the government. So assuming Seattle checked into my past at all, they should find nothing except I was an MP. Most MPs don't do the kind of stuff I did, the kind of stuff they need to worry about. Hell, my discharge papers don't even list the organization I was really with."

"So it's good, right?"

"Hell if I know. I may have let some stuff drop to Bill. I can't remember. If *he's* the one involved, or if he passed it on…" He shook his head. "I need to think."

"You need to stop driving yourself nuts. It is what it is."

He looked at her. "Speaking from experience?"

"You better believe it," she said hotly. "Dammit, Buck, I watched my mother die. Do you honestly think I don't understand that there are some things we can't do a thing about except endure them and get through them?"

She went to him again, gripping both his forearms this

time, making him look into her eyes. "We'll deal with it. We'll find a way."

It took him a minute to batter down his anger and self-disgust, but he did it. Somehow, looking into those violet eyes, eyes that ought to be accusing but instead reflected a genuine concern for him, got through his fury. He'd just told her he had endangered her through his own sense of hubris, but all she wanted was for him not to feel bad about it. She was extraordinary.

He knew he was lost then. Utterly lost. Whether or not he ever solved this mess, the only thing that mattered was keeping Haley safe. She mattered more to him than drugs, crime, all those things that had been his obsession for so many years until he'd gotten burned so badly he told himself he didn't care anymore.

Because he did care, about Haley. Even if he never saw her again after this week, he had to know that she was going to be okay, that he'd left her no worse off than she had been before he'd barreled into her life.

He shook free of her grip, but only long enough to pull her into his arms and kiss her. He wanted her. Damn, he wanted her more than he could remember wanting anything. Yesterday had only whetted his appetite for her and her loving.

He was going to steal these minutes for them, and just for them. He was going to love her the way she deserved to be loved, and he was going to leave her with the best memory possible before he set out to deal with these cruds.

Because he was going to deal with them, if for no other reason than to protect Haley. And when he left this damn town, he wanted her to remember something good about him. Something truly good.

There was only one thing he could give her to do that: himself.

Sweeping her up into his arms, he carried her to her bed. When he felt her arm wrap tightly around his neck, and felt her lips kiss his cheek, he knew the only true goodness he had known in a long, long time.

He didn't deserve it, not considering how he had set out to use her at the beginning. But deserve it or not, he was going to leave with this memory of her.

Or die with it.

Chapter 12

The world vanished in an instant. A strange kind of tunnel vision came over Haley as Buck set her on her feet beside the bed. All the things she'd been thinking about, like how silly and reckless she was to want a man who was a rolling stone, vanished as need burst forth into her mind and body as if nothing else in the world existed.

He stood gazing into her eyes, holding her by the shoulders. "Be sure," he said quietly. "Be very sure. A woman gets a first time only once. I want it to be the one you *really* want."

A momentary shyness poked up through the heavy sensual miasma that was fogging her brain. He knew she was a virgin. Somehow that embarrassed her, even though she had already figured he must have guessed. But to have it out in the open, and spoken… Her cheeks warmed.

"It's okay," he murmured. "It's okay. Everyone has a

first time. It should just be the right time with the right person. That's all I'm asking, Haley. To be the right person and the right time. Because if it's not, neither of us will forgive ourselves."

She nodded and lifted a trembling hand to cup his cheek. "I've wanted you for a long time."

"So I wasn't the only one eyeballing over the last few months?"

The question caused her to laugh nervously. "Sometimes I just wanted to stare at you, but I never could."

"Oh, baby," he said, "I stared at you all the time. I had to slap down my own thoughts again and again."

"Then stop slapping."

He studied her, then nodded. "You can change your mind at any time. I mean it. And talk to me. Let me know what's right, what's wrong."

"I'm not sure I know."

"You'll know when you feel it," he promised.

"You'll…show me?"

"What?"

"How to please you?"

"This is going to be a totally mutual delight." He smiled faintly. "All the way. Trust me."

"I *do* trust you."

Something passed over his face, as if her offer of trust troubled him in some way, but then he leaned in and kissed her.

Had she just been feeling shy and embarrassed? No longer. His kiss swept that all away as his tongue plunged into her and teased nerves inside her mouth that she never would have imagined could feel so sensual. She tipped her head back to welcome him deeper, and he took the invitation immediately.

His hands began to prowl her body, first her neck,

sending exquisite electric shocks running through her, then along her shoulders, more calming, then to her breasts, where he squeezed. She gasped and arched helplessly at the hot tide of pleasure that stoked. He kneaded gently, continuing to kiss her, moving from her mouth to her cheeks to her throat, then eased the pressure to brush lightly across the peaks of her breasts.

Her nipples responded instantly with flame. Who would have guessed such a light touch could feel so exquisite?

She grabbed his shoulders, needing support as he teased her along the path of passion. She lost all sense except that delightful brushing that promised and never fulfilled.

Almost before she knew what was happening, her shirt was pulled over her head. She gasped at the suddenness as cool air touched the skin of her back and belly, but almost before she absorbed that, she felt a twist on her back and her bra fell away.

She looked down and saw her naked breasts exposed to him, saw his dark, callused hands caressing that intimate flesh, felt the heat begin to pool like a huge weight between her legs. And with each touch of his fingers, another bolt of electricity shot through her. The sight alone would have driven her to the brink, but the touches took her so far it was almost painful.

The urge to hurry grew in her even as everything in her body seemed to become lethargic, as if the very fire of passion drained the strength from her.

"Easy," he murmured. "You have such beautiful breasts. Just enjoy the pleasure they give you."

"The pleasure *you* give *me*," she whispered, mesmerized by the sight of him touching her so intimately. Her eyelids were growing heavy, too, like the rest of her, but she didn't want to stop watching him touch her. The intimacy of his touch combined with seeing it excited her. Little murmurs of delight began to escape her, and lethargic or not, her body began to move. Every cell tugged her toward him.

He bent, and she gasped as his tongue flicked her engorged, reddened nipples, making them ache even more. Fiery ribbons ripped through her at each touch, and then when he pulled back and looked at her breasts with evident satisfaction, she thought she would melt.

The dampness of her nipples felt exquisite in contrast to the heat in the rest of her body. She thought it couldn't get any better. But then he leaned in again and began to suck one of her breasts.

Ah! The pleasure was intense beyond imagining, and it instantly weakened her. She grabbed his head, holding him closer still. As if he sensed her need, he caught her hips in his hands and swung her around until she rested on the bed. She almost cried out at the loss of his mouth on her breast, but he didn't leave much time for regret.

His hands went immediately to her feet, pulling off shoes and socks, then to the clasp of her pants. In no time at all, he had stripped her bare.

Her eyes fluttered open and she saw him standing there, looking down at her. She read pleasure on his face, as if he liked what he saw, and somehow it prevented her from feeling anything but delight in being so exposed to him.

Then his fingers flew to his shirt, working buttons until he could toss it aside. For the first time she saw his powerful, naked chest and arms. He gleamed almost like bronze in the morning light, and she had some hazy thought of gods and statuary when she saw how perfect he was.

Then he reached for the snap of his jeans, and she listened to the sound of the zipper opening, the ratcheting sound somehow the most exciting one in the world at that instant.

He bent, and when he straightened, she could see him in every detail, the way he could see her. He was gorgeous. Perfect. She hardly even noticed the dimple near his waist, nor the shiny smoothness of a small patch of scar tissue.

And his manhood. He was big and hard already, and some little voice in her head wondered how this union could even be possible, but it was drowned swiftly in new sensations as he dropped beside her and half covered her with his body, beginning to worship her with his mouth, starting at hers, and working his way slowly down, finding sensitive places she hadn't dreamed existed, from the side of her neck to the hollow of her throat.

She shivered with longing and reached for him, needing to give him all that he was giving her.

A small, smothered laugh escaped him, and he rolled back. "I'm all yours," he said huskily. "Learn me the way I've been learning you, if you like."

She most definitely liked.

More emboldened than she'd ever felt, she rose on her elbow and began tracing his planes and hollows, learning what could make him groan and, better yet, what could make him writhe.

His skin proved deliciously smooth to her touch, warm and almost satiny. Running her hands over his shoulders and chest was a sensual delight unlike any of her imaginings. When her own needs demanded she move on, she discovered the tiny, hard points of his nipples, and from the way he reacted she guessed they were as sensitive as her own.

Surprised, wanting to make him feel what he had made her feel, she leaned forward and lapped at them like a cat. A shudder tore through him, a groan escaped him and she knew an instant sense of feminine power. This large, strong man could respond helplessly to her. The feeling was heady.

Her courage grew and she dared to give a gentle nip to those hard little points. From the way he stiffened and groaned, she knew he loved it.

But there was more to learn, and now that she felt secure in herself, she moved her hands lower, across his smooth belly. She felt the dimple and the scar tissue, and for an instant she almost snapped out of her mood. He'd told her he'd been shot. That must be what it was.

Something warned her not to let go of the moment. Questions and talk were for later. For now all that mattered was wringing every bit of pleasure out of this incredible sharing.

She dropped a kiss on his belly, loving the sound that drew from him. And there was more.

If he'd ever felt this suspended on the welder's arc of need before, Buck couldn't remember it. Haley's explorations, so innocent yet so provocative, were driving him nuts. It was all he could do to hold still and submit to her wishes, to wait for her to find whatever she wanted and needed, to learn him as he had already learned her.

He knew the delightful secrets waiting for him between her thighs and forced himself to be patient. This was her first time, he reminded himself, and she needed to dictate the pace.

The thought almost vanished when all of a sudden she wrapped her hand around his staff. His entire body jerked with hunger and pounding need. Damn, he didn't know how much self-control he had left.

"How…?"

He barely heard her whisper. It took a moment to penetrate. Dimly he understood her question, and reached down to guide her hand, showing her how to stroke him, how to lift him to insanity.

What he would have given to have her put her mouth on him there, but he didn't suggest it by word or deed. Too soon, he thought dimly. She was a virgin. Some things needed to wait…

Then shock hit him. He looked down and saw her drawing his staff into her warm, wet mouth. Her tongue ran along him until he thought he would explode. Excruciating pleasure zapped him, and he endured as long as he could before finally, gently, lifting her away before he lost it.

He drew a couple of deep, shuddering breaths, hanging on, barely.

"Did I do something wrong?"

"God, no! It's too good."

He absolutely loved the smile that tipped the corners of her mouth when she heard that. She started to lower her head again, but he stopped her.

"Just a second," he insisted. "Just a second. This is one thing we're doing together, at least this time."

She pretended a pout, but when he nudged her shoulder, she rolled back. Then he turned, pawing on the floor for his jeans, and pulled out a foil packet. He held it up, letting her know.

He tore the packet and began to roll the protection on, letting her watch, letting her learn. Then he turned again and leaned over her, sprinkling kisses on every part of her he could reach.

"I might hurt you a little," he warned.

"I know."

Okay, then. He devoted himself to arousing her to a fever pitch, sucking her breasts, stroking her between her legs until she was wet and her hips were heaving to meet his hand. Her response inflamed him to the very same heights of need.

Only then did he rise over her and settle between her legs. Taking as much care as he could, he parted her widely, then positioned himself. With one long thrust, he drove home.

He felt her stiffen, heard her gasp. He stopped immediately. "Haley?"

"It's okay. It's okay."

Then her arms wrapped around his shoulders, pulling him closer. He began to move inside her, cautiously at first, but her response was so clear.

She was riding the wave with him. Higher and higher they rose, until they reached the crest. Everything inside him seemed to explode, as if all that he was jetted into her.

He heard her cry of completion at almost the same instant. It drove home to his soul.

She lay there surrounded by him, by his arms and his legs, cradled in strength, and all she wanted to think about was their lovemaking, as if by replaying it countless times in her head she could engrave every detail in memory.

She felt so good, so replete, so relaxed, and even that minor moment of pain had vanished so quickly it had left no lingering ache.

She could have lain there forever, reliving the past hour, reveling in it. She didn't want to move, she didn't want to think about anything else. She had found heaven in his arms, and she clung to it.

Eventually Buck stirred. He kissed her gently, brushing hair back from her face. "How do you feel?" he asked.

"Like I've been to paradise."

He smiled and kissed her again. "Me, too. And I'd love it if we could just stay here forever."

She heard the *but* without him speaking it. They didn't have that kind of luxury, not with all that was going on. She knew that, and felt a little silly for having wished it. Unfortunately, she knew that reality vanished for no one.

He rose and went to the bathroom. She lay in the bed, knowing she needed to get up, needed to clean up, needed to face whatever this day would bring. The memory of White Shirt, as Buck had dubbed him, came back to goad her.

La-la land was not a safe place to go right now.

He emerged from the bathroom, bent to sprinkle kisses on her and grabbed his clothes. "I'm sorry, Haley. I need to call Gage. Once we get this settled…"

She nodded, accepting the implied promise, but not believing it. Once this was settled there'd be nothing to keep them together. They'd each go back to their separate lives.

But she'd always have this memory. Always. And if that was all she ever had, she was determined not to regret it.

He went out to the other room. She climbed out of bed and headed for the shower. She supposed under other circumstances there might have been some pillow talk, but these weren't other circumstances. Buck was worried for her. Frankly, she was more worried for Buck.

Since the moment he'd told her that one of his bosses might be in on this, she had known in her heart of hearts that he was probably in a lot more danger than she could be. She was nobody, after all, and while Buck kept harping on all the reasons he was worried about her, she knew that Buck was the one they must consider a real threat. He was a former cop of some kind. She was just a waitress who might or might not have seen something.

When she emerged showered and dressed, Buck was still on his phone, and making a fresh pot of coffee. She sat at the table, looked at all the food, and realized she was ravenous. The eggs were beyond hope, but the rolls weren't, so she dug in. A slice of cold ham provided a tasty accompaniment.

"Okay," Buck said finally. "See you in a bit."

He joined her at the table and offered her fresh coffee. She accepted gratefully.

"Gage is going to help us out," he said.

She almost questioned the *us* part, but then realized that was ridiculous. This might not be her investigation or her case, or anything approaching it, but she was in it up to her neck. "How?"

"He's got Identi-Kit software we can use to put a face on White Shirt."

"Anything else?"

"Yeah. Some of the local cops are going to be helping."

She looked up from her roll. "Why? I thought you didn't want them."

"I didn't. Not at first. But this thing is snowballing. Gage is going to pick just a few people he's sure can keep their mouths shut and we're going to give them White Shirt's face. And...well, they have to get involved now. The tox screen came back. Ray was poisoned."

The roll fell from Haley's fingers as shock drove her stomach down to her toes. "So it's true," she whispered hoarsely. "It's true."

"I'm sorry, but yes. It wasn't just a crazy accident."

"So they really will murder." She stared blindly, seeing nothing, only now facing how much she had refused to believe that someone she might know had committed murder.

What kind of mental game had she been playing for nearly a week? Acting like she was in a play rather than reality? Pretending to think there was a possibility that Ray had been murdered but absolutely believing he hadn't been? Role-playing? Total denial?

"Haley, nothing's changed."

"Everything's changed." She focused on him. "Everything. We've been talking about it but I've been acting *as if,* if you get my meaning."

"I think that's normal."

"No, that's delusional. I've been play-acting."

"This would be more than most people could take in if they haven't dealt with it before. Babe, there's a point at which the mind just balks. Some things take time to process, that's all."

She shook her head, looked down at the roll, then reached for her coffee instead. She was relieved to see that her hand didn't tremble. "Reality-check time."

"You've been taking a helluva big reality check since this began. Cut yourself some slack, Haley. The mind isn't a bunch of computer circuits that operate in a logical, linear fashion. It has its own methods of dealing with things and absorbing them. I'd be shocked if you hadn't had trouble with this."

He glanced at his watch. "Do you know a guy named Ransom Laird?"

"Sort of. He has a sheep ranch up north of here. And his wife is a novelist."

"Well, we're going to meet him at the library in a little bit."

"Why?"

"To talk to me about alpacas."

She knew what that meant, and another stone fell into her stomach. Claire. Claire had poured Ray's coffee. Claire had talked to White Shirt for no good reason that she could figure out. Claire had tried to find out what Buck was doing here. She didn't know what would be worse, learning Claire was involved or that the Listons were. Either answer would transform her world forever.

As if it hadn't already been shaken to its foundation. Ray was dead. Murdered. And they needed to find out who had done it.

That was enough of a shake-up right there.

Miss Emma, as everyone had called Emmaline Dalton since she'd become librarian nearly thirty years ago, greeted them warmly. A lovely woman in her late forties, she was blessed with a warm smile. She took them to a private reading room. "Ransom should be here soon," she promised.

Apparently Gage had told his wife something about what was going on, at least a small part of it.

"Gage's wife is a beautiful woman," Buck remarked, as if he could sense Haley's nervousness and sought to relax her.

"Yes, she is."

Ransom arrived then, a guy in his fifties with blond hair and a beard, both silvered a bit with gray. He introduced himself to Buck, gave Haley a quick, friendly hug and sat at the table with them.

"Gage said you want to know about alpacas."

"I want to know a little more than that," Buck said

frankly. "Like what Murdock Bertram is doing with them and could they be causing financial problems."

Ransom sat back, frowning thoughtfully. "I take it this is some kind of investigation?"

Buck nodded.

"I'm won't ask questions then. Just understand I don't know Bertram well. We've talked a few times about his alpacas. They're very expensive alpacas."

"Why would he want to do that?"

"Championship stock is worth a lot of money, as much as fifteen thousand or more per animal. It really comes down to the quality and color of the wool."

"So he could make a lot of money?"

"Eventually. If you want championship stock, the outlay is huge. Growing a herd can take years, because alpacas seldom have more than one kid at a time. For most people, it's a loss for a long time before you see any profit."

"So," Buck asked, "if you had to judge, would you say Bertram might be financially strapped?"

"I don't have access to his books." Ransom stroked his beard. "Looking at it from the outside, though, I can't figure how he's paying for all those alpacas. I know how well I'm doing with my flocks and I can extrapolate. My guess is he's gone into debt to buy those animals."

"I saw at least four alpacas in his barn," Buck said after Ransom left. "There may have been more, but I didn't get much of chance to look."

"Four alpacas at about sixty thousand dollars?" Haley's tone was utterly disbelieving. "Possibly more? I always knew he was better off than a lot of folks around here, but not by that much."

"So a minimum sixty-thousand-dollar investment in

a handful of livestock, which strikes me as a hairy bet. I'd rather put my money in the stock market. And given that losing a single animal would put you down, I'm not sure you'd get very good terms on a loan. So what do we know now?"

"That Murdock Bertram is buying very expensive alpacas."

"And that a fellow sheep farmer doesn't seem to think it's a very wise bet. Which is not to say it couldn't turn out okay. And for all we know, Bertram had that much in savings or something."

"It's possible. But maybe he suddenly came into some money, too."

Their eyes met and held, and Haley felt an irrepressible shiver of sexual excitement, even though this was exactly the wrong time.

"Ah, don't look at me like that, babe," he said softly, reaching out to stroke her cheek lightly. "We've got life-and-death stuff going on here. Much as I want to drag you to my cave right this minute, I can't."

She understood, but that didn't mean she had to like it. She restrained a sigh and asked, "What's next?"

"We wait. Gage should be here soon."

"Why don't we just go to his office?"

"High profile," he answered. "He can come here to visit his wife without raising a single eyebrow."

She should have thought of that, but her thinking seemed to be a bit scattered this morning. "What's Gage coming for?"

"He's bringing a laptop with Identi-Kit on it. We're going to try to give a face to White Shirt."

Now this was more like it, Haley thought. After days of struggling around blindly, they at last seemed to have a real plan.

She still found herself shying away from the news about Ray having been poisoned. The shock of that still rippled through her, and she felt the stirrings of denial trying to take root. No way was she going to allow that now.

Things had gotten too dangerous. For her, for Buck, it didn't matter. She could no longer even remotely pretend that murder wasn't in the equation.

Chapter 13

It took an hour with the Identi-Kit, as Gage had to make frequent adjustments, but finally when he turned the screen toward her she gasped. "That's him!"

Gage smiled and saved it. "There we go, then. I'm only giving this to a few of my deputies, so don't expect immediate results." With a nod, he left.

She and Buck lingered a while in the reading room to ensure no one might even remotely think they had been here to see Gage.

Just as they decided they could leave, Buck's phone rang. He pulled it out and frowned. "My boss."

Haley immediately froze and waited.

"Yeah, I'm about to take my lady to lunch," he said. A pause. "Look, your shipments aren't my problem. You already told me they're not my problem. Fine by me. No, I won't come back early. I told you, I met a lady." Another pause. "Then fire me. I can drive for someone else."

He disconnected and blew a long breath.

"What was that about?" Haley asked. "Are you fired?"

"Not yet. They seem to be working up to it, though."

"But why?"

"So they can discredit me if necessary. Claim I'm a disgruntled employee. And they certainly want to know if I have any information I haven't passed to them."

"Do you?"

"Plenty. I'm a cop, Haley, or I was. I don't discuss investigations, especially with interested parties."

He paused, clearly thinking about something. A minute later he said, "Let's go get lunch on the off chance that he has someone check out what I just told him."

Haley was struck by an idea as they headed for the City Diner. "You need to have a fight with me."

"What?"

"A public fight. Then you can pretend to leave town and they'll think the coast is clear. They're probably a lot more worried about you than me, and I have to be at work tonight anyway. So if you drive off in a huff, maybe they'll think the coast is clear again."

He was silent for a few minutes. "First, that puts you at risk. Second...I need to be nearby."

"I'm not saying you can't be nearby. But there has to be some way you can hide your truck and make it look like you've left. And I can call you as soon as I see anything. You wanted to use my car anyway."

He didn't answer.

"Buck, you said it's obvious they want you out of here. So let's make it look like you're on your way back. Then maybe they'll get down to business again and we can find out who they are."

He didn't answer, so she left it alone. She wished she knew where she stood with him, whether he was just concerned she might get hurt or if she meant something more to him.

But even more than that, she was worried about him. Hell, he'd gone trespassing on two ranches even after her warning about how dangerous it was in a place where people had to protect their own property.

But no, he'd gone anyway, and now he was giving his boss reasons why he wouldn't come back even if it cost him his job.

God, she'd die if anything bad happened to him, but she didn't know how to tell him that. Letting him know how much she cared about him might only upset him, or worse, distract him. Whatever he decided to do, his mind had to be fully engaged. Now that they knew the truth of Ray's murder, she was absolutely certain that Buck could wind up dead, as well. He was just one man, facing this mostly alone.

Just as they found a parking place, he said, "I'll think about it, Haley, but I'm concerned about you."

"What can they do to me at work? Nothing. And I really don't know anything. When I talked to Jim about it, I told him I didn't really see anything, and he seemed to believe me. So it's *you* they're worried about. That makes two phone calls now trying to pull you out of here. Think about that."

"I am. I said I'm thinking. Give me some time. I'm rearranging the puzzle pieces. Let me see where it gets me."

With that she supposed she had to be content. At least for now.

But she didn't have to like it.

Chapter 14

Much as Buck hated to admit it, Haley might have a point. Two phone calls, both designed to get him out of the area. If they had ever been worried about what Haley might know, that seemed to be taking a serious backseat to what he might uncover if he hung around.

If her estimation was correct, then him appearing to leave town might get things rolling again.

But hell, even the slight chance that they might be worried about Haley worried him. There was still the possibility that White Shirt had been outside her place, but he might have been looking for Buck.

That was when he realized he was calculating ways to cover his bases. All of them, most especially Haley. Which meant he had just about accepted her idea.

Because it made sense. They seemed more eager to remove him from the area than anything. But he'd never forgive himself if anything happened to her, and if it did it would be because of him and his harebrained idea to use her as cover.

Crap, he could be such an idiot sometimes.

Before they climbed out of the car, he pulled out his phone and called Gage. "If I wanted to make it look as if I'd left town, where could I hide my truck?"

He felt Haley's gaze snap to him. "Haley had the idea that the thing these guys most want to see is me leaving. And considering I've had two calls from my boss about getting back to Seattle, and the last one was practically a threat to fire me if I didn't, she might be right."

When he closed the phone, he had some answers, but he still wasn't feeling entirely settled.

"Let's get lunch," he said. "I need to think some more and Gage has some ideas he wants to work on. Then we'll decide."

She turned off the ignition. "You know I'm right."

He was delighted at the exercise of authority on her part. This was the woman who'd given him a good argument when he'd first met her, but for the past few days she'd been almost subdued, as if she were a passenger on this train.

"If you have ideas, I want to hear them," he told her. "But after lunch. We have to consider every possibility we can think of, Haley."

"So you don't want to fight over lunch."

He looked at her, drinking in her lovely face and violet eyes. "Not over lunch, no. If we do that, it'll have to be tonight at dinner. At the truck stop. Until then we've got time to think this through and plan. I don't want to do anything half-cocked."

"Do you ever?"

"Sometimes," he admitted. Like his decision to use her as cover. God, what had he been thinking?

Well, clearly he hadn't been thinking. That simple thought of using her, common to his previous career, sickened him now.

Then another thought struck him: Bill had actually tried to call him off before. Not just these last two calls, but the first one when he'd wanted Buck to pick up Ray's load and return to Seattle. Then the resistance to giving him LoJack information. Did they really not keep those records? Or had Bill been trying to put him off?

Certainly the information Bill had eventually sent had proved to be darn near useless, no matter how he looked at it. But there was still that attempt to get him to bring Ray's load back before he'd even started his return from Denver. Probably the first salvo to get him away from here.

When he thought about that, he felt a little better about using Haley as cover. Crap, he'd revealed her to Bill, but at the same time, they might have already known because of Claire. If that was the case, then getting him to come straight back to Seattle would have left them a clear field to take care of Haley one way or another.

So maybe he hadn't been such an ass after all, even if his thinking hadn't been perfectly clear. While exposing her more, he might have actually saved her.

He'd like to believe that, but right now he wasn't sure. The grimness that began to settle over him was the worst he had felt since leaving the army. All he had were strands of suspicions and weaving them together was taking him down the rabbit hole to places where any number of possibilities might play out.

He needed, he thought, one more thing. One more useful thing. He hoped he'd get it in time.

Haley noticed something at the diner. It was amazing she noticed anything at all, considering that their lunch mostly involved Buck staring at his plate. She understood he was preoccupied, but it didn't make her feel good, not after their lovemaking just a few short hours ago. Her head jerked a little as she realized how very little time had passed since then, yet so much had happened it seemed like ages ago.

She looked around the diner while she waged an internal struggle with her deepening feelings for Buck, which he didn't at all seem to reciprocate, and considered all the things that might be threatening them. She caught sight of three men sitting together in a booth. She saw them looking at her and Buck. And she knew at once they weren't local.

She looked quickly away, as if her eyes had been skimming the room absently, and focused on the sandwich in front of her. She took another nibble and let her eyes wander again.

One of the men was staring their way. The instant she looked his direction, his own eyes darted elsewhere. It was too obvious.

"Buck?" she said uneasily.

"Hmm?"

"Don't look, but there are three strangers sitting in a booth to the right. They're not from here and I've caught them staring at us."

Buck never twitched. "Okay, concentrate on eating." He forked some broccoli into his mouth. "What do they look like?"

Keeping her attention on her plate, she described them as best she could from memory. Ordinary, really, except one had a thin scar on his cheek. They'd done a better job of fitting in than White Shirt had.

"Exactly where are they sitting? I'm going to need to take them in fast."

She told him the exact booth.

"Are you done?"

"I can't eat."

At once he looked up and around. When he saw Mavis he signaled her, but Haley noticed that he scanned the entire diner as he sought Mavis.

"Got 'em," he said as Mavis approached. "Don't look at them again."

"Okay."

Her insides fluttered as they packaged their meals. Buck threw a tip on the table, scooped up the bag and helped her from her seat. Then, never glancing at the guys, he slipped an arm around her waist and guided her to the register, where he paid.

He helped her into her car, bending to kiss her cheek before he closed the door. He was just getting in on the passenger side when the three men came out. He appeared to ignore them, but Haley, who forced herself not to even glance at them, couldn't help gripping the steering wheel so tightly that her knuckles whitened.

"Easy," Buck said as he fastened his seat belt. "Nothing's going to happen. Not now. Let's go to your place."

She couldn't help it. She glanced at the three men again and saw them climbing into an almost-new blue pickup two parking spaces down.

Buck spoke. "Let's see if they follow."

As she backed out and headed toward Main Street, it seemed that they wouldn't. But before she'd gotten three blocks along Main, the truck appeared behind them at a distance. Buck was watching in the side mirror.

"We've got a tail," he said.

"I see that." Her voice was tight.

"Just drive as you normally would. They'll probably drop us once they see we're going to your place."

"Why would they?"

"Because I told my damn boss I was staying here to woo you. We stick to the story."

The story. Yes, it was just a story, but hearing him say it out loud hit her stomach like a punch. She argued with herself yet again, telling herself there was no time or room for this right now, that more important things were happening, that it was never meant to be anyway. Buck would move on as soon as he figured out what was going on here. He'd never made her a single promise except to keep her safe. He'd never murmured those sweet nothings that might have meant he had feelings for her.

No, he'd made love to her, and she'd heard often enough that that was meaningless to men, even though it seldom was for a woman.

She tried to loosen her grip on the wheel, paying attention to following her usual pattern and speed. She glanced Buck's way, as if she was talking to him. He did the same.

From the outside it probably looked as if nothing unusual at all was going on. Inside, though, the tension was thick and almost stifling. She could hear her own breathing, and that wasn't normal.

God, she just wished they could tumble into bed and forget all of this! A childish wish.

She parked in her usual slot. The blue truck seemed to have disappeared. She was just beginning to relax as Buck helped her out of the car. Maybe it had been nothing at all, sheer coincidence.

Buck took her hand, carrying the bag of food as they walked toward the building door. Just as they were about to step inside, she heard the rumble of an engine and glanced toward the street.

The blue pickup eased by. None of the three men inside it looked at them.

"No coincidence," Buck muttered as they walked inside and began to climb the stairs.

"No," she agreed, her insides twisting nervously. "No, it wasn't. But what does it mean?"

"That they've either called in reinforcements or I underestimated the size of the gang."

"Why would they call for reinforcements?"

"Because I haven't left."

That didn't ease her mind any to think that she wasn't the one they were after. For the first time she faced the fact that she cared more about what happened to Buck than to herself. She looked at him after they entered her apartment and felt her heart squeeze with a longing and a fear for him unlike anything she had felt since her mother died. This was different somehow, though, and she didn't quite know why. Perhaps because she'd anticipated her mother's passing for so long?

All she knew was that looking at Buck made her ache so painfully she could hardly stand it.

He quickly dealt with the mess they had left from breakfast, then put the lunch bag in her fridge. He grabbed the garbage sack from her waste can and tied it off.

"I'm taking this out to the bin. I'll be right back."

She doubted his purpose was that innocent. He wanted a look around. Fingernails driving painfully into her palms, she merely nodded and watched him go.

What could she do? Not a thing. Not until they decided how they were going to handle this. Not until they had some kind of plan.

She sank slowly onto her desk chair, drew a steadying breath and dug the heels of her hands into her eyes. When had this become so freaking real? When had she gotten her heart all tangled up with a drifter to the extent that fear for him had her stretched as tightly as if she were on a rack?

She could no longer fool herself. Death waited, just as it had waited for Ray. She only hoped it wouldn't be for Buck.

Taking out the trash was such an ordinary task it wouldn't draw a second look, but it gave Buck a chance to scope things out. He already pretty much knew the layout of the immediate area—he always made sure he had a good mental map—but it also gave him a chance to find out if the guys in the blue truck might be watching from somewhere.

His question was answered as he tossed the bag over the edge of the large commercial bin. Three blocks up, the pickup had parked along the curb. No one was visible inside it, but that meant nothing. If he was the one on the stakeout, he'd have abandoned the truck for now, too.

It would be odd for three men to just sit in a truck like that for too long. Plus, they'd have a better view of whether Haley's car pulled out from other vantage points. All they had to do was keep someone near enough the truck to move it fast.

Yup, he thought as he closed the bin and headed back inside. They had a tail. There was no other alternative to Haley's plan: a big fight and him storming out and pretending to leave town. The two of them were trapped in dangerous treacle, and any attempt to escape it would let the bad guys know how much they knew.

Back inside Haley's apartment, he took one look at her sitting in her desk chair, and some shell inside him really began to crack. She appeared pale, frightened and pinched, and her violet eyes seemed to have almost doubled in size.

He crossed to her immediately and knelt before her, drawing her into his arms. "I'm sorry," he murmured. "I'm so sorry I dragged you into this. As God is my witness, I'll keep you safe."

"I'm not worried about *me,*" she said, her voice as tight as wire. "Buck, they're after *you*. That's obvious now. You've got to at least pretend to leave. *Please!*"

"I will," he said, lifting a hand to stroke her silky hair. "Tonight. I'll work out the details, you can give me a hard slap at the diner and everybody on the planet can watch me rumble out of this town. But I'm not leaving. You've got to understand that. I can't do that."

"Why not? It's not your job to solve this. Gage and his deputies can take over now. You've got to protect yourself."

He caught her face between his hands and kissed her, at first hard, then sipping gently from her lips. "I can't leave now. Not until I'm sure it's rolled up and you're safe."

"They don't care about me anymore." But her arms crept up, twining around his neck. "Buck, I'm scared to death for you."

"I can take care of myself. But I wouldn't be able to live with myself if anything happened to you."

"I'll be fine," she insisted. Then she buried her face in the side of his neck, and the gesture touched him deeply. Her warm breath on his neck made him shudder with longing. At what point had he moved past doing a job to having a personal stake in this?

He didn't know. Such moments could rarely be defined, he supposed. He just knew that nothing had ever felt as good as holding this woman, feeling her face pressed to his neck, feeling her concern and caring for him in every muscle of her body.

One kind of tension eased out of his body, to be re-
placed by another. He needed her. Not just wanting, but
needing. Once this was over, she probably would want
to get on with her life, but that was a wound he'd have to
live with. Too late to prevent it now.

He sighed. "I want you," he murmured into her ear.
"But we could get interrupted if someone calls."

Her arms tightened around him. "I don't care."

At that moment neither did he.

He lifted her, carrying her, loving the way her body
curled into his, the way she clung to him and softened,
giving him the ultimate trust. She made him feel like a
very different man from the hardened one his past career had forced him to become. She made him feel as if
it was okay to be other things, too. Tender things. Kind
things. Good things.

In a way it was easier this time. They knew one another, shyness was gone. They undressed themselves
quickly, then slid beneath the coverlet to embrace. Twining together, skin against skin, had never felt so good
to him.

She had slipped past barriers he had built a long time
ago, and he swelled with a huge need to give to her everything he could.

But the cell phone he had dumped on the table beside
her bed couldn't be forgotten. He had no idea how much
or how little time they had, and he didn't want these moments to be shattered by a phone.

It seemed she felt the same way. Their earlier experience had taught her a lot, and her impatience matched
his. No time to worship or adore, no time to linger and
discover. Hands flew over one another, mouths followed
eagerly. And when he lifted her over him so that she

straddled him, she simply looked down at him with hazy delight.

He captured her hanging breasts in his hands, kneading them until her nipples turned hard and rosy. Then he lifted his head and began to suck. A deep groan escaped her, and her hips began to rock against his, her already-damp sex cradling his, driving him up the slope of passion as if he were riding a rocket.

He would have liked to draw it out, would have liked to drive them both as close to the edge of madness as he could, but that damn phone remained at the back of his mind, a reminder that time might be short.

When he struggled to get a foil packet from his pants, she grabbed it from him, gave him a delightfully impish look and insisted on rolling the protection on him herself.

That was sweet torture, and he looked down between their bodies to watch.

"Like this?" she asked as her hands enfolded him.

"Exactly," he managed to say thickly. *Exactly.*

Then she lifted her hips and he reached down to guide himself into her. She sank onto him with a soft moan of pleasure. He drew her down, one hand on her hips to encourage her movements, the other on her shoulders to bring her breasts near enough to lick and suck.

Her hands clenched the pillow on either side of his head as their hips rocked together, each plunge to her depths drawing a soft cry of pleasure from her.

He kissed her, licked her, nipped her everywhere he could reach, and the movement of her hips told him just how good she was feeling. Faster and faster she moved, as if straining toward the goal, and each of her movements carried him higher with her.

Then, just as he thought he was going to crest without her, he felt the shudders begin to run through her, heard her moan of pleasure, and the paroxysms of her body swept him over the top with her.

She collapsed on him, sweaty and warm, and he wrapped his arms and legs around her to hold her tightly as the aftershocks tore through them both.

Never had he felt so good or so drained. Or so much like he had finally come home.

"The guy's getting anxious," Jim said into the phone. "The stuff is on the road. Having it sit around is causing him problems. He owes people. That Devlin guy needs to go."

"He has to if he ever wants to drive a truck again. Just a few more days. Tell your guy we'll go as soon as we can."

"I want out of this."

"Then you should have stayed out of my wife's honeypot."

Jim closed his eyes, furious that he had fallen into that snare. Furious that Claire had basically set a trap for him once she had guessed he had money. Furious that she had wheedled enough information out of him to give it to her husband, and then her husband had threatened him with telling Betty Liston things Jim didn't want his mother to know. "Keep your woman happy and she won't be looking to leave you."

"She wanted money," Bertram said. "I've got money now. But that's all she wanted *you* for, you idiot."

As if Jim cared. One stupid affair on his part and he'd been paying ever since. It had to have been a setup.

This mess had even cost him his brother, not that he cared that much. Ray had always been an ass to him. But he wasn't going to let anything happen to his mother. "I'm out of this after the next load. You can work it yourself."

"Will the guy agree?"

"I'll make him. I'm not wasting any more time up here to make you rich." Tough words. He wished he was actually as certain as he sounded, that he could turn the course of this fast-moving locomotive.

Silence. "We'll see. What about the Martin girl? You're sure about her?"

"She doesn't know anything. Both your wife and I agree on that."

After a moment, Bertram spoke again. "Devlin will be gone in a couple of days, if not sooner. I've got the company ready to turn the screws on him."

"Okay, then. A couple of days at most, but that means unless we can find a way around this, a shipment is going to make it to Denver in the morning. Do you have any idea how much trouble that could cause? I'll tell my guy he needs to get someone on it there. But you better be right. This is one dude you don't want to make mad."

Bertram laughed. "I've made him a lot of money. I can make him even more. Tell him to stuff it."

Right, Jim thought as he hung up the phone. Right. Tell the guy to stuff it? When he'd already sent three men up here to deal with the problem if it didn't go away fast? Bertram had no idea who he was dealing with.

But Jim did. He had a dead brother to prove it.

Chapter 15

The first call was from Ransom Laird. He'd stopped by the Bertram place to talk about getting into alpacas himself since the wool market was down.

"I was right, he's got about eighty grand in the alpacas he has and he's thinking about buying more. He explained being able to buy them by saying he used his savings."

"But you don't believe it?"

"No."

Another piece snapped into place. Bertram was it. The question now was how the Listons were involved, and when he thought of Jim Liston's big, fancy and very expensive sports car, he could see a huge link.

Jim knew people in L.A. and apparently was making a lot of money. One guy with money, and another who needed it.

It was a long way from proving a court case, but the puzzle began to look nearly whole.

Gage called a while later. It was possible to ditch the cab. One of his deputies would help.

"We're having a fight tonight," Buck said reluctantly to Haley. "Almost as soon as you get to work, while there are enough people around to take note of me roaring out of town. I'll be back, but I don't expect action tonight."

He didn't add that the appearance of those three men today might mean someone was planning to take him out before the night was over. He could deal with them if he needed to.

Haley nodded, her face tightening. "Okay. But what if there is?"

"Then I'm going to have to move really fast."

"You'll be careful?"

"All I want to do is follow the box truck, find out where it's going. That's all I *can* do. I'll leave the rest to Gage."

Something in her eyes said she didn't quite believe he would do nothing but follow. But that was his plan. He needed to scope things out so Gage would know what he was up against, not play superhero himself. Doing that might only blow the whole thing. All he needed to do was get concrete information to the sheriff.

Nobody needed to know how badly that chafed him.

Haley was nervous, even though she knew she didn't have much to worry about tonight. Buck had been pretty certain that if they'd been delaying shipments because he was poking around, it would take them at least a day or two to respond to his departure. So nothing had to happen tonight except their fight.

"I'll have to stay in hiding until this is over," he said again. It must have been the third or fourth time he'd mentioned it. It almost sounded like an apology, as if he didn't want her to think he was truly going away, or that he wanted to be away from her.

She understood. She wasn't happy about it, but she figured they were running fast toward the end, whatever it would be. As sweet as he'd been to her this afternoon, as close as he had held her, she was just a stop on the road. She couldn't regret it, even though his leaving would hurt.

"Quiet argument," he reminded her as they approached the motel. "I'll come in when it's still light enough for anyone who's interested to see me drive away. I'll be back here well before dark."

"I've got it," she said, hoping her voice didn't sound nervous. A low-voiced conversation that nobody was supposed to actually hear, her sounding angry, him getting angry, to wind up with a slap... God, she was worried she might not be able to carry it off.

He'd checked to make sure his number was in her cell phone and hers in his. If there was a transfer, she was to press his number, then hang up as soon as the call connected. His caller ID would identify her and he'd know the exchange was coming down.

It sounded so simple. And it wasn't supposed to happen tonight. She drew a couple of deep breaths. There was only one thing she had to worry about, and that was getting through their little scene.

Then tomorrow and the next few days she could worry about the rest.

"You'll do just fine," he said as she let him out at the motel. "Just fine." He squeezed her hand before climbing out of the car, but offered no kiss. Of course not. Things were supposed to be getting rocky between them.

She remembered what he'd told her, and didn't follow him with her gaze as he climbed out and walked to his room. Instead, she did the first part of her job: she hit the accelerator so hard she tossed gravel with her tires, then stopped just long enough to scan the state highway before squealing her way across it and into her parking space at the back of the diner.

Angry. She had to look angry, as if they'd had a fight.

She slammed her car door loudly when she climbed out. There were only a few rumbling trucks in the lot, but the slamming of her door was even louder. She could see heads in the restaurant turn her way.

Angry, she told herself. *I'm angry. Furious. Buck is a scumbag.*

She felt her face tighten into something like anger as she forced herself to stomp inside.

"Whoa!" said Hasty as she brushed past the counter to the lockers in back. "Wanna talk?"

"No." She made sure to bang her locker door, as well. The stage was now set.

When she emerged, tying her apron into place, she was surprised. "Claire's not on tonight?" she asked. They always worked the same nights. Instead she saw Meg at the far side of the place.

"She called in sick. Are you sure you feel well enough to work?"

"I'm just mad," she said. "I'll get over it."

Then, before he could question her any further, she grabbed an order pad and headed toward the tables in her section. The girl she was relieving was a new hire she didn't know all that well. "I got it, Jo," she said tautly.

Jo took one look at her and scrambled to hand over her order pad so Haley could deliver the bills.

Fear ate at Haley, making it hard to hang on to the pretense of anger. Buck was so sure he could take care of himself, but she kept remembering those three strangers. One man couldn't stand up to three, could he?

Around six-thirty, a wave of trucks began to pull into the lot. She glanced out, saw nothing unusual, but caught sight of Buck coming across the highway. Only a short time now. It was as if a fist clenched everything inside her.

She glanced out the window again as she wiped a table beside it and down the road a distance saw that blue pickup again.

Her heart slammed. What if they were here to take care of Buck? Put him out of the way? But daylight protected him for now.

She turned away from the table and went to take an order from a couple of familiar drivers who always ate together. They joshed with her, and finally asked if she was feeling okay. "Boyfriend problems," she said shortly. "I'll be fine."

"Well, take it easy," one said kindly. "These things work out if you let them."

"I'm not sure I want it to work out." Which effectively put an end to that conversation.

She heard the bell over the door and knew without turning that it was Buck. Showtime. God, how was she supposed to do this?

Then she remembered Maude and Mavis at the City Diner, and the way they slammed things down. Holding the image in her mind, she went get a cup and a napkin-rolled set of utensils. Her mouth drawn tight, like Maude's, she stomped over to Buck and slammed the mug and silver down. Maude would have been proud of her.

"What do you want?" she asked rudely.

"Coffee, biscuits and gravy," he said, his face flat.

She turned without another word, calling the order out to Hasty as she scribbled it on her pad and stuck the duplicate to a clasp for Hasty. Then she grabbed a pot of coffee and returned to Buck's table. She poured carelessly, letting some of it splash.

"Now," he muttered, then before she knew what was happening, he grabbed her wrist.

From there it got easy. She glared at him. "Let go of me!"

"Not until you calm down." He kept his voice low, and she was sure almost nobody could hear him.

She yanked her wrist free and he let go, probably a good thing, because she could see some nearby drivers stirring, as if they were about to come to her rescue. That wasn't part of the plan.

She leaned down, keeping her voice tight and low. "Eff you," she said.

"Do it," he answered in the same low, tight voice.

Straightening, she drew her arm back and slapped his face hard. "Get out of here, Buck Devlin! I never want to see your face again, not ever. You lowlife, lying…" She ran out of words as her voice rose, but thank goodness she didn't have to come up with any more of them.

He rose instantly, tossing a bill on the table as if it were trash. "Trust me," he said, his voice level and tense, "if I ever see you again it'll be too soon!"

With that he turned and stormed out.

To her horror, she realized the entire restaurant had gone dead silent. Feeling just awful and equally embarrassed, she darted her gaze around to see a lot of gaping faces. Then one of the drivers actually started to applaud.

All of a sudden the place was full of hand-clapping and whistles of approval. "You tell him, Haley," someone called.

She shook her head. "Sorry," she said, her voice thickening for reasons that had nothing to do with anger, and everything to do with having made a public display of something she didn't feel, from having made Buck look bad to his fellow drivers. "I'm sorry."

She certainly hadn't anticipated this reaction and didn't know what to do about it. But no one seemed to feel she needed to apologize.

"Get the lady a dinner on me," another driver called to Hasty.

But Hasty had another concern. He motioned her over because he couldn't leave the food cooking on the grill unattended. "You need the night off?"

"I'd rather work."

"Then sit a minute until it quiets down. You sure you're gonna be okay?"

"I'm going to be very okay in just a few minutes. Really. It's going to feel good once I stop shaking." A lie. When had she become so good at lying?

So she slipped onto a stool, Hasty put a piece of pie and cup of coffee in front of her, and the restaurant quieted back to normal. Then she heard a cheer and looked.

Buck was leaving. There was no mistaking his big cab roaring out of the motel parking lot. A couple of the drivers clapped and one gave her a thumbs-up.

Done. Now she just had to live with the sick feeling.

Buck roared out of town with mixed feelings. On the one hand, he wanted to grin at how well Haley had carried that off. On the other he hated leaving her behind, especially when he roared past the blue pickup truck. Only one guy was visible now, but he was sure the other two were around.

He'd have to take care when he made his way back.

Then he realized he'd have to take even more care. Damn, the truck had pulled a U-turn and was following him. He hoped all they wanted to do was make sure he was going for good, but the farther they followed him, the more difficult they were going to make his rendezvous.

He settled in a little above the speed limit, as if he was still angry, and waited. His concern built, but a little more than four miles passed and they finally dropped off and turned.

Not good. Yes, he wanted them to assume he was headed back to Seattle, but he wasn't happy that they were heading back to town. What else might they intend to do?

He finally reached the road Gage had told him about. No one was in sight, so he pulled onto it and bumped along for nearly another mile. Then he saw a sheriff's car with Gage and Micah waiting beside it.

Pulling up alongside them, he parked and climbed out.

"Okay," Gage said. "I'll take you back and drop you off just a mile outside of town. Micah here will take your truck to a motel down the road, in case they've got the LoJack on."

Buck nodded. He liked the plan. "We've got a wrinkle."

"Three guys in a blue pickup," Gage said. "We didn't miss them, believe me. So far they seem to be mostly interested in you, though, so I'm not expecting any trouble now."

"At least not until another switch comes."

"Tomorrow, right?"

"That's my guess," Buck agreed. "I doubt they want anything to go through to Denver because they can't off-load here."

"You better let your boss know you're on the way home as soon as you've got signal."

"Yeah." He did that, lying on the backseat of Gage's

car as they drove toward town. Meanwhile his truck continued west with Micah at the wheel.

"Bill? Yeah. I'm on my way back. What the hell do you care? The lady didn't want me." He listened to the yammering from the other end. "Right now I'm feeling too damn mad to drive far, so I'll probably crash for the night. I'll let you know when I'll be there."

"I'm glad you're coming, Buck," Bill said. "I'm getting hell for having one truck off the grid."

"Well, you won't get much more hell." Buck disconnected and lay on the seat, thinking about that brief conversation. Bill had sounded relieved, but he'd also sounded sincere about getting hell for having a truck out of action. So maybe it wasn't Bill. Maybe it was one of the suits.

For now he could only wonder.

Gage dropped him at the appointed place, a woodsy turnout. No one else was in sight. Grabbing his duffel, Buck thanked him and began to slide out.

"Remember," Gage said. "You can follow them, but that's it. Any trouble, give me a call."

"Thanks again." Then Buck melted into the woods and began to trot toward the truck stop. Not that he expected anything else to happen tonight, but being so far from Haley was making him nervous.

It didn't even ease his mind to know that she was surrounded by people right now, that nothing could happen to her.

He'd always found it hard to trust, and right now he was having trouble trusting himself and his own instincts.

He was too worried about Haley.

The truckers, Haley realized, had a grapevine as good as Conard City's. She had no idea what had passed among them, but they seemed to handle her with kid gloves even when the next wave arrived.

She felt the cell phone in her pocket vibrate once, Buck's signal that he was back near the truck stop. Some of the tension slid away and she found it easier to chat with her customers. Still, even as she relaxed, it seemed they were all going out of their way to be extra nice. Once or twice she had to remind herself that she'd just *pretended* to have a fight with Buck.

Not that she was anywhere near unfazed. She wished she had some idea of how things would unfold.

Then the three guys from the blue pickup came in for some pie and coffee. Her nerves ratcheted as tight as an overstressed spring, and she was grateful that Meg waited on them. She wasn't sure she could have.

Then she noted something odd and wished she could tell Buck about it. When they left, they all got into different trucks: one in the blue pickup, and the other two into separate SUVs. One after another they drove off to the east. Maybe they were done. She wiped tables and wondered as midnight approached. Two more hours on her shift, and she was beginning to feel amazingly tired.

"You need to leave early?" Hasty asked her as things wound down to near emptiness.

"I'm fine, really. Bills to pay. Besides, I'd rather be busy."

"Guess I can understand that," he agreed, patting his breast pocket and indicating he was about to go out back for a smoke. "I guess I misjudged that Devlin guy."

"Why do you say that?"

"The way he looked at you. I could've sworn the love bug had bit."

Haley's heart squeezed. "Guess not," she said stiffly.

"Not what he seems, huh?"

"Who is?"

Hasty left it at that and headed out the back door.

Not five minutes later, she saw the white box truck pull up outside in the empty lot. Her heart began to race like she'd just run a marathon. Tonight? Was it going to be tonight?

She waited a minute to see if the driver climbed out, but he didn't. As if she hadn't noticed a thing, she kept wiping tables and bussing dishes.

Then she remembered and turned away from the windows to pull her phone out enough to select Buck's number, sending the signal to him. As soon as she saw the connection was made, she disconnected, slipped the phone back in her pocket....

And felt her keys. Oh, God, she hadn't left her keys under her car seat as Buck had asked, because they hadn't thought anything would happen tonight. How was she going to get them to Buck? What if they did a transfer? She couldn't go out in that lot to give him the keys, and he couldn't show up in here.

For the first time, quivers of full-blown panic struck her.

Chapter 16

Buck's phone vibrated in his pocket. He took just long enough to send Haley an answering vibration, then pulled his ski mask down. He slipped through the woods toward the back of the parking lot.

Tonight? They must have sent those three guys to take him out so they wouldn't have to skip this delivery, because that stuff had to have been readied for shipment yesterday. Now that he had appeared to clear out, they were going ahead.

Haley must be feeling like a wreck. He'd practically promised her there'd be nothing to worry about for another day or two. How wrong he'd been.

Dressed all in black, his face concealed by the mask, his knives and certain other apparatuses appropriately placed and concealed, he found a vantage from within the trees to watch the parking lot.

The box truck was there, but nothing was going on.

Not yet. There were still other trucks in the lot, so they'd have to wait.

He settled down on the dirt, figuring he had at least some time. Three big rigs, one box truck. At least two of those rigs had to pull out before they could handle the switch.

He wished he could look in the Listons' barn right now and see if that tarp-covered box was gone. It was probably in the back of that white truck right this instant, waiting to resume a much-delayed trip to Denver.

The minutes absolutely dragged by.

When things started popping, they popped fast. Two of the rigs pulled away, taking to the road again. Then, as if on cue, the box truck moved, backing up until it was only a few feet from the back end of the remaining rig. A rig from his own company.

Rear doors opened and the two drivers, one of whom was White Shirt, dropped a metal ramp between the backs of the truck and covered it with cargo blankets. He watched, unmoving, as they wrestled a crate off the rig and then wrestled one back onto it from the box truck. The banging Haley had remarked on from the last time was kept to a minimum, as if they had learned something, and the blankets did a damn good job of silencing the exchange. Not perfect, but good enough that no one would probably look out from the restaurant.

He glanced toward the one window he could see from his vantage point and noted that only three people remained inside: Haley, another waitress he thought was Meg, and Hasty. He glanced at his watch and saw that Haley had slightly more than an hour left on her shift, and she was doing a good job of not even looking toward the parking lot.

Ten minutes, he figured. They'd have the switch done in about ten minutes. Then, after they pulled away, he was going to have to dash to Haley's car and follow that box truck.

Haley felt sicker by the second. Even though she didn't look, she heard just enough to suggest the cargo exchange was happening. She and Meg sat at the counter, chatting with Hasty, who was busy cleaning the grill. All she could think of, though, was the fact that Buck was going to run to her car to follow that truck and he wasn't going to find the keys.

"You don't look so good," Hasty remarked, glancing over from the grill.

"I'm feeling a little puny," Haley allowed.

"Maybe you should go home, girl. I won't hold it against you. You know that."

"I know." She gave him a wan smile. "Give me a minute to see if it passes." Most especially to wait until the trucks pulled away. If she went out there now, she'd catch them in the act they were trying to conceal. As soon as they were sealed up again and at least one of them took off, she could put the keys in the car for Buck. Being out there when nothing was happening would certainly look innocent enough.

At long last she heard the diesel roar. A glance over her shoulder told her the rig was pulling out. The door on the back of the box truck was now closed.

"I'm going out to my car to get an antacid," she told Hasty.

"I have some here," he said, holding up a roll.

"I don't like those," she said quickly. "I like the kind without sugar. I'll be right back."

She slid off the stool and headed out the door. Her car

wasn't parked that far away. She reached it and pulled
open the passenger-side door to open the glove box. As
she did so, she tossed her keys on the floor, where Buck
would see them. She heard the other truck moving, but
managed not to look at it. She knew he had to back up
and turn to get out of the lot front-end first, given how
he had parked, so she didn't think anything about it when
she heard the truck draw closer.

Straightening, she closed the glove box, checked to
make sure the locks weren't engaged. Then she slammed
the door.

When she turned around, she realized the box truck
had pulled up right beside her, its passenger door open.
Fear instantly dried her mouth and sent her heart into
high gear.

"Get in," White Shirt said. "Now."

She was staring down the barrel of a gun.

Buck moved a little closer. He was horrified to see
Haley come out of the restaurant and go to her car when
the box truck still remained, but as he watched, he quickly
realized she must have neglected to leave the keys in her
car, since they hadn't expected activity tonight. Smart
woman, he thought with admiration.

He watched her open the passenger-side door and
reach for something in the interior. The box truck started
up and backed up in a wide turn, perfectly natural given
the way he'd been parked.

The truck blocked Buck's view of Haley and her car as
it did so. He tensed and edged closer, heard gears shift,
as if the truck were slipping from reverse into low gear.
Normal. It seemed to pause for a half minute, not long,
but long enough that every muscle in Buck's body coiled.
Then, before he could move, it was driving out of the lot.

Haley was gone.

Before the truck reached the highway, Buck was running in top gear, dashing between the remaining trees over the rugged ground. He pulled the cell phone from his pocket as he ran, and hit Gage's number. It didn't connect.

Dammit. Reaching Haley's car, he looked in and saw the keys on the floorboard. He glanced over his shoulder and saw the box truck disappearing east along the highway. He couldn't lose sight of it. Losing sight of it meant losing sight of Haley.

Cussing silently, furious with himself, furious with the whole damn universe, he grabbed the keys and slid into the car, turning over the ignition and tearing out of the parking lot. The box truck was just a couple of blocks ahead.

He tried Gage again. Still no answer. He hesitated. If he called the emergency number, a dozen cops might converge on that truck. Their appearance might cause the driver to hurt Haley. At the very least, it would blow the case out of the water, because he doubted the driver was going to give up his confederates.

But mostly he was worried about why the guy had snatched Haley. What he intended. What he might do to her. He couldn't risk something happening to her. If that meant he had to find a way to get her back himself, then he'd do it, because he wasn't going to risk a bunch of local deputies getting involved when they didn't know what was going on.

That left Gage. He hit the number again, heard it connect, and then heard the beeps that said he'd lost signal.

Dammit! They were reaching the far side of town now, the truck just far enough ahead of him that it wouldn't know it was being tailed. He had to keep it in sight because Haley was in there.

He punched Gage's number again and this time reached voice mail. He left word swiftly, telling Gage about Haley, warning him to be cautious, then tucked the phone in his pocket, knowing he was going to try again in a few minutes. Gage had said he'd be available all the time. He'd get the message, he'd get help and come. In the meantime *someone* had to know where that truck was going, or they'd never find it or Haley.

For the first time in a very long time, Buck felt real fear. His mouth had turned dry as sand; his hands on the wheel were damp. Adrenaline made his heart hammer hard and fast and everything except the moment and the truck ahead of him seemed to recede. Some corner of his mind registered that he was terrified, but the terror couldn't reach him. Not now, not yet. Adrenaline had put up its wall.

Eyes on the truck. The command rode through his mind like a mantra. Come hell or high water, he wasn't going to let that truck or Haley out of his sight.

Haley sat pressed to the truck's passenger door. Her first thought was that when he slowed to turn onto the highway, she'd fling herself out, but before they even reached the end of the parking lot, she heard the automatic locks snap shut. When she pressed the button, nothing happened.

"You won't get out," White Shirt said. "You try anything, I'll shoot you."

Leaning against the door, she looked at him, looked around the small cab and realized this damn truck was built more like a car. He had automatic transmission. *Auto!* So he was able to drive with his right hand on the wheel and keep the gun lying on his lap, his left hand on the grip, the muzzle pointed straight at her.

Any hope of catching a moment where he had both hands doing something else evaporated.

She was breathing heavily, her stomach knotted with fear, and she thought of Buck, hoping he had seen what happened. He *must* have seen. And he must be following right now. She glanced in the big side mirror but couldn't see anyone behind them as they pulled through town.

That didn't mean Buck wasn't following, she assured herself. It just meant she couldn't see him. It was a dark enough night. If he was driving with headlights off…

She looked at White Shirt again. "Why are you doing this?" She hated the way her voice quivered.

"You know who I am. You saw me with Ray."

"I never saw you before!"

"Don't lie. You looked right in my face that night."

"What do you want with me?"

"You don't want to know."

That scared her as much as that gun pointed in her direction. In fact, it scared her so much she didn't care if he managed to take a shot at her. If she was moving, he might miss the important parts of her. Buck had survived being shot, after all.

She felt for and pressed the window control button, determined to climb out at the very next turn. It didn't respond either. He had everything locked up, all the controls on the far side of him.

"Please don't hurt me," she begged. "I don't know what you're talking about, but even if I did, I'd never say a word to anyone. Have I been talking like I know something about anything?"

He laughed. "You've been hanging with that cop guy."

"What cop guy? You mean, Buck, the driver? He just wanted to get in my pants." God, it hurt to say that, but desperation was lending inventiveness to her lies.

"Did he?"

She didn't answer. Her eyes roamed the cab, looking for something, anything to use against him. Hell, he didn't even have any trash lying around.

"Just let me go," she implored, hating the desperation in her voice. "Whatever you think I know, I won't say anything."

"Just shut up," he growled, "or so help me I'll hit you so hard you'll see stars."

So she fell silent, sure that a man who could kidnap her at gunpoint wouldn't hesitate to beat her. Her nails dug into her palms as she tried to force herself to think.

There had to be something she could do. Something.

Take the ride, she told herself. Keep quiet, stay alive until they got where they were going. Then she might have an opportunity. If not, Buck certainly couldn't be far behind.

Knowing that death might only be a few miles away, she felt a whisper of amazement at how much faith she had in Buck.

A guy she really hardly knew. Yet she believed that somehow, like a superhero, he would rescue her. Maybe she was crazy, but she clung to that hope like a lifeline while her eyes roamed, looking for a weapon, a way, a means…anything that might help her escape this man.

Oddly, a kind of peace began to steal through her. A kind of calm unlike any she had felt before. She wasn't afraid of dying, she realized. Only of how.

Which meant she had to find a way to take this guy on. Because if this was the end, then she wanted it on her own terms.

Of all times for cell phones to fail, Buck thought in disgust. No matter how many times he called, he got

Gage's voice mail, and then when he finally got desperate enough to call the emergency number to get them to contact Gage, he got a message that all circuits were busy. Angry, he tossed the phone on the seat beside him, and focused on the red taillights ahead of him. A dark night, a late hour—it wasn't hard to follow that truck at a safe distance.

Not right now, anyway. He just prayed nothing would happen, that the guy didn't know he was being followed. And he wished there was just a little more light out here. He could follow those damn taillights right into a ditch, because he was driving without headlights. One wrong move and he'd be useless to Haley.

Tension kept him bent close to the wheel, kept his eyes narrowed as he tried to keep his eye on that truck and judge from its movements if there were any bends in the road ahead. He'd driven this road with Haley and he thought he knew it fairly well, but it wouldn't be the first time his mental map screwed up on him.

He wondered what awaited them. Wherever this truck was going, there'd undoubtedly be other people. Those three who'd been hanging around town today? Or were they gone, their purpose served when he left town? He had little doubt at this point that there'd been a lot of pressure from somewhere to get him out of the way. He hoped they considered that done.

But why the hell had they dragged Haley into this?

He should have listened to his own damn instincts, and he gave himself a mental kick in the butt. One thing to miss that he'd been sent out here on a wild goose chase, but another to make the assumption, once he figured out they wanted him out of here, that Haley had dropped off their radar.

Hell, she'd seen White Shirt outside her apartment.

Foolish to assume he'd been trying to find out where
Buck was. But who the hell could have imagined that
she'd get kidnapped right out of the parking lot like that?

He couldn't have. In fact, thinking it over, he had to
believe it was an impulse on the part of White Shirt to
do it. That couldn't have been planned. Except he'd sat
there after the other truck pulled away. Not long, as it
happened, but what if he'd been planning to get Haley
when her shift ended? What if he'd intended to wait another hour if necessary, follow her home and do her there?

A crime of opportunity he couldn't have foreseen. But
foreseen or not, he now had to fix it.

Just then a huge tumbleweed, maybe six feet in di-
ameter, rolled out onto the road. Before he could avoid
it, it had stuck itself to the front end of the car, blocking his view.

He jammed on the brakes, cussing a blue streak. With
every second, Haley was getting farther away.

Much as she struggled to think of something, Haley
came up with no ideas. She'd have to find a way to do
something when they stopped. Glancing over at White
Shirt again, she wished she had the nerve to reach over
and pull the keys from the ignition. But his left hand was
still on the butt of that pistol in his lap, and the barrel was
still pointed directly at her.

She'd need a better opportunity. She just prayed she
would find one.

Buck pulled the tumbleweed loose, most of his attention on the taillights that were growing ever smaller. His
hands got scratched up on the dried, sharp branches, but
he hardly noticed. At last he tugged it free and tossed it.
The wind picked it up again and carried it straight into

a fence, where it tangled even as he was climbing back into the car.

He jammed the accelerator, the car protested, tossing gravel, then gripping the road. Still, it went. Risking his neck, he pushed it up over fifty on the road he couldn't really see, willing the distance between him and those taillights to close. It seemed to take forever, but gradually they got larger again.

Then the truck turned. In that instant Buck knew exactly where they were going. Plans began to roll around in his mind. He could do this.

He just had to do it before they hurt Haley.

The Liston farmstead! Haley recognized it even in the dark and from a distance. The house lights were all off, the family still sleeping, but there was a dim light emanating from the barn.

She didn't know whether this was bad or if it could have been worse. She *did* know she was disappointed in Mr. and Mrs. Liston, although she guessed she wasn't really surprised about Jim. Not with that fancy car. Not with that certain slickness she had detected. No, she guessed she knew how he made his money now, and it wasn't selling cars.

But some of her calm seeped away as they turned into the drive and bounced toward the barn. She had no idea who would be waiting. Jim? Most likely. Those three guys? Maybe. Whether she could do anything at all depended on who was there, what was available and what opportunities she might see.

Buck had done this kind of thing for a living, and she wished desperately that he was there to guide her. As it was, she couldn't even tell if he had followed. She'd caught no sight of a car behind them, and given the dubious state of her car, it was entirely possible that even if he had followed it had broken down. *Please,* she prayed, *let it at least make it this far.*

As they rolled toward the opening barn door, she decided that her first need would be to delay whatever these guys intended for her. To find some way to put them off, or make it more difficult to deal with her. She had no real experience of fighting, so she'd have to rely on her wits, wits that had never been tested in a situation like this.

Into the dimly lit barn. The first person she recognized was Jim Liston. Then her heart sank as she saw the other three men. Five men, one with a gun on her.

God, what was she going to do?

The truck rolled to a stop. White Shirt set the brake without turning the engine off and pointed the gun at her. "Get out," he said.

She was about to comply when the door opened. She nearly tumbled into Jim Liston's arms.

"Haley?" He sounded shocked. Anger suddenly filled his voice. "Dammit, Cal, what were you thinking? She wasn't involved in any of this! Now we've got a problem."

"She saw me," White Shirt said, his voice flat and cold. "I don't leave witnesses."

"My God!" Jim took Haley's arm and helped her out of the truck, none too gently. "You can't do this! If this woman disappears, they won't stop looking until they roll up the whole operation!"

The three other guys responded to that, straightening. But it was not Haley they looked at, it was White Shirt. And they didn't look happy.

"You're going to cost us millions," Jim shouted. "You damn fool!"

White Shirt was evidently getting the message. He

still held the gun, and now he leveled it at the three men. "She's mine. The rest is your problem."

"You just made her our problem," one of the three men said. He was tall and lanky, and a thin scar ran down his cheek.

"I won't talk," Haley said quickly. "I promise I won't talk. I don't even know what's going on!" Calm had completely deserted her, but now adrenaline was rising in huge waves.

"Get over here." Jim grabbed her arm and dragged her over to a few bales of moldy hay. "Sit and don't move. I swear, Haley, you give any of these guys cause for concern and there's nothing I can do."

"I just want to go home. I told you, I don't know what this is about." God, for an instant she loathed how craven she sounded.

"Then shut up." Jim shoved her down onto the hay and grabbed a rope. He seemed to have a lot of experience tying people up, because he quickly bound her wrists and ankles, and then tied them together behind her back.

She would have loved to fight. Would have loved to jump, screaming, at just one of these guys, but even as her heart and mind shrieked a desire for action, a more sensible part realized it would only get her killed.

She lay on her side on the stinking, prickly hay, watching, fearful and furious all at once. And behind her back, she struggled to free her hands. The rope began to bite into her and rub her raw. She hardly noticed the pain.

"Let's get this damn load down," Jim said. "Haley can wait." He turned once more to cuss at Cal—White Shirt—before the five of them went to the rear of the truck and rolled up the door.

A ramp was pulled out, and Haley peered over her shoulder, watching as Cal and two of the other men pushed the crate down it. She wiggled her hands some more, wondering if she was imagining that the rope was loosening.

Looking around her in the dim light, she hunted for weapons. Any kind of weapons. Because she didn't believe that after all of this they would be able to let her go, no matter what she promised.

Buck pulled Haley's car off the road into a copse of trees about a half mile from the Liston place. On this chilly, dark night, even at that distance he could see light coming from the barn, even though he couldn't make out any real detail. He pulled on his outer gear swiftly, masked his face and checked his knives and the fine wire he had hidden behind his belt. Two knives and a garrote. It might be enough.

He paused just long enough to try his cell. He got a bad signal, but he reached Gage's voice mail again. He left his message in as few words as possible.

"Liston place. They kidnapped Haley."

Then he turned the phone off, jammed it into a utility pocket on the leg of his pants and set out at a dead run.

The rules had just changed. Haley was in danger. Damn the law.

He'd break every single law on the books to save that woman.

Hell, he'd die for her.

Chapter 17

The men were busy inside the barn and clearly not concerned that anyone might be watching. Buck crept up to the back side, away from the open door, and began peering through grimy windows.

Having the light inside made it a whole lot easier to see the interior. No flashlight bounced back at him off the cloudy glass. While the filth on the windows didn't exactly help, it no longer prevented him from seeing anything.

His heart slammed when he saw Haley tied up and lying on the bales. He could tell she was trying to free her hands without moving too much. He wanted to run in there and scoop her up immediately, but he wasn't that stupid and he was better trained than that.

Tamping down every bit of patience, seeking the cold and calculating part of him that would help them both survive this night, he began to prowl around the outside of the barn, learning where everyone and everything was.

There were five men in there, he soon realized. Not bad odds. He'd faced worse in his day and faced men who were better trained than most of these goons. Still, it wouldn't pay to underestimate any of them.

Jim and another tall man, Scarface, stood to the side and watched as the three others struggled to move the crate out of the way so the truck could back out. It was headed for exactly the spot where he had suspected a crate was hidden under the tarp the other night.

From the pigpens came squeals and other sounds of disturbed pigs, but no light went on in the house. The senior Listons evidently wanted to know nothing about what their son was doing in the barn. Good.

Oddly, only one man, White Shirt, appeared to be armed. He thought about that for a moment and found it hard to believe. Did they really all feel that secure out here? Including the three who had come from out of town?

He was reluctant to believe it.

Coming around to the side of the barn farthest from the road, Buck saw the blue pickup and two black SUVs. He crept up on them and tried the doors. Two were locked, but the third one was not. Standing on the passenger side, he didn't think he could see a key in the ignition.

While the men inside struggled to move the heavy crate, he quietly opened the door and was grateful the ignition-key alarm didn't sound. Then he leaned in and began to search.

He found two pistols in the glove box, both Glocks. He pulled out the magazines and tucked them in his pocket. Then he took both guns and emptied the chambers. Useless now. That's the way he liked them.

Both the other cars were locked, which was fine, and they didn't have car alarms. Very stealthy, these guys. He found some pieces of metal, jammed them into the door locks and hoped that they hadn't somehow improved cars so that jamming the locks wouldn't prevent keyless entry from working.

He checked out the barn again and saw that Haley was still on the bales, still tied up. The men were busy trying to pry the crate open now without doing obvious damage. Five minutes?

He took the time to check Jim's car. It wasn't locked either and contained no weapon. He took a moment's delight in ripping some wires from under the dashboard, putting the car to bed.

He had just moved back to the barn to plan his move when he saw headlights coming down the road. Hell.

He checked out the interior scene again, assured himself that no one was paying attention to Haley yet, then drew back into the shadows, waiting. In a last-minute decision, he decided to grab one of the Glocks from the unlocked SUV and reload it. Quietly.

God knew what was going to happen next.

A white Suburban turned into the Listons' drive and came bouncing boldly to the door of the barn. An older man, Murdock Bertram, he assumed, climbed out.

"I see things are back on schedule," he said as he walked into the barn. "Who are these guys?"

"My guy sent them," Jim said. "I told you he didn't like delays."

"Well, obviously nothing is delayed then, is it? Is the shipment okay?"

"We'll see in a minute." The men were still prying the crate open, taking forever because they couldn't damage it.

Then Murdock swore. "What the hell is that girl doing here?"

"Ask him," Jim said, pointing to White Shirt. "He screwed up."

"She *saw* me," White Shirt argued. "No way I'm leaving a witness."

"Well, now she's seen *me,* too," Bertram said. "She's seen all of us. You damned fool! You can't just disappear someone around here. Not someone like her. She doesn't even take mountain hikes. They'll be looking for her before tomorrow night." He swore again.

"I'll make it look like an accident," White Shirt said.

"Like I believe that."

"I swear," came Haley's quivering voice, "I won't say a word. Who would believe me, anyway?"

A pang pierced Buck's heart as he listened to her. He hated hearing her plead for her life and hated himself for having put her in this position. Although maybe he hadn't. Maybe White Shirt had wanted her since he learned she had reported the cargo exchange to the cops. And where would he have learned that? From Claire. The wife of the man who was standing there right now, cussing.

"You freaking idiot!" Bertram said. "I ought to put you six feet under. Nobody would miss *you.*"

Buck peered in through the window nearest the door. His mind slipped into gear again, figuring sight lines, vectors, stamping himself a mental image of where everyone was standing, including the one guy who had a gun.

They finally got the crate open. Buck judged there was no hope of the cavalry arriving in time. It was just him. Blood flowed to every part of his body as it readied. He was going to need to be explosive, and if there was one thing he'd always been, it was explosive.

He squatted, stretched, shook himself loose.

"You'd better go put those Canadian plates on your car," Bertram said to White Shirt as one of the others pulled some packing foam loose and revealed a cavity containing two large black leather bags.

Game time, Buck thought as the man headed toward the barn door.

He waited, plastering himself against the wall until the guy rounded the corner. Then, almost faster than the eye could see, he slammed the blade of his hand into the guy's windpipe, and the fingers of his other into his solar plexus.

White Shirt dropped without a sound, strangling silently, unable to suck any air through his crushed windpipe. The solar plexus had just been added protection.

Down to five. He picked up the dying man and dumped him behind one of the vehicles. Then he resumed the position.

"Go see what's taking him so damn long," Bertram finally snapped. "God, how long does it take to screw on a license plate?"

It was Scarface who came this time. He paused at the corner of the barn, trying to adjust his eyes to the darkness of the night. Buck didn't give him time.

His hand snapped out to grab the guy's collar and yank him around into the darkness. Again the blade of his hand to the throat, a satisfying crunch.

Four to go.

But he couldn't wait any longer. In another minute everyone in the barn would realize something had gone wrong. They wouldn't come out singly, and he wouldn't put it past any of them to get nervous enough to use Haley as a hostage.

She lay on the bales. Near the edge. He just hoped she was in a condition to obey a barked order.

Hefting the Glock, he made his way to the door.

Haley heard Buck's voice, and for an instant she froze in disbelief. Then the words penetrated. "Haley, hit the floor!"

At once she rolled off the bales, getting the wind nearly knocked out of her. She struggled against her bonds and felt one wrist come free. She hardly noticed it was now wet with blood.

Twisting, she tried to work at the ropes and in the process saw Buck, practically a blur because he moved so fast, going after the four guys. God, he was outnumbered! She fought harder against her bonds, trying to pick a knot apart with one hand, and heard a gunshot.

Time seemed to stop. She froze and stopped breathing. Then, lifting her head, she looked and saw one of the men on the floor, a gun nearby.

And Buck. Moving like a ninja or a karate expert or something. She'd never in her life seen a real person move like that. He seemed to be everywhere at once.

The three remaining men converged on him, but at least two of them were next to useless as far as she could tell. A roundhouse kick caught Murdock Bertram in the side of the head. A punch to the gut brought Jim to his knees.

The last guy, though, looked like he knew how to fight. She fought harder against her bonds, needing to help, to do something, and got her other hand free.

It was almost with pleasure that Buck saw the last guy knew what he was doing. The rest had been almost too easy, and he had a little mountain of fury he needed to work out.

It never entered his head he might lose. He never lost. He'd been trained to take on the best of the best.

They circled each other, getting ready, looking for opportunity. The other guy's hand flashed toward his belt and a knife came out. A switchblade.

Buck pulled his barong from his own waist and the fight engaged. Jabs and parries, one after another, never holding still, almost dancing like boxers. A flash as the other guy's knife stabbed toward him. He jumped to the side and the blade met air.

And then he saw his moment. The other guy was slightly off-balance now, his feet out of position. Buck moved to the right and snapped a foot into the outside of the man's knee, hearing the crackle and pop of tearing ligaments. His attacker crumpled with a scream of pain and rage that ended when Buck drove the heel of his hand into the man's jaw. The attacker was unconscious before he hit the ground.

Buck waited, breathing heavily, for someone to move, to come at him again. Then he heard the most beautiful sound in the world.

Haley asked, "Need some rope?"

A week later, Haley sat at the counter at the truck stop, sipping coffee, eating blueberry cobbler and being questioned by Hasty as fiercely as any of the cops who had talked to her. Well, maybe more so.

"I want every detail," Hasty said. "I knew something was going on, but I didn't know what. And when that Jim Liston came in here and started asking questions, I called him, you know."

"You did?"

"You better believe it. I told him I didn't care what was going on in my parking lot, but he'd damn well better stay clear of you and make sure nothing happened to you."

Haley felt astonished. "Really? You knew something was going on?"

He snorted. "I don't miss much, but keeping my mouth shut is the way I keep my business. But look at you," he said, pointing to her bandaged wrists. "They hurt you."

"Well, Jim didn't," she said fairly. "I think he was trying to protect me." Which was as kind as she was going to be.

"He better have been. I can't imagine how terrified you must have been."

"I was," she admitted. "But maybe not as scared as I could have been. I knew Buck was coming, and I thought the sheriff wouldn't be far behind. Only it turned out that something was wrong with the cell-phone tower, so only Buck was coming. But he was enough. Quite enough."

"I heard he killed two of the guys. Is that true?"

Haley hesitated.

"He was protecting you," Hasty said kindly. "In my book that makes it okay. You don't have to tell me, but I want all the details."

"I can't tell you everything," she answered. "I'm not supposed to say too much and anyway, I don't know *everything*. I guess it's not all finished yet."

"Then for God's sake, give me the outline. I never would have figured Claire for a criminal."

"I'm not sure she is." Haley sighed. "It's a mess, Hasty."

"Just tell it however it comes out."

"From what I can tell, Murdock Bertram needed a lot of money."

"Alpacas," snorted Hasty.

"That was at least some of it. From what I heard, when he saw Jim come up last spring, he figured out Jim was making a lot of money."

"That car of his kind of advertises it."

"It does," Haley agreed. "So anyway, he put Claire up to getting Jim to telling him how. Getting him in on a deal."

"I don't want to know how he did that."

"Neither did I, but it wasn't pretty. Anyway, Claire had this thing with Jim, found out what her husband wanted to know. Then Murdock threatened Jim's family. His mother, actually. Jim loves his mother."

"Not enough, judging by what happened to his brother."

"Jim didn't do that. I don't think he had any idea Ray would get killed. But somehow Bertram had this contact in Seattle at the trucking company, which helped get the whole ball rolling, and he got Ray a job to keep him quiet about what was going on at the Liston place. Other drivers were involved, though, because it would have been too obvious if only one driver was delivering mixed-up shipments. That's what Buck is working on back in Seattle. See? I told you I don't know everything."

"It's enough," Hasty said, leaning an elbow on the counter. "Keep going or we'll get another wave of drivers in here. So Ray shot his mouth off about coming into money and that's what got him killed?"

"Evidently. Claire denies she knew she was poisoning him when she poured his coffee that night. She swears Bertram told her it was just some stuff to make him sleepy so he'd pull over somewhere, because they wanted to have a talk with him."

Hasty shook his head. "If she believed that, she's dumber than I thought. Then what?"

"Buck came to town. And unfortunately, Bertram's contact in the trucking company let him know they'd asked Buck to look into things. That put a hold on the shipments of drugs until they figured out how to get rid of Buck. Buck's supervisor was panicking because one of his bosses wanted Buck pulled out immediately, saying he was exceeding what they wanted him to do and they were afraid of liability issues. So it wasn't his supervisor, that much I know."

Hasty nodded. "Someone higher up. Makes sense. The supervisor notices something, wants to get to the bottom of it, and makes enough noise they can't ignore him. So they drag in some guy who they don't think will do much to make it look like they're doing something."

Haley nodded. "That's what Buck figures. He said toward the end that he thought he might just have been a cover story. Like I was for him."

Hasty's face softened. "He coming back?"

"I don't know." She looked down at her plate, biting her lip and fighting back tears. God, she was tired of being constantly on the edge of tears.

"I'll go find him for you."

At that a jagged, sad laugh escaped her. "I don't want him that way, Hasty. You know that."

"I know." He reached out and awkwardly patted her shoulder. "So it was drugs?"

"Oxycodone, like Buck figured. Each pill is worth hundreds on the street. And evidently Bertram knew a way to get them into Canada without a border check. So that was what he offered the drug dealer in L.A." She paused. "You should have seen what was in that bag, Hasty. I've never seen so many pills and so much money all together at once in my life!"

"Hard to imagine," Hasty agreed. "Okay, I think I get

it. The supervisor in Seattle figures out something bad is going on. His bosses agree they need to check it out, even though one of them is involved. They send Buck thinking he'll just breeze through and that will be the end?"

"So it seems."

"They sure misjudged that man." He pursed his lips thoughtfully. "The rest I get, sad to say. End result, your friend Buck helped stop one huge drug operation."

Haley nodded. "He sure did. They're going to have a hard time figuring out everyone who was involved."

"I just wish they hadn't gotten Ray involved," Hasty remarked. "That boy wasn't a bad apple. Now the Listons have lost both their boys. A damn shame, and all over some stupid money. Root of all evil, mark my words."

Buck had gone to Seattle as soon as Gage was through with him. The other end of the operation needed to be cleaned out. Haley understood why he needed to go. She understood everything except the part where he neglected to say he'd be back or he'd call.

Apparently he was done with her.

But when she remembered the look in his eyes that night and before he left, she shivered a little. There had been death in his dark eyes, no mistaking it. He was a man who wasn't going to rest until he'd settled it all. At some point this had ceased to be an intellectual exercise for him, the way it had seemed at first. It had become personal.

Because they had used him? Or because she had been kidnapped? She didn't know and had no way of knowing, although as the days passed and she heard nothing from him, she began to think she didn't figure into it at all.

Which wasn't fair, she told herself a few days later. He had come after her and saved her, and she had no doubt that he wouldn't have taken action against those guys if she hadn't been endangered. He'd said so himself. She'd heard it more than once: he was going to find out what was happening and who was involved so Gage could clean it up.

Instead he had needed to start the cleaning himself. Because of her.

Given that White Shirt had kidnapped her simply because she had seen him with Ray, she figured it might well have happened anyway, so she ought to be grateful to Buck for saving her.

But gratitude was hard to feel when she was hurting so badly. She had no regrets, though she couldn't help feeling used and tossed aside without a backward glance. She honestly hadn't figured him for that type of man, even though she'd been telling herself all along that he was going to leave.

But leave without a word? Without an explanation? That was the worst cut.

Late in the evening the week before classes started, she sat outside in the twilight, working on looking forward to starting her much-anticipated practical nursing work next week. She was now so close to her dream of working in a hospital and taking care of people.

That was what really mattered, she told herself. Not the restlessness at night when she couldn't sleep for thinking of Buck. Not the way he had left. Not her aching, breaking heart. She had a whole life ahead of her, and she needed to remember that Buck was responsible for that.

The knock on her door didn't surprise her. Since news of her kidnapping had erupted throughout the county, plenty of her neighbors had taken to dropping by, often with a plate of dinner, sometimes just to chat for a few.

Almost like a wake, she thought with bitter humor. As if someone had died.

Well, people had died, but not her, and the fact that her heart wanted to die was something no one else knew. Not really. Sometimes she saw these unannounced visits as a kind of apology from people who were used to looking out for each other and felt they had fallen down on the job this time. Certainly everyone seemed worried about how she was doing.

And this was the reason she loved living here.

The instant she opened the door, shock froze her, then washed through her in cold and hot waves. She stared at Buck Devlin and went light-headed.

"Haley?" His tone was worried. The next thing she knew, he'd wrapped her in his arms to steady her, kicked the door closed and carried her to the armchair, where he sat holding her. "Are you okay?"

She gasped, shock draining away before a flood of anger. "No," she said, pounding his chest with her fist on each word. "I. Am. Not. Okay."

"Haley—"

"How dare you leave like that, without a word or a call? How could you treat me like a disposable tissue? The least I deserve…the least…" Her voice broke and along with it the dam that had been holding it all in. She began to sob, deep, wrenching sobs drawn from the anguish she had been carrying for weeks now.

"I'm sorry," he murmured. "Oh, God, I'm so sorry."

"Why?" she demanded on a fresh sob. "Why?"

"Because I didn't know," he answered, holding her tighter still.

"Didn't know? Didn't know what you thought of me?"

"Didn't know if I was going to prison."

The word stopped her between one sob and the next.

Her heart grew so still she wondered if it would ever beat again. "Prison?" She could barely squeeze the word out. "How? Why? You never... They... Buck!"

"Shh," he said, rocking her gently. "Shh. Things got messy. I killed two men, Haley. That never gets overlooked."

She tilted her head, trying to read his face, but she could see only one side of it. "You saved me!"

"That's true. But I still killed two men. Then this drug operation was international and it crossed state lines. So the feds got involved, and the Canadians got involved, and the guy in Seattle who was part of this did a pretty good job of setting me up as a participant."

"Oh, my God," she whispered.

"It's okay now," he said, squeezing her. "Gage helped a whole lot. So did my boss, Bill. It's all okay. But it took time, and, Haley, I couldn't tell you anything. They wouldn't let me talk to anyone. Even if I could have, I wouldn't have wanted you worrying about it. I figured if I wound up in jail you were better off not even knowing about it."

She started crying again, but this time quieter tears as she clutched his shirt, pressing her ear to his chest and soaking up the steady rhythm of his heartbeat. He could have been jailed? The thought horrified her beyond bearing.

"It's okay now." He must have whispered the words a hundred times as he held her, rocked her, stroked her hair. Gradually exhaustion and relief took hold, quieting her until she simply lay against him, her cheeks stiffening with drying tears.

"Okay?" she repeated, her voice hoarse.

"I'm a free man again. I just want you to tell me one thing."

"Yes?"

"Do you want me? Because if you don't I'd better leave right now. I can't guarantee anything will ever pry me from your side again. Life is hell without you."

After so long believing he had left her without a word, it was hard to believe what she was hearing now. She found the energy to push back a little, and this time he turned his head so they stared at one another.

"I mean it," he said. "So before I lay my heart at your feet and tell you you'll never get rid of me, this is your chance."

Her heart began to lift, as if it were filling with helium. "Truly?"

"Truly. I love you. It was hard enough going last time. I'm not sure I can do it again, Haley. So do you want me?"

She lifted her hand to touch his cheek. "Yes."

"Be very sure. I'll still be driving. I'll be gone for days at a time. It's not the easiest life for a wife."

"I'm sure," she said, and threw her arms around his neck to bury her face against him. "I thought I was going to die from losing you. I don't care if you have to be away as long as I know you'll come back."

"I can guarantee that. I love you, Haley Martin. Like I never thought I'd love anyone."

"I love you, too," she answered, as sure of that as of anything in her life.

He smiled then, and the man who seldom smiled seemed to light up from within.

A new day was dawning for her and for him.

* * * * *

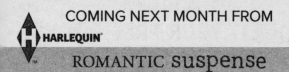

REQUEST YOUR FREE BOOKS!
2 FREE NOVELS PLUS 2 FREE GIFTS!

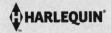

ROMANTIC suspense

Sparked by danger, fueled by passion

YES! Please send me 2 FREE Harlequin® Romantic Suspense novels and my 2 FREE gifts (gifts are worth about $10). After receiving them, if I don't wish to receive any more books, I can return the shipping statement marked "cancel." If I don't cancel, I will receive 4 brand-new novels every month and be billed just $4.49 per book in the U.S. or $5.24 per book in Canada. That's a savings of at least 14% off the cover price! It's quite a bargain! Shipping and handling is just 50¢ per book in the U.S. and 75¢ per book in Canada.* I understand that accepting the 2 free books and gifts places me under no obligation to buy anything. I can always return a shipment and cancel at any time. Even if I never buy another book, the two free books and gifts are mine to keep forever.

240/340 HDN FVS7

Name	(PLEASE PRINT)	
Address		Apt. #
City	State/Prov.	Zip/Postal Code

Signature (if under 18, a parent or guardian must sign)

Mail to the **Harlequin® Reader Service:**
IN U.S.A.: P.O. Box 1867, Buffalo, NY 14240-1867
IN CANADA: P.O. Box 609, Fort Erie, Ontario L2A 5X3

Want to try two free books from another line?
Call 1-800-873-8635 or visit www.ReaderService.com.

---

* Terms and prices subject to change without notice. Prices do not include applicable taxes. Sales tax applicable in N.Y. Canadian residents will be charged applicable taxes. Offer not valid in Quebec. This offer is limited to one order per household. Not valid for current subscribers to Harlequin Romantic Suspense books. All orders subject to credit approval. Credit or debit balances in a customer's account(s) may be offset by any other outstanding balance owed by or to the customer. Please allow 4 to 6 weeks for delivery. Offer available while quantities last.

Your Privacy—The Harlequin® Reader Service is committed to protecting your privacy. Our Privacy Policy is available online at www.ReaderService.com or upon request from the Harlequin Reader Service.

We make a portion of our mailing list available to reputable third parties that offer products we believe may interest you. If you prefer that we not exchange your name with third parties, or if you wish to clarify or modify your communication preferences, please visit us at www.ReaderService.com/consumerschoice or write to us at Harlequin Reader Service Preference Service, P.O. Box 9062, Buffalo, NY 14269. Include your complete name and address.

HRS13

Copper Lake on a pretty spring Sunday was at its best. It was welcoming. Peaceful.

It was home, Stephen realized. It had been luck that brought him here, and now he wanted to stay. He belonged.

If only Macy felt the same.

They turned the corner, where a couple of tables and chairs flanked the coffee-shop door. Stephen held the door for his girls.

His girls. He liked the sound of that.

"Did you sleep well last night?" he asked after dragging a chair to the two-person table for Clary.

He looked back at Macy in time to see her shoulders stiffen slightly. If he hadn't spent much of the past six days with her, he might have missed it entirely.

"I did. It was nice having Clary to cuddle with." She gazed across the street, then met his eyes again. "But when I got up this morning, I couldn't find my keys. I leave them on the kitchen island. I always have. But we finally found them on the mantel underneath the wedding portrait."

He faked an accusing look. "Were you planning to scratch out your faces with the keys? 'Cause I've got to tell you, car keys weren't made for destroying canvas and oil."

Her smile was unsteady. "I don't remember putting them there."

He wasn't sure why that was so important to her, but he shrugged. "You forgot. You were preoccupied. It happens all the time."

"I'm not normally forgetful."

He curled his fingers around hers. "But this isn't a normal time for you, is it?"

"No," she agreed with another weak smile.

Stephen couldn't help but wonder why the incident troubled her more than he understood. But if there was a subtle way to ask, he couldn't think of it, so he just went with straightforward. "Tell me why it bothers you so much."

Her gaze drifted away—not an obvious shift, as if she didn't want him to see her eyes, but he would bet hiding was exactly the reason. "You'll think I'm crazy. The hell of it is, I might be."

Is Macy crazy? Or is something more sinister at work in Copper Lake? Find out in COPPER LAKE CONFIDENTIAL

Available April 2013 from Harlequin Romantic Suspense wherever books are sold.

HARLEQUIN®

ROMANTIC suspense

Look for the second book in Elle Kennedy's
The Hunted miniseries!

Dr. Julia Davenport spends her days saving
lives, but when she stumbles upon a shocking
government conspiracy, the only life that now
needs saving is her own. Teaming up with
Sebastian Stone was supposed to help her
stay alive, but Julia doesn't expect to feel such
overwhelming passion for the sexy soldier.

SPECIAL FORCES RENDEZVOUS
by Elle Kennedy

Available April 2013 from Harlequin Romantic Suspense
wherever books are sold.

Heart-racing romance, high-stakes suspense!

HRS27819